ALL YOUR LIES

OCS FRANCIS

PROLOGUE

There's a bright moon. I could do without that. It feels like a searchlight. Like they know I'm coming.

I tell myself over and over there's nobody else here. Just me and them. I can see a few specks of light, but they're a long way off. No witnesses, no one to get in the way. Just like the plan.

Except it doesn't feel like the plan. The plan was just an idea, almost like a joke at first. But now it's real, and now I'm locked into it.

I tell myself it'll be easy. It'll be fine.

I approach through the trees, my boots crunching underneath me. I stop and listen. Nothing. Silence.

Come on, come on.

I keep going, out of the trees and across the grass. Then I can see someone approaching. I freeze. I almost run. Then I understand. I'm just looking at my own reflection, perfectly captured in the dark glass of the building in front of me.

I step forward a few more feet, watching the way mirror-me moves. It gives me an out-of-body experience. Like I'm just watching all this. Like someone else is going to do it. Then I know I can go through with it.

I feel the weight of the rock in my hand, and the switchblade in my pocket against my leg.

It's time to finish this.

B enedict Raine is dead.

Amber feels a lurch in her stomach. It dips and dives. It's a sensation full of colour and contrast.

Benny is dead.

She raises her head from her phone, looking out across the low, flat sweep of Port Meadow. It is a perfect carpet of faded green beneath the thin blue of the evening sky. She looks back at the headline.

Photographer Benedict Raine dies aged 62.

A small herd of horses grazes a little way in front of Amber. As if as startled as she is, one of the animals breaks from the group, trotting away and shaking its head. It accelerates into a canter, and another horse follows. Then another and another until the whole group is off, a blur of legs and flow of manes.

There is something primal about this wild space so close to the city. Something free and open when everything else feels as if it is closing in.

Amber had stopped for a moment just to take it all in, reaching into her bag for her camera. But her hand found her phone first, and absentmindedly she started checking messages, flipping through Instagram, then scrolling down the headlines.

There it was: Benny is dead.

She finally plucks up the courage to click on the headline.

Celebrated photographer Benedict Raine has died at the age of 62 after a road accident, reads the first line after today's date — 1 February 2020.

Next is a short statement from his family and a brief résumé of his career that makes him sound as if he personally won a series of wars rather than just having photographed them. Finally there are some tributes that are already flowing in from Twitter.

Everyone's your best friend once you're dead, thinks Amber. A road accident, though. A lifetime in wars, riots and revolutions, and that's how Benny went. Amber finds herself hoping it was quick, hoping he had no realisation of how he was dying. Benny would have hated the banality of it. She isn't sure where that sympathy has come from.

Towards the bottom of the news article is the one photograph by Benedict Raine that everyone knows, even if most couldn't name the photographer. It's of a Lebanese boy, the survivor of a sectarian massacre, staring into the lens with his Kodachrome blue eyes. It was on the cover of *National Geographic,* and if it didn't make Raine as a photographer, over the years it cemented his myth. The look on the boy's face is one of fear and devastation. But there is something else in that expression too: a righteous anger and a seed of vengeance.

Amber puts away her phone and tries to absorb the news for a few moments. It bounces around off her insides. She walks on, looking up at the sky, vast and empty. She pauses at the edge of the meadow and pulls out her camera. She flicks through the pictures she's taken today. It's a displacement activity, something to dislodge the tumbling feeling in her stomach. She has been in town photographing the climate change protests, and is pleased with the shots: the parade of painted faces, the mouths wide in dissent, the clutter of waving placards.

As she looks at all these people, she has a flash of a different face in her mind's eye. It's a face she can neither forget nor fully remember. Deep, strong blue eyes and a lost look. That's all she has left of that face now. It's a fragment that always comes back to her when she thinks about Benedict Raine. Of all the faces she has photographed, this is the one that won't ever leave her.

THE HOUSE IS empty when Amber lets herself in. A clutter of clothes on the bedroom floor tells her Johnny is out for a run. She is glad of that. She is still feeling startled and raw from learning the news about Benny. It isn't something she wants to talk to Johnny about.

She goes to her computer, downloads the photos from the day, and imports them into her editing software. She starts to sort them, but the activity can't hold her. She knows what she wants to do. It would be better not to, but she does it anyway. It's an itch that has to be scratched, a wound she can't help picking.

She types Benedict Raine's name into Google. The results fill her screen, and she drinks it all in. About the man, about his death. She wishes this could be the end of it — that after this she could look away forever. And she wishes the fragment of that face in her memory would go now too.

The past is supposed to be small and far away. But Amber's memories often feel more like viewing a scene through a long lens. The object in view is large, filling the frame. Everything else — the background, the context — is blurred and harder to see. It is not like the wide angle of the present, with everything crowding into frame and focus at the same time.

The last thing she watches online before shutting it all off is a clip on YouTube. It is an interview Raine did with a minor TV arts show just a few weeks ago. The studio is dim around his pale, brightly lit face. The interviewer is half in shadow, an exaggerated distance away. It gives the sense of an interrogation.

Benny looks a little reduced from the man she remembers in the flesh. He is slimmer than any of the slightly saggy portraits that fill up the image search. He sounds different as well. His voice is weaker than she remembers. It still has that smooth drawl and that manner that would seem supercilious if not undercut by humour and self-awareness. But it is a little tired, hoarse, and occasionally cracking. His slightly crumpled glamour is still all there: a linen suit, open-neck white shirt, a wave of blond hair flopping down on his forehead, and the careful stubble on his chin with a grey glisten to it.

The interviewer asks him about retirement. Raine gives a snort and reaches for a glass of water. It is strange to see him drinking anything other than whisky. He puts the glass down and looks hard at the interviewer.

'I'd be lucky to make it that far,' he says very seriously, his voice all gravel. He breathes in and smiles. 'In my line of work, that is.'

'Time at least for a memoir?'

Raine pauses before he answers, the fingertips on one hand rubbing together. 'I think, perhaps, it's time to tell it all. Let it all out into the open.'

'Warts and all?'

'Warts, boils, melanomas.' Raine laughs, but his eyes look deadly serious. 'But that's not for a memoir. That's probably for the confessional. I think it would be cleansing to confess everything.' He puts a slow weight into the last two words. But then he cannot hold the look of the interviewer, who raises his eyebrows.

'Confessional? Haven't you always been an avowed atheist?'

Benny takes a second or two to gather himself. Then, as if glad of the tangent, he begins a long and circuitous answer about his views on matters of faith.

Amber has seen enough. She closes the browser and flips the lid down on her laptop, sitting in the silence for a moment.

She is glad Benny's death came so soon after the interview. Glad he didn't follow up on his promise to tell it all. Because among all the feelings that have been crawling around inside her, there is one that now surges to the front. Among the guilt and fear and disgust, the strongest feeling she has now is one of relief. A sense of freedom. The knowledge that the one other human who knows the truth about what she did all those years ago is now dead.

Then the feeling flips on its head. She is thinking about her phone glowing with notifications in the small hours two nights ago. The message, the missed call.

She is thinking: *What if Benny has already told the truth?*

2

BENNY

Monday, 22 January 2001

It would be hard to forget the first time I met Amber Ridley. Except apparently I did forget that. I'm told I met her when she was nine and then eleven. I have no memory of either occasion. Well, I suppose she made more of an impression aged twenty-one. I know, I should be ashamed of myself. I was forty-three after all. I suppose I am ashamed, a little anyway.

I do remember when I first properly laid eyes on her, when I really noticed her. Nineteen years ago now. It was one of those moments one wishes one was holding a camera. A perfect capture, then it's gone.

She was sitting in the corner of a café on the South Bank, the low winter sun coming in through the window, throwing perfect Rembrandt lighting on her face — half glow, half shadow. She had a hand up to her forehead, a freshly lit cigarette between her fingers. The smoke floated up, drawing curves in the sunlight.

I was pleased to see she was a smoker. So many young people were such puritans. They're even worse now, I think: full of righteousness and moral certainty. She didn't strike me as that type. It was partly my projection, of course, but her brow held a restlessness to it, framed in long dark hair flowing freely onto her shoulders. I noticed a small tattoo on the inside of her wrist. I wanted to touch that skin immediately.

The moment was broken by Florence MacRory calling my name across the room.

'Benny!' She waved in that animated way of hers, her head going back a little and her disobedient auburn curls bouncing.

'Hello, Freddie, how are you?'

Florence was Freddie or Fred to just about everyone who knew her, and had been since I'd met her as a student. I can't even remember why. She didn't care about the misunderstandings it sometimes created. In fact, I think she revelled in them.

We exchanged our usual social kisses, and I turned my attention to the woman beside her.

'And you must be Amber.'

Amber's posture changed — I detected a slight tensing of those shoulders. A little nervousness at meeting me? Perhaps. If it was, it didn't show fully as she stood and shook my hand.

'Delighted,' I told her. 'The prof here has told me a lot about you. Nice to finally meet.'

That was when she told me, a little pointedly, that we had in fact met before. Twice. It had been through her father. He had been a middle-distance colleague of mine for a few years, but I didn't remember him well. Amber told me about our second encounter. It had been a garden party. I had a sudden flash of a shy girl in a patterned dress clutching a camera being thrust towards me, but that could have been my mind's invention.

I offered a deliberately exaggerated apology. Amber laughed. A little with me, a little at me. No, there was no doubt that we would get along.

'I enjoyed your talk,' she said.

'That's very kind of you to say.' I'd delivered a guest lecture on her course that day. Freddie had twisted my arm to do it, then told me there was a student of hers she wanted me to meet. She was someone very promising, in her final year, in need of a little mentorship.

'I loved what you said about thinking of a photo as part of a story. About it not just being a moment, but the way it can hold all the things leading up to that moment, and sometimes even following it. I'm sorry, you put it better than that.'

'Oh, I was probably quoting someone else. I can't claim to be a natural with words.' This was awful false modesty, but as modesty goes, I find this is the best type.

At this point, Freddie made one of her left-field interjections, the sort that would usually have engaged me. But I can't remember anything about this one — it sailed in and out of my head without touching the sides. I was paying attention only to Amber now.

Her eyes caught mine. It was just the quickest look, half a smile, the flicker of an eyebrow. I felt we already understood each other. Then Freddie tailed off, losing her way without anyone to join her, and Amber and I got a better chance to talk.

She started by asking me some questions about myself, but I batted them off. I was much more interested in her — in her work, that is. She'd even brought a small portfolio along. Freddie provided a little running commentary, as if keen to let me know she should take some credit for her student's development. But they really were good, strikingly so. Amber had an eye, and I could tell she already had courage. She didn't flinch from beauty or ugliness.

I gave her my card as we left. I told her I'd be very happy to offer whatever advice she needed about the industry, even provide a little mentorship when I could find the time. I was just about to head off to Beijing, but I hoped to be back in a few weeks. I knew we would both be very glad to meet without her tutor present.

Look, I don't want anyone to think I'm a complete monster. I really was her mentor. I really think she learned a lot from me in that time. I learned a little too. But it was a mistake to introduce her to my wife, and to invite her and her boyfriend to those long boozy dinners at our London flat. It was a mistake to suggest to Amber when she graduated that she should apply for money from my wife's foundation for young photographers. I was foolish to think these attempts to insert her legitimately and visibly into my life would protect me against temptation.

I did resist for a while. More to the point, Amber resisted. It was a full nine months. Then something changed over a series of weeks. Both of our relationships faltered, fell into bad patches. Both of us were stupid enough to get drunk with only each other for company, foolish enough to let the other know how we felt. It broke the paper-thin barrier between us. There was no going back after that point.

Until then, I really should stress, it was entirely above board. But then it was below board. Or rather, below sheets. And up against walls, and in the shower. Snatched moments in cheap hotels. All a little sordid, I know.

But I'd like to make it clear she knew exactly what she was doing. Nothing between us happened without consent. I made no offer, and she made no demand on me. There were no strings attached, no quid pro quo.

I'm sure it would all be seen very differently these days.

As I said, I'm not a monster. But I've never pretended to be a saint either.

And there was no way I could have known where it would all lead, and the damage it would do.

3

AMBER

'Isn't it supposed to rain at funerals?'

Johnny is looking up at the speckless blue. It's unusually warm and bright, a prelude of spring, and he fidgets in his heavy coat and suit.

These strange hot days out of place in the year don't give Amber the simple pleasure they used to. But for all that, she thinks Johnny looks very beautiful in his get-up. His mother's dense black hair and warm brown skin, his father's smoky eyes. He's wearing his bespoke three-piece suit, grey with the faintest check. She knows why he wanted to give it an outing. It is a release from recent months when they barely seem to have gone out or seen friends. They have been telling each other that this is the year that they will go out more, travel again. But Amber isn't so sure about that now.

It is nearly three weeks since she saw the headline on her phone. Three weeks since that late-night call.

What the hell am I doing here?

She watches the crowd flowing out from the church. She and Johnny had arrived a little late and slipped in at the back, then made their exit as the final organ piece swelled into the nave. The neat rows of heads are now a muddle of faces. It is quite the gathering: the great and the good of photography and journalism, a smattering of celebrities, even the odd politician.

Amber was surprised to be invited. Surprised and increasingly apprehensive. Perhaps she is catching the guilt from the service. For most of it, she found she couldn't take her eyes off the ornate arch in front of the choir stalls, flanked by vengeful angels, their wings tipped with fire.

'The Catholic Church comes into its own at funerals, doesn't it?' she says to Johnny.

'Hmm?'

She swerves from her own thought. 'It must be an enormous comfort. If you believe all those words.'

Her husband looks sceptical. 'Did he though? I mean Benny.'

'I guess funerals aren't really for the dead,' she says, thinking of her father's funeral, the way she does at every one of these occasions. It was a quarter of a century ago and it still feels like yesterday. A bleak, gunmetal day, a deluge falling on an ugly squat crematorium. Johnny is right: it is supposed to rain at funerals. The sun knew it had no right to shine that day.

The letter of invitation to this one arrived via Amber's agent, handwritten by Benny's widow, Genevieve. It spoke of how highly Benny and Genevieve had always thought of Amber's work, and of how Genevieve had been sorry they had lost touch. It would mean a great deal if she would come to the funeral.

It should have been easy to make an excuse and not go, but somehow Amber didn't find it was. Benny is dead now, and Genevieve is a widow. Whatever else has gone before, that much is true. And Amber is sorry, in her own way, to have lost touch with Genevieve. In her ignorance of what went on between Amber and Benny, Genevieve showed a generosity to Amber that she did not deserve.

So she is not here for Benny, Amber tells herself. She is here for Genevieve. But she knows there is something else too. It is a need to see that Benny really is gone. And more than that: to know that he went without ever saying a word to his family or friends.

Among all the faces, Amber spots her old college tutor, Freddie MacRory, chatting with the war correspondent Tim Vance. It is years since Amber has seen Freddie. The whirl of her hair is a little greyer, but no more restrained. She must now be the age Benny was, but she has lost none of the striking presence of those full lips and aquiline nose. Freddie was a little chaotic as a tutor and — as Amber came later to realise — not a very good photographer. But she was fun and warm and a bit mad in all the best senses. She is dressed now more brightly than anyone around her, as if she has come to the wrong event. But Freddie was never sombre or conventional.

Despite all the fond memories, Amber lowers her eyes, hoping not to catch Freddie's. She is feeling a sharp stab of the lingering shame about where the introduction to Benny led. On the surface of it, Freddie wouldn't have disapproved. She was always unembarrassed about her own many lovers, raising the middle finger to the men for their double standards. She was probably Benny's lover too, at some point in their lives. Indeed, it was partly this closeness with Benny that makes Amber feel uncomfortable now. It was the sense that of all the people Benny could have confided his secret in, Freddie might be one.

Amber turns away. She is feeling stiff today, and she stretches her back. Her lightly swelling stomach protrudes from her jacket as she does so. She brings a hand instinctively to it, then pulls her coat back around it as if embarrassed. Johnny catches the action and gives her a funny look.

'It's ridiculous,' she says, 'but I feel kinda self-conscious being pregnant at a funeral.'

Johnny shrugs. 'One in, one out.'

'Johnny!' She flicks his arm with her order of service, but she is smiling.

'Besides, you're hardly showing. People might think you just ate a big breakfast.'

'Are you telling me I look fat?'

He turns to face her. 'Yes, my darling, you look wonderfully, beautifully tubby, and I adore it.' He reaches out and takes the edges of her coat, opening it a little. As he does this, she feels a momentary twinge low down towards her pelvis. It is the tiniest expression of discomfort that flickers across her face, but Johnny spots it. 'All okay in there?'

'It's fine, J,' she says. It comes out like an admonishment.

'Sorry.'

'You've got to stop doing that, though.'

'Doing what?'

'You're not going to make it another four months if you panic every time I get the tiniest little cramp.'

'I wasn't panicking. I'm just...'

'I know. So am I. All the time.' And that's all that needs to be said about how they're both thinking about the small life inside her. About how precarious it feels. Amber always knew she would spend her twenties avoiding having kids. But she didn't expect how hard it would be when they finally tried. The trying and trying. The IVF they couldn't really afford. The hope and the false hope. The twice that she ventured far into her first trimester before it all came crashing down. The giving up. The accepting that they couldn't. Telling themselves it was probably for the best with their busy lives.

Then this. Forty years old and getting careless. And right

now, just over twenty weeks pregnant. A perfectly normal scan just three days ago. Halfway there. In less than a month, it will be viable. In two months, if it can find its way out, it will be safe. It will be a baby. It will be their child.

A group of mourners are drawing close. There is an elderly couple shuffling along, stooped and slow. Next to them, a solitary old lady with a vacant look on her face is being pushed along in a wheelchair by a teenager on the cusp of womanhood. The group stops for a second to talk to well-wishers. The teenager lifts her hands from the wheelchair and starts to fiddle with each of her fingers in a way that reminds Amber of Benny. She must be his daughter.

A woman catches up to the party, then steps ahead. It is Genevieve Bayard-Raine, as elegant as she always was. Dark brown hair with the subtlest touch of highlights, not a strand out of place. A long midnight-purple coat and a green scarf. Still very beautiful, in that stern way she always had, amplified by the effect of the occasion.

She heads for Amber and Johnny. Amber feels a wave of weakness pass over her: not knowing what she will say, worrying about what will come out of her mouth. Genevieve moves closer to the couple, her hands open.

'I am so glad you could come.' The edge of her French accent is still there, although less sharp than when Amber first knew her.

'I'm so sorry for your loss,' Amber says, the words feeling empty. She thinks Genevieve is about to shake her hand, and can't help but think about how the government keeps telling everyone to wash their hands all the time. But Genevieve keeps moving forward and leans in to give Amber a short, firm hug.

'I expect hugging will be banned soon enough,' she says, drawing back quickly, a light, sad smile on her face, her usual steel gone.

'A beautiful service,' Amber finally says. The cliché feels leaden in her mouth, and Genevieve looks unconvinced.

'If it had been up to Benny, we would have buried him in a bin bag in the North Sea. But his parents...' She nods her head up and back to indicate the elderly couple still moving slowly a way behind her. 'They still think they could save his soul. I'm sorry, I shouldn't be so flippant. And, you know, Benny, he had more of a spiritual hinterland than most people supposed.'

Amber thinks about this for a second, and that phrase of Benny's from his final interview flashes into view. *I think it would be cleansing to confess everything.* Perhaps if he told anyone, he told a priest. Priests weren't allowed to tell anyone else, right?

'How long has it been?' Genevieve is saying across Amber's bubbling thoughts. 'It must be a decade if it's a day.' And she turns to Johnny, asking him about his music, reminiscing about how she used to love hearing him play the old piano in their London flat.

Amber examines Genevieve. She barely seems to show any sign of grief, but you can never tell these things from the outside. She remembers at her father's funeral she felt almost a sense of relief, something lifting from the days of crushing despair that had come before it. Soon after though, the despair was back. And worse.

Genevieve switches back to Amber. 'Look, there's a bit of time before I have to go off to the cremation.' Her face grows more serious. 'There's something I'd like to talk to you about.' And Genevieve starts to move away, signalling that they should follow. Johnny throws Amber a look, flicking up his eyebrows, but all she can think about is whether either of them ever knew, ever guessed who Benny really was to her.

The trio moves away from the church towards a clutch of trees overlooking the Victorian graveyard. Amber tries to control the sinking feeling in the pit of her stomach. She knows it is ridiculous to be nervous. What is Genevieve going to say to her here, in front of Johnny? And after all this time. Her affair with Benny ended over eighteen years ago, and she knew Genevieve for a good seven or eight years after that. There were countless times in all those years that she could have accused Amber of sleeping with her husband. There were countless times Amber could have confessed. There were times she almost did.

But each time she didn't tell, it became harder the next time. Because to tell that one secret would have been to tell everything. How it began, how it went on, and worst of all, how it ended.

4

BENNY

Friday, 9 November 2001

L ife is once, forever.

I've always liked that line of Cartier-Bresson's. It was his way of saying that when you capture a photograph, there's just one chance to get it. It's a fleeting, fluid moment, and then it's gone. But if you catch it, it becomes indelible, eternal. It's true of all the things we do. We act in the moment, and we can't go back. We can't create that moment again, and we can't erase it. All its consequences are permanent.

It's easy to see now that I shouldn't have taken Amber to the cottage. But I didn't know then what I do now. For that matter, I didn't know on that Friday in November what I would by the Sunday morning. Not entirely.

The cottage belonged to my old pal Tim. He was in the country even less than me in those days, and he never asked any questions about who I took there when I borrowed the place for the odd weekend. He called it the *Sandcastle*. Not because it was grand — it wasn't — but because its front door was almost on the beach. A small track ran down to the sands proper, just at the point that an old wooden groyne jutted in from the sea towards the grassy dunes. There was even a little wooden rowing boat tied to a post at the top of the beach, and at high tide you only had to drag it a little way and it was in the water. On calm, clear nights you could take it out and just bob under the stars.

My car crunched to a halt outside the cottage. It had taken three hours to get up from London, and my hands were numb from the vibration of the drive. I was driving the '63 Corvette. It probably stood out a little too much. Amber had been quiet for the last part of the journey, and she stayed that way as we unloaded our bags and a box of food and went inside.

The old part of the cottage was stone, with a new wooden extension with big plate glass windows looking out to sea. The other three sides were shielded by a dense ring of tall trees, so that even across the flat sweep of the fields and the beach, it was almost invisible until you were right up close. There was an old stone chapel a few hundred yards down the lane, and a small café and farm shop just beyond that. But the nearest houses were nearly a mile away. I coveted the hell out of it, but Tim never wanted to sell. And it was probably better that it never became part of the Bayard property empire.

'I need a drink, a big one,' said Amber as she put down the food box. I was surprised to see her hands were shaking. She looked disconcerted by it too. She held them up in front of her, examining the effects of the stale adrenaline in her system. It was something I'd experienced myself enough on the job. After an explosion, the near-miss of a gunshot, or the surge of an angry crowd. Sometimes the shock doesn't hit you in the moment. It can hide away for a little while, then crawl out later to leer at you.

I went to her and took her hands where they met her wrists. I held them firmly, pressing into the fleshy pads beneath her thumbs. I brought her hands up to my mouth and kissed the ends of her fingers.

'Hey, we're here. We're not dead.' I widened my eyes at her. 'Unless you're a ghost. Will you haunt me, my darling?'

'That's not funny. We could have been a lot less lucky.'

That much was true. But getting lucky was my life a lot of the time. And I couldn't take full responsibility. It was Amber who had provoked me.

It was just past Norwich, about two and a half hours out from London, that Amber started glancing in the passenger-side mirror. I pretended not to notice for a while, but it started to irritate me. Was it something about my driving? I know I was going quite fast, but there's no other way to drive. Was she worried the police might stop us? Finally I asked her.

'I keep seeing the same car behind us. Since we left London.'

'You think we're being... followed?' My voice was full of false drama and B-movie intonation.

'Don't take the piss. Seriously. Dinged front end and a big rust patch — I keep seeing it behind us.'

'It's Friday. Lots of people are driving to the coast.'

She sank down in her seat and crossed her arms, a sulk on her face. A few seconds later, as the road straightened from a bend, she shifted back up.

'There!'

I looked in the rear-view mirror. There was a car behind us, that much was true. I couldn't see anything remarkable about it, but it was quite a way back. It looked like one of those low-down sporty hatchbacks, but not a new one.

Maybe a late eighties model. I didn't doubt Amber's observational skills, but I meant what I'd said to her. It didn't mean anything. Lots of people went up to the coast. She was just being twitchy.

But I'd been driving too long. I was bored. I was willing to play along.

'I guess we'd better lose him then,' I said, keeping my B-movie voice. And I squeezed some more revs into the engine. Gently at first and, once I could see the lie of the road ahead, I pushed my foot down hard. I felt the weight of my body and the punch of the engine.

Out of the corner of my eye, I saw Amber's hand reach out onto the dashboard. I allowed myself to glance across. I thought maybe she was smiling just a little. I pressed down harder. The straight gave way to long slow winding curves. I took the racing line along them, pushing faster and faster.

Then a twist, dropping right down through the gears, and flooring the accelerator as the road opened.

'Okay, enough already,' said Amber, though she was grinning now.

'Not sure we've lost him,' I said, and kept up the speed. Straight through a village at double its thirty limit. I knew there were no speed cameras here.

'Jeez, Benny.'

I laughed, looking over at Amber. Her face still had excitement all over it.

The road rose and narrowed out of the village, but I was sure I knew this stretch.

I was wrong.

The blind rise I'd forgotten about fell away, and the other car was coming right at us. It was too late to stop. If I braked hard, I would probably still hit him, and I'd lose control. I held my breath and jinked the car just a little to the left. I swear there was an inch between him and me as I passed, the other side of my car rasping on the hedgerow. The Doppler blare of his horn fell away behind me. I glanced at him disappearing in the mirror; then my eyes were back on the road.

The next seconds hit me like a series of static images stuttering together. The cyclist in front coming from nowhere, shiny in Lycra; my foot onto the brakes; the road suddenly a little slick in the cold; the loss of control and the car sliding out; fighting the wheel as the back end twisted behind me. I felt I had it, but I was still moving at the cyclist. He must have heard me, because he looked up and back. I thought he was going to tumble off for a moment, but he managed to brake hard and skid to the side of the road. My car was still twisting. Down on the brakes again, skidding right round, and finally we were still, sitting right across the road.

In the cottage, Amber took her hands back from mine and put them over her own mouth.

'Look, we're okay. I'm sorry.' I almost tried to justify myself again, but I stopped. Still, she had been enjoying the ride. She couldn't deny that. She bunched her shoulders and moved away from me. 'Please, let's not. I didn't bring you here to argue.'

'*Bring* me here. Huh.'

'What's that supposed to mean?'

'Never mind. Just... maybe I shouldn't have come. This whole thing is... Whose is this place anyway, if it's not yours?'

'Oh, don't you worry about that. Look, we should have that drink.' And I fished out a bottle of wine from the box.

'Yeah, okay.' But she walked further away from me, towards the big windows that looked out to the sea.

I knew what was going on. This mood of hers wasn't just about our near miss on the road. It was because this was our first time away together. There had been a few nights in hotels, but one of us would always arrive late or leave early. Never at the same time.

I knew this weekend was taking things up a notch, and it was registering hard on the Johnny-meter. That was my little name for how much she talked about her boyfriend. I never spoke about Gen when I was with Amber — why would I? But she spoke about Johnny. I suppose it was her way of keeping me at a safe distance. A little mention here and there didn't bother me. But the more she spoke about him, the bigger I knew her doubts were.

Johnny was a musician: piano, trumpet, guitar. Taiwanese nose flute for all I cared. The type of smug bastard everyone groups round at the end of the night, smoking joints while he strums away in the corner. He was a little older than Amber, but still much younger than me. They had been together for a couple of years, but she liked to downplay it. She wasn't sure their relationship was going anywhere. He was off touring with his band again. She wouldn't be surprised if he was playing around as well. She said if the band got signed by a proper label, that was bound to be the end of her and Johnny.

I recognised this kind of talk for what it was. All the things she said were probably true, but they were excuses too. They were her attempt to justify our affair in that part of her moral universe. I didn't really see the need to do that on my part. I knew I was doing the wrong thing by Gen, and so did Amber. She knew I didn't intend to leave my wife, and she knew she was free to walk away at any moment.

The trouble was, I didn't want her to. I felt that more strongly all the time. Of all the girls, all the women, I didn't want her to go.

I wished I was free, but knew I wasn't. I was being squeezed out of shape, but I couldn't break away. I wished I could keep her, and I wished I could hold onto everything I already had. I'd do anything to make that possible, anything.

5

Amber often wishes that she never met Benny. And if she could not have that wish granted, she wishes that the last time she had anything to do with the Raine family was the day she came back from that cottage by the sea. Her bloodstained jumper stuffed in the bottom of her bag, she stumbled into her flat and never wanted to hear the name Benedict Raine ever again.

But here she is, turning into the driveway of his farmhouse.

It has been a little over half an hour's journey to get here, just on the edge of the Chiltern Hills. Even as she drives up to it, Amber can feel that *farmhouse* is far too modest a word for this place. At the end of a well-maintained drive is the main building on the estate: three floors of sandy-grey stone, a mossy slate roof, and the spent tendrils of wisteria spreading along almost the length of the building.

When people said the Raines were rich and successful, it was often added that it was Benny who was successful and Genevieve who was rich. Benny never lived within his means, but he did live within hers.

Amber passes a gardener as she finds the spot where Genevieve asked her to park. A white van is there, its back open to a man pulling out power tools. Next to the van is a vintage-looking duck-egg-blue Vespa scooter, straight out of a Fellini movie, and a small modern motorbike.

The well-tended gardens in front of the house are dotted with sculptures. They are not ones Amber would have chosen if she had the money that Genevieve does. Strange curved cocoons stand upright like alien sentinels. Giant metal mobiles twist like contortionists in the breeze. A big copper face rises from the ground and stares empty-eyed at those who approach.

Amber finds herself nagged by a sense of familiarity, as if she has been here before. But she knows she hasn't. When she first knew the Raines, they had only just bought this place, and she and Johnny only ever went to see them at their spacious London pad. And after that, she only ever saw Benny on what was supposed to be neutral ground. She had no way of knowing that one of those places would turn out to be hostile territory.

Pushing the feeling of familiarity from her head, she checks her phone for messages. There is one from her friend Kay, but she swipes to ignore it. She's already put Kay off once since the funeral, and she still isn't ready to talk to her about all this. She puts the phone away and sees the front door of the house open. It is Genevieve. Her hands are open in front of her in the same way she approached at the funeral. She is sporting a well-put-together trouser suit and a crisp white blouse.

'On your own?' she says as Amber climbs out of the car.

'Johnny's coming later in the day, if that's okay?'

'Of course, of course. So glad you could both make it.'

'Excited to be here,' Amber lies. She feels she is only partly here by choice. The idea that Genevieve put to her at the funeral does hold a certain morbid fascination; she cannot hide that fact from herself. But mainly she is feeling railroaded once again by obligation and her own secrets.

She might not have wanted to hear Benny's name again, but it wasn't just up to her. The photography pond is a small one, and the Raines are big fish. For all the impossibility of staying lovers, even friends, after that Norfolk weekend, it was also hard to cut Benny and Genevieve out of her life completely. A sudden severance risked too much attention, and Genevieve's hospitality and generosity made a slow move away almost as hard. Too frequent refusals created a suspicion of their own. But with each occasion that Amber accepted something from Genevieve, it doubled the guilt and hardened the secret, until they settled into a new sort of orbit. It took Amber years to fully drift away.

Amber grabs her bag from the boot of the car and is ushered inside. The hallway resembles more a lobby to a country house hotel than a home. It is spotless and perfectly ordered, with a cluster of fine art and photography prints immediately visible on the nearest wall. The wide staircase curves up ahead of them, and she can hear someone playing Chopin on a piano in another room. There is a small table with a hand sanitiser dispenser and some art catalogues.

'This is Sam,' says Genevieve.

Amber looks up from the table to see a man she didn't notice before, or hear arrive — as if he has just materialised from the fabric of the house. He is tall and slim, sporting a fashionable crest of hair and calculated tailoring. Without thinking, Amber sticks out her hand, but he keeps his to himself. Instead he gives a small *namaste* bow, his body moving in a fluid little dance.

'Sam is my... well, my *factotum*. I've never liked the word assistant. If there's anything you need, just ask Sam.'

'Be delighted to help,' says Sam, a lilt in his voice that

Amber can't quite place. 'Great pleasure to meet you.' He speaks with the kind of earnestness that can only be fake.

Amber understands now that she has not come to someone's house — she has come to a business headquarters. This is the heart of Raine plc, the Bayard Foundation, the hub of all of Genevieve's property, art and financial endeavours.

At the funeral, Genevieve had got straight to the point as she led Amber towards the graveyard. It was about Benny's archive. Most of the well-known material had been catalogued for years. But Benny was a late convert to digital photography — a stubborn refusenik as Genevieve put it — and he had left a huge unsorted archive of negatives and prints that had never been absorbed into the main collection. It was a mixture of professional and personal material, and Genevieve thought it would make for an interesting retrospective of his lesser-known work. She spoke about it all in a very businesslike way.

'Can I ask, why me?' Amber had said, finding herself not able to look directly at Genevieve.

Genevieve paused and, as if following Amber's eyes, looked up through the trees at the cyan sky.

'There's something indelible about film, isn't there?' said Genevieve. 'I think you understand that. You know I've always rated you, and Benny always spoke highly of you. And it's your film work that I really love.'

Amber shoots with digital cameras for her more immediate work — there is simply no other way to do the job. But for anything that requires more permanence, she always turns to film. She trained on it, and she stayed with it. Celluloid was barely dead for a decade before it started its renaissance, but Amber never let it go in the first place.

It is partly the end result that satisfies her: that texture and grain she has never quite been able to fake digitally, and those vintage lenses with all their beautiful flaws and idiosyncrasies. But it's also the process: the slowness and precision that it requires; the knowledge you don't have shots to waste; the preciousness of every decision about subject, light, composition. It is even about the soft mechanical clunk of the older cameras she uses. It has a physicality to it, giving consequence and permanence to each shot.

'I'm really flattered,' she told Genevieve at the funeral. 'But I'm a photographer, not an archivist. I'm sure there are better qualified people.'

'Sure, sure,' said Genevieve, as if she agreed on the technicality, but that Amber was missing her point. 'We can get help in if you need it. But it needs someone good to direct it. And I'd also like that to be someone Benny would've trusted with his work.'

'That's very flattering,' said Amber, thrown into a new twist of emotions.

'I think it's a shame you and I lost touch. I'm glad I was able to help you when I did.'

'And I was very grateful.'

The thing Amber regretted most in the years after the cottage was taking money from the Bayard Foundation, Genevieve's philanthropic fund. She suspected strongly that Benny had engineered it. She assumed it was money to assuage his guilt and buy her silence. But it was also money she needed to keep going when she and Johnny were penniless, when her mind was at its most disordered, when the secret inside her was tearing up her mind and body.

'Look, I don't want you to feel pressured about it,' said Genevieve, stopping at a moss-covered gravestone. 'Why don't you at least come and take a look? You can meet Benny's assistant, take stock of things, see what you think. Why not come up on a Friday? Then you two can stay for the weekend. It would be nice to have some people in that big old house.'

It might have been easier to say no if Johnny hadn't heard

all this. Amber wasn't able to invent a lie or stave off the moment when she could have mentioned it in passing later to Johnny. It was not like the days she'd had in 2001 to think of how to explain the deep cut in her hand.

And it would definitely have been easier to say no if Genevieve hadn't next said out loud the amount of money she was offering as a consultant day rate — just to come and take a look. Amber and Johnny both knew it was money they couldn't afford to turn down with the year they'd just had, and the baby on the way.

Johnny never made a packet from his music. His band never did get signed, and they went their separate ways after a while. But he has always been a glass-half-full type, and he talks about not getting signed as a good thing — making him abandon what he calls his *rock star delusion* and moving back to his first love of jazz. Since then he's always just about got by gigging and as a session musician.

The house they live in isn't even legally theirs. It belongs to Amber's mum, imprisoned in a care home with early-onset dementia. Amber and Johnny do not have much. Each other. Each other and this new life.

'C'mon, let's at least go for the weekend,' Johnny said at the end of an argument that Amber did not want to be having, because every sentence that continued it would contain more lies. 'I'm sick of staring at these four walls. It feels like we haven't been further than the Botley Road since last year. Be like a little holiday. Maybe chez Raine has big creaky beds we can have lots of noisy sex on and feel like naughty teenagers.'

'You're such a romantic.' But she liked that bit of this idea.

She knew she should close her eyes to all this. She should run away.

But she knew too that Genevieve's request was made in

innocence. And Benny is dead now. He is gone. He cannot touch her. He cannot be allowed to take any more from her. She decided she would inch towards it, her eyes wide open.

6

AMBER

Genevieve leads on down the hallway into the house. Amber misses what she says next because on the wall she sees a huge face looking down at her.

The black-and-white print almost fills the wall, top to bottom. It's of a teenaged boy. Grubby, pockmarked cheeks, tatty clothes and eyes burning. The subject is in command of the picture, the lens a little underneath him so the viewer is defied to look squarely in his eyes. There is none of the sentimental voyeurism of a lot of photography of street kids. His name is Luiz. Amber knows this because she took the photo. Behind him are more faces, younger children, and the whole scene is caught in the inner frame of a halo of a broken chain-link fence. It looks staged, as if the figures behind Luiz have been choreographed to perfectly fill the space around him. But Amber knows it is a real moment — the result of trust, patience, and quiet observation.

'Benny always loved that one,' Genevieve says, seeing Amber has stopped. 'That whole series, in fact.'

Amber finds she cannot respond. She feels slightly

hijacked by the emotions the image is stirring in her. She thinks about Luiz from time to time, about the fact she tried to draw attention to his world, about how the series won her awards and was displayed in prestigious galleries. And how she donated a sizeable chunk of the money she made from these shots to a project helping Luiz's *barrio*. But none of that helped Luiz. He was shot dead by the police less than two years after the photo was taken.

'There's something so truthful... so forgiving about that series,' Genevieve is saying.

Truth. Forgiveness. The thoughts stab at Amber, and she looks away from Luiz's eyes. She sees those other eyes briefly in her mind — the ones from all those years ago that will not leave her — then they are gone as the two women move on through the house.

Genevieve shows the way into a large stone kitchen, warm from a deep red AGA in the corner, full of the clutter of normal life, and Amber finally feels she is in someone's home. At the kitchen table, there is a form of long hair and a onesie slumped over a mobile phone.

'This is my daughter, Yvette,' says Genevieve.

The onesie slowly unfurls, and Amber recognises the young woman from the funeral. Wide grey eyes under full brows and the sulking pout of a bored teenager. When she registers Amber, she looks embarrassed to have been inter-rupted in this state, and her movements quicken. She is upright, flicking her hair from where it has settled on her shoulder.

'Yeah, hi. It's Yvey,' she says pointedly, then adds, 'as in *ee-vee*,' stressing out the length of the syllables, as if this is very important.

'Hello, Yvey. Amber. Pleased to meet you.' There is a dry silence between them. 'I'm very sorry about your dad.' The words clunk in Amber's head, and she is glad that Genevieve rescues her from further conversation by telling her daughter to go and get dressed.

Genevieve offers Amber a coffee, and they sit for a few moments. Amber is lost for anything to say. She wants to ask about Benny's death, but doesn't dare to. She has gleaned he crashed while out riding his motorbike, but that's all that has made the news. She didn't even know he had a bike. Was he going too fast? Was it a hit-and-run? She remembers the drive to the cottage with Benny: tearing along, adrenalised, out of control, their near-death experience.

'Let me show you the studio,' says Genevieve finally.

Amber is expecting to be led back into the house, but Genevieve goes out through the large French doors at the back of the kitchen. Amber follows, and they are in a cottage garden glowing in the morning sun, busy with early flowers. A path runs across the garden and into the green-brown stripe of a young beech wood. Genevieve leads further into the trees and, as the trunks thicken with age, the light becomes less. The path starts to wind, but it is still well-laid stone underfoot. Then the beech gives way to a patch of silver birch, and the sun is on their faces again. They are in a large round clearing, a reservoir of light cut from the gloom of the woods.

At the centre of the clearing is the studio. Its hybrid construction is evident immediately. One end of it is an old stone cottage, its windows still there but all black, boarded up from inside. Expanding from the stone structures is a large, modern square, its sides made almost entirely from huge slabs of glass.

The setting and construction of the whole thing immediately make Amber think of another building. She almost says it, like the reflexive jerk from a hammer to the knee. It reminds her of the cottage by the sea.

She clenches her jaw to stop the thought, and Genevieve

fills the silence. She talks about how they had to fight the local Council about the design because the original cottage was listed, and about how Benny used to love the seclusion of this spot. Genevieve talks about Benny almost as if he passed away at a great age a long time ago.

They go on inside. The glass box houses a large digital editing suite and a living area with seating, an enormous television, and a small island kitchenette. It is mostly well ordered, but on one side there are rows of cardboard boxes, stacks of mounted prints waiting to be hung, and a chaos of paperwork and old folders. It is very bright, and Amber sees the glare of light falling on the large computer monitors. As if reading her mind, Genevieve touches a switch on the wall, and the glass becomes in an instant opaque, diffusing the excess light.

'Smart glass — a little Bond layer, don't you think?' says Genevieve, laughing. She switches it back, then waves at the digital editing suite with a few words of explanation. She walks to the back of the glass square to a large door that must be the original front door of the old cottage. It is a heavy wooden thing, with a big iron lock, from which a large key protrudes. Genevieve twists the key — it gives a satisfying mechanical clunk — and opens the door. In front of them is a short white corridor with a narrow slatted wooden staircase and another door at the end.

'We completely redid the innards,' says Genevieve, walking ahead and opening a door at the far end of the corridor.

Through this doorway, Amber can only see perfect darkness. Genevieve hits a switch by the door, and the room flickers into existence. It is clinical in its whiteness, the absent patient attended only by the big umbrellas of studio lights in softboxes. There are stacks of reflectors in one corner, a trolley with a computer, and a shelf of various photographic paraphernalia. There are no windows, and this is the only way in. Sealed for perfect light control.

But Genevieve has flicked the lights off as quickly as she turned them on.

'He never used this much, but it seemed a facility to have,' she says flatly. 'No one goes in there these days,' she adds and closes the door, as if this had been the site of some terrible act and she doesn't want to dwell in here.

Get a grip, Amber tells herself. *Stop jumping at shadows, stop examining everything for deeper meaning.*

'And upstairs,' Genevieve is saying now, 'is why you're here.'

Because of how they are positioned in the corridor, Amber climbs the stairs first. She opens the door, again into darkness. She feels around and finds the lights. This time they don't flicker on brightly, rather fading up gently, pushing the darkness away. The room is bathed in a dim yellow light, revealing row upon row of shelves that stretch to the back of the room. Each shelf is jam-packed with box files, envelopes, metal canisters. They are shoved in at every angle, piled on top of each other. There are even what look like tubs of film, still undeveloped.

Amber steps between two rows of shelves, feeling now how cold the room is. It is that draughtless dry chill of careful temperature control. She pulls down a box file. It is laden with layers of envelopes. She takes one out and opens it: stuffed with strips of negatives.

'Is this room all negatives?' she asks. A film negative is not a large thing — an inch by an inch and a half. Amber cannot imagine how many thousands — tens of thousands — there must be in here.

'Some contact sheets, a few prints, a lot of slide film for his colour work. And yes, a great number of negatives.' Genevieve looks almost embarrassed. 'I'm afraid Benny was a bit of a hoarder. Never very good at...' A change comes over her, a moment of frailty crossing her face. It is as if a crack has opened and her grief is leaking out.

Amber remembers something Benny always used to quote at her. His little mantra about not missing the moment. To never flinch from the shot. Because that vanishing moment can become eternal.

Life is once, forever.

And now, looking at this chaotic glut of an archive, she realises she only ever half understood what he meant.

It was as if, for Benny, nothing could be thrown away or be allowed to die. Everything must be kept. Every shot, every frame, forever.

7

BENNY

Friday, 9 November 2001

We wrapped ourselves in all the layers we could find and took our chairs out onto the deck beyond the windows to enjoy the last of the day. We didn't care that it was cold. It was too beautiful an evening to sit behind glass.

We both had cameras with us. I had the Nikon I carried everywhere. Amber was fiddling with an Olympus that was at least five years older than she was. It was an all-manual beast. When I first saw her with it, I told her using something so antique came across as a bit of an affectation. She told me it belonged to her father. That shut me up.

Amber finished a cigarette and stamped it into the sandy ground. She raised her camera and pointed it south-east along the coastline. The sun was setting behind us, but its last bits of light caught on the tips of the low waves, and the red-yellow ripple of the sky reached like tendrils towards the darkening sea. She must have caught my expression out of the corner of her eye.

'What?' she said.

'Thousands of pictures of sunsets, all of them irredeemable clichés.'

She lowered her camera, looking put out, but she still let me lean over and kiss her. As I uncoupled from her, I reached down to my camera at the base of my chair.

I'd loaded the roll of film into the camera earlier. It was black and white and a fast film — one for low light. I had that type of film in because I already knew the pictures I wanted to take tonight.

I held my camera up and pointed it towards Amber. Her skin still gave a glow in the dying day. I squeezed the shutter, but as I did, she moved her hand up in front of the lens.

'I'd rather not be an irredeemable cliché, thanks.'

I lowered my camera. 'What's that supposed to mean?'

'Maybe not as many as my sunsets, but I don't suppose I'm the first or last in your collection.'

'My *collection*?'

'I'm not fucking you because you're Benedict Raine, you know.'

'Well, I hate to disappoint you.'

'You know what I mean. I'm not another groupie who–'

'You think I have groupies? Should I be flattered or insulted?'

'Look, Benny...' She tailed off, but I knew what she was trying to say. She wanted to ask again if there was more to this than hotel trysts and clandestine weekends. Part of me wanted to be able to say there might be more, could be more. In fact, what that part really wanted to say was that I hadn't felt about anyone like this since I met Genevieve. But, no, she knew the deal. This was what it was.

'I don't just bring anyone here,' I told her.

'Anyone?' she came back at me with. 'No one in particular springs to mind?' It was if she was daring me to say my wife's name. But there was so much we couldn't say to each other.

My glass was empty, and so was the bottle at my feet. Amber's glass was still almost full. I got up to get more wine, my camera still dangling from my shoulder. I slid open the door to the deck and left it that way as I went into the kitchen. As I fished out another bottle, I turned to see Amber perfectly framed in the open door. She was looking down the coast again, towards the colour in the sky, her profile against the waves beyond. I put down the bottle, raised my camera, and took a quick picture. I don't think she registered it.

She wasn't entirely wrong in what she had said. She was very perceptive. *Collection* wasn't the right word, though. That sounded so sterile and sinister. But she was right that I liked to capture these moments. I liked to hold onto a little bit of time I wouldn't ever get back, with people who wouldn't or couldn't stay with me. I could tell myself all I liked that I could find a way to keep Amber forever, but really I knew that any time I saw her could be the last.

I took another frame. If I couldn't keep all of her, I could keep a tiny piece.

8

Amber comes blinking down the stairs from the archive. She and Genevieve were there for some time discussing the extent of the work. Amber has agreed to at least spend some of the weekend getting a feel for what is there and deciding if this is a job she can do. This seemed enough to satisfy Genevieve.

They emerge back into the glass box to find the digital editing suite now occupied by a man staring intently into the monitors. He has a mop of white-blond hair, like a lamp above his black skinny jumper. Amber thinks immediately of Andy Warhol. He has earbuds in and barely moves as the two women enter the room. One monitor has photo editing software open, displaying a catalogue view of rows and columns of images. The other monitor is a mess of folders. The man's mouse is jumping between the two, selecting folders and scrolling through the catalogue as if he's looking for something.

'I see Mika has joined us,' says Genevieve to Amber loudly in a way that feels more closely directed at the man than her. But he still doesn't look up. Genevieve goes on, now talking about Mika as if he isn't here. 'Mika is... was Benny's assistant. He hasn't been with us long. I'd hoped you'd be able to work together on some of this, but unfortunately he's decided not to stay with us.'

Mika finally cracks his shell and swivels round on the chair. The sense of Andy Warhol evaporates immediately. He is boyish, handsome, tanned. He has a light brown stubbled goatee. His eyes are a piercing blue.

'Hiya, sorry, just finishing something,' he says, and gives Amber a quick smile.

'I'll leave you two to it,' Genevieve says, and Mika says nothing else, swivelling back to his work.

Mika brightens once Genevieve has left them. He makes Amber a cup of tea in the kitchenette and pulls a Diet Coke out of the fridge for himself. As he delivers the tea, he slides a crisp business card across to Amber. It prompts her to pull one of her own out of the back of her phone case. It is old and tatty, and she feels a little embarrassed by it as she hands it to Mika.

Mika wanders off towards the sofa by the big TV, and they start to chat. He's young, in his mid-twenties. He was only hired as Benny's assistant a few months before his death. He seems like the soul of indiscretion.

'Yeah, I was pretty surprised to get the gig,' he is saying. 'I mean, Benedict flipping Raine, right?' He sucks in some air.

'You say that like there's a *but*?'

'Man, there's always a but. I've worked for some massive butts.' He laughs at his own bad joke. 'Seriously though, I was, like, his third assistant in two years. He'd been going through them.'

'How so?'

'Quit, fired, resigned. Divorced, beheaded, died for all I know.' He laughs again, a juvenile little snort. 'I'm here for just another week, then I'm off to work for someone a bit more, y'know, not dead.'

'You should be kinder to Genevieve. She's just lost her husband.'

He looks admonished, like a schoolboy. 'Yeah, I guess. But man, she spends all day breaking my balls, and she expects me to stick around for the rest of my notice.' The chided look gives way to a sadder one. 'Truth is, I liked working for Raine. He was a dude. Look...' He hauls himself up from the sofa. 'I'll show you what I've started.'

He gives Amber a tour of the digital editing suite and hard drives. It's almost as packed as the negative archive, but unlike the hard copies, it's all perfectly and logically ordered.

'This was a bat-shit crazy mess when I got here,' says Mika. 'Like, what the hell did the last dude do all day?' He goes into the editing software and navigates to a folder. 'I even made a start scanning in a few negatives.' He gestures at the big, slightly ancient scanner set up a few feet away from the screens. It's a model Amber has used before. It's old and obscure, but she knows you can get consistently great results from it if you know what you're doing.

Mika clicks a folder, and a grid of images pops up on-screen. Even at that scale, the look of film is distinctive in colour and tone.

'Can I take a look?' Amber asks.

Mika jumps up from the seat, and Amber slides in. She double clicks an image, and it fills the screen. Then she zooms in, moving the cursor around to examine the detail. She does this a few more times with some other photos in the set.

'Okay, most of these are all right, but have you checked the hypertone settings on some of the more contrasty ones?'

'Say what?'

'Look.' She gestures, and Mika leans in. 'That weird halo

effect on the highlights.' She points to a bright part of an image. It's subtle, but there's a slight banding round a bright area of the image where it meets a darker shade.

'Oh... uh... is it? I thought that was the film.'

'No, not the film — it's across a lot of these. See.' She points at a zoomed-in portion of another image to show him in detail. 'I'll have to rescan some of these.'

'Sure, if you think so.' Mika makes a sharp breathing noise and goes back to the sofa and his Diet Coke in a low sort of sulk. Amber doesn't say anything, just smiles to herself. Boys with tech, never as clever as they think they are.

It's a slow morning, moving boxes and sampling strips of negatives. Mika helps half-heartedly, but seems more interested in his phone.

Amber lays out the negatives in rows on a large lightbox embedded into a table next to the computers. She starts to pick over them with a magnifier. She can barely see the wood for the trees, but every now and then she finds an image of Benny's that reaches out and pulls her in. The praying soldier before a battle — then the same face hours later, shattered and hopeless. The scramble of protesters running from tear gas, their eyes streaming. A small child holds a handgun up against their own face.

A little after midday, Mika says he's going into the local village, Radlow, for his lunch. He pulls himself into some motorbike leathers that have been sitting in the corner and grabs a helmet. He reads the look Amber is giving him.

'Yeah, I know. Sometimes I think it's why Raine hired me, so we could talk bikes.'

'Yours is the bike out front? Or the scooter?'

'The scooter? C'mon.' He flashes a cocky smile. 'Don't

worry, I'll ride carefully.' And he leaves Amber alone in the room, thinking again about Benny's last hours.

Her mobile buzzes with a message. It's not a number she knows, but it's signed off as Sam. There is lunch ready for her in the kitchen.

As she goes back towards the house, a strong wind is blowing, and the dense stripe of beech trees shudders.

A quicker, more definite movement catches her eye. Something is running, small and low down. Then it stops and looks up at Amber, eyes shining. It is a small deer. She and the animal are locked together for a moment. Then the deer tears off, leaving just the wind in the leaves.

There is no one in the kitchen, just a spread of sandwiches and salads laid out under plastic hoods like a corporate buffet, and a note from Sam saying she should help herself. So she sits and eats in silence, taking in the kitchen, which does not seem to have a mark of Benny anywhere in it.

As Amber is finishing her lunch, Yvey comes in. She doesn't say much, but Amber can feel her eyes on her, as if she wants to say something but can't pluck up the courage. Sure enough, when Amber gets up to go back to the studio, Yvey follows a little distance behind through the door into the garden.

'Mind if I tag along?'

'Sure.'

Yvey runs to catch up, a darting quality to her movements. She reminds Amber strangely of the deer. She is pretty, and she will be very beautiful like her mother, but there's an uncertainty to her slightly elfin face, as if she's not yet comfortable in who she is.

'I've followed you for a bit,' she says. Amber doesn't quite get the phrasing, and the mental image unnerves her. Then Yvey holds up her phone. It clicks into place.

'Oh, I see. On Instagram?' She laughs.

'I really like your work.'

Amber pulls out her own phone from her pocket. She doesn't post very regularly on Instagram. She should do a better job at it. She should be better at social media all round. She should have a YouTube channel like all those men who rabbit on for hours with endless unboxings and tech reviews of the latest gear. It would make her more money than her actual photos.

She opens her own Instagram account and flicks to her followers. Then another piece falls into place: she remembers the strange way Yvey insisted on how her name should be said. She scrolls through her followers and finds the account: @_e_v. 'Oh, you're *EV*.' She laughs again. 'I follow you too. I like what you do.'

'Really?' Yvey sounds disbelieving. 'You're not just saying that?'

'Honestly.' It is the truth. Going on the average teenager, Yvey's Instagram should be a wall of selfies and party videos, but it's not. It's full of video art: short clips and loops of abstracted shapes and patterns; minimalist hyperlapses of racing shadows and changing skies; stuttering, horror-inflected crawls through the undergrowth.

Then Amber places the feeling she had when she arrived — the sense of familiarity to this place. She quickly scrolls through EV's images, and now she can see in the pictures fragments of the farmhouse and grounds. She scrolls back up to the latest post, one she hadn't seen before. It is taken at night in the studio clearing. The lights of the studio are full on, and the magic glass is open. The camera moves around the clearing in a sweeping motion, accelerating and decelerating in bursts. The shot is overexposed so the studio is white-bright at the centre of the image. Like a lighthouse, a burning beacon in the darkness.

9

AMBER

Yvey sits cross-legged on the floor, looking out at the clearing, throwing questions at Amber as she sorts through another box file. *How did she get started in photography? What advice does she have? Should Yvey stick with going to university? Should she take a year out and go to art school?*

Amber finds herself not able to give advice. In part because of how changed her professional world is from when she started, but mainly because her thoughts keep looping round to when she left college and Benny became her mentor, then her lover. And about how her career was nearly destroyed before it had begun by her mental collapse after the end of their affair. And how Genevieve's unwitting generosity was part of her salvation.

She tries throwing the questions back at Yvey, asking what she enjoys about her studies. She is in her final year at school, eighteen in the summer. But Yvey doesn't much want to dwell on talk of her current school, which she only moved to last year. She makes a glancing reference to the move being unexpected, and Amber detects something in her voice that implies it was against her will, the result of something she doesn't want to talk about.

Finally, stuttering and uncertain, Yvey asks about Benny. Amber knows these questions have been coming. She knows this girl might want to connect with someone who knew her father.

'What was my dad like when you knew him?'

Unlike when she looks at Genevieve, Amber can see the grief in Yvey's eyes. She remembers being Yvey's age, only a few years after she lost her own father. Almost the age she was when she met Johnny. Just a few years younger than when she was with Benny.

That thought feels shocking. Yvey seems still so much like a child. But Amber remembers how mature she felt she was at that age. How finally confident that she was ready for the world. It felt like such a time of possibility. Before everything had narrowed, broken her a little.

'Your dad was...' She struggles to find the right answer. She wants to be able to speak honestly, but is caught between two sentiments. She wants to be kind to Yvey, and to be able to talk about the talent and charm Benny had. Because despite everything, she can still make herself remember those things.

But the other feeling is there too, with its different set of answers. She wants to warn Yvey against men like her father. She wants Yvey to understand that sometimes you have to know the hard truth about the people you love.

Amber sticks to her script. She tells the simple story she tells anyone who asks about her and Benny: about his mentorship, about the generosity of the Bayard Foundation, about how they gradually lost touch. She has got it down pat. But it still hurts a little to lie to Yvey.

'When did you see him last?' Yvey asks.

'Years ago.'

Yvey looks disheartened, as if she had hoped that Amber might be able to give her something else, something recent, to hold onto. As if there are bits of Benny's memory scattered around the world, and she can collect them. Amber knows the feeling; she remembers that part of grief.

'I'm really sorry. I wish there was something I could say.'

'S'okay. I know you get it. Your dad died when you were young, didn't he?'

The question is jarring. 'Yes, how did you know?'

'Uh, dunno. I read it in a profile of you, I think.'

Amber doesn't remember talking about it publicly, but maybe the fact made it into someone's write-up. Not that she has given an interview in years. Her years of bright young promise feel a long way behind her.

'How did he die?'

'He drowned,' Amber says simply, and the feeling of that day is right there in the room with her. It was one of those childhood holidays that Amber was too old for. She didn't want to go to Cornwall with her bickering parents. She wanted to be with her mates.

She remembers not blaming her dad for going swimming rather than sitting on the beach being nagged. She had begun to suspect he only took up triathlon to have more time away from her mum. They didn't hate each other, but they didn't love each other either. They had married too young. They were staying together for the sake of the children, Amber could already see that. But she was fourteen; her brother was eleven. Her parents didn't need to do that. She just wished they would end it, go their separate ways. She loved them both all the same, especially her dad. His size and strength. His compassion. His determination.

He was a good swimmer, confident in the sea. He knew what he was doing when he went out beyond the shallow of the bay, past the craggy headland. He wouldn't have put his life in danger like that. He wouldn't leave her like that.

But they said he must have underestimated the tide.

She remembers running up and down the beach, calling out at the sea. Then shouting, then screaming. The sky seemed to fall in on her, the rocks around tumble and crush her.

They didn't find his body for three days.

And the memory mingles now with a later one. This time she is on the ocean herself, tipping in a small boat in heavy darkness. Her hand is still bleeding into the makeshift bandage she has wrapped around it. She is keeping her eyes on the dark horizon. She is being sick over the side into the black water. She knows she has to go through with it, but she still can't bring herself to look down into the boat.

Yvey's voice cuts into the memories. 'I'm sorry to bring it up. I just thought you were someone I could talk to about this. I'm sorry, it's just I miss my dad and...' She sniffs back tears and stands up with a quick spring of the legs.

'It's okay. I understand, I really do. I know you want to be able to change what happened. I know you're probably angry.'

'Dad was sick, you know. He tried to pretend he wasn't. But I know it was really bad.'

'Sick?'

Yvey doesn't answer. She is looking at a faint shape moving behind one of the panes of glass that Amber has switched to opaque to block out the glare. The glass slides back a little way, and Mika comes in.

Was he dying? Amber wants to ask Yvey. She sees Benny in her mind, not as she remembers him, but in that last interview. Physically reduced, his voice tired and cracking.

Yvey is standing now, looking away from Mika. They don't say anything to each other. It's as if they can't even make eye contact, just as Mika was with Yvey's mother. Yvey gives Amber a thin smile and slips out into the clearing.

Amber goes to the glass and watches as Yvey walks away. The silver birches around the entrance to the tunnel through the woods stand like the ghosts of trees. Yvey disappears into them, back along the path to the house.

10

AMBER

Johnny is holding Amber's hand as they walk between the trees. The ground underfoot is soft and mulchy. They come to the edge of the beeches and find a small hut surrounded by stacks of wood ready for chopping with a heavy old axe leaning against the logs. They stand in the slanting sun, their silhouettes stretching out with the trees onto the open field.

Johnny arrived late in the afternoon, driving one of those rental cars you book on an app, and Sam showed them both to their bedroom. Johnny sat on the edge of the bed and bounced a few times, but it didn't creak. Then he nosed around the en suite, which was full of huge mirrors and a big bath. He came out, making his eyebrows dance at Amber. He grabbed her for a kiss, which lengthened and deepened. Then she pulled back.

'Sorry, you probably need to get back to work.'

'No, let's just go for a walk.' She'd had enough of craning over negatives. Her back was sore, and she was starting to get a headache. She did want to be with Johnny, just not some-where she could feel Benny's shadow falling across her. So they walked the extent of the grounds and ended up at the edge of the beech wood.

Watching their shapes in the sun, she squeezes his hand. Then she pushes her body into his, letting him wrap himself around her.

'I love you, Johnny Copeland,' she says.

'I love you too, Amber Ridley,' he replies, reciting his half of their little in-joke about their names. It had never occurred to either of them that Amber should change her name when they were married, but members of their family still sent letters to Mr and Mrs Copeland.

'How is Lump?'

'Lump is fine.'

'Are we really going with Lump?' says Johnny, popping the *p* of the word. 'Can't we do better than Lump?'

Amber doesn't answer, just hugs Johnny tightly. She knows the dehumanisation of her pregnancy is a survival mechanism. They don't even know the sex of the baby; they have chosen not to. *She* has chosen not to. Johnny would have been happy to know. He says he doesn't mind what it is, but Amber knows he wants a boy. He probably wants at least three boys so he can start a band, but it's a little too late for that.

Being a dad is something Johnny has always craved. More than Amber craves motherhood, she sometimes suspects. Maybe her desire for a child has been chipped away at, failure after failure. But if the life inside her makes her fear as much as hope, with each passing day it has brought her closer to Johnny. She is glad they have stuck at it despite her doubts.

She saw what happened to her parents, marrying young, marrying too soon. She hadn't wanted to be like them — to stick with the first man she fell in love with when she was barely twenty. But she had. She sometimes wishes she met

Johnny ten years later. Then she could have delayed falling for him, and avoided betraying him. Even if the betrayal, and everything that flowed from it, was what made her realise just how much she loved him.

'How's the archive?' asks Johnny, sensing her reluctance to talk about the baby.

'It's interesting. I'm not sure I'll take the job — I'd rather be taking my own photos than sorting someone else's.'

'Okay,' Johnny says simply, as if he has decided not to fight her about this. 'There'll be other work.'

She feels relief and is decided. She'll do what she can this weekend, give Genevieve some initial thoughts, recommend someone else for the job, and that will be the end of it. This will be the last time she has to think about Benedict Raine.

'I'd like to do a little more this evening. Then I'll come in for dinner. There's a grand piano in the house. I'm sure Genevieve wouldn't mind if you–'

'I found it. Sexy little Bosendorfer.' He grins and wiggles his fingers.

They walk back to the clearing together, and Johnny heads down the tunnel of trees towards the house. The path is lit now, a line of LED lights along the ground snaking into the thicket.

Mika is leaving the studio as Amber comes in, togged up in his bike leathers.

'Cool to meet you, yeah,' he says. 'You coming again?'

'Not sure. Probably not. Unlikely before you're off.'

'Well, good luck, yeah. Don't let Genevieve be too much of a bitch to you, will you?'

And he slips out through the crack in the glass, bouncing his helmet in his hand.

Amber sits back down at the table with the lightbox where she has been reviewing negatives. She has a file open she'd been working on when Johnny arrived. It's really early material, from when Benny was just starting out in the late seventies, and a lot of the negatives are in poor condition. But there's a beautifully bleak sequence of a vanished English industrial landscape: grime and soot and hard, lined faces. And another from a similar period taken in Belfast. Kids playing feet from the rifles of British soldiers. Angry young men throwing rocks and bottles. Hard eyes staring out from under balaclavas.

She goes down another layer of envelopes in the box. There is a free-floating strip of negatives sandwiched between envelopes. She picks them out.

Immediately it is clear these are not like the others. They are not as old and of a different film stock. Black and white, Ilford 3200. A fast film: one you would use for shooting in low light.

Holding the strip up to the light, Amber can see it's from the beginning of a roll of film, partially blacked out, with only two and a half clear frames. She lays it out on the lightbox and bends over it with the magnifier. The first image is unclear, half-burnt out by exposure outside the camera. It looks like the blur of someone's hand half-covering the lens. The owner of the hand is not in focus, indistinct in the background.

The next two are clearer.

She feels her breath tighten as she sees what they are. She doesn't want to believe it. She glances around her. The studio is silent and empty. She takes the strip of negatives to the scanner and loads it in. The machine clicks and whirrs, gives a small beep, and the images materialise on the monitor.

There are two pictures, almost identical. They are of a figure sitting in profile, framed in the rectangle of an open sliding door. It is a woman holding a wine glass. Even in negative Amber can see who it is.

Blood swirls in her ears. Her chest is constricted.

The photos are of Amber sitting outside the cottage by the sea, framed in the open doorway.

Just some photos of her, she tells herself. That's all they are. A couple of lost pictures in the wrong box, that's all. They don't say much, not on their own. Not without the rest of the film.

The rest of the film.

She plunges back into the box file, emptying its contents out onto the table. She opens every envelope, holds every strip up to the light. But there is nothing more.

She stands and looks out into the clearing. The light is fading fast. She flicks the switches, turning the remaining transparent windows to opaque, as if she can shut out the world. As if she can imprison in here all the secrets that these photos hold. Not just what they show, but what came next.

11

BENNY

Saturday, 10 November 2001

I drank too much that first night to do what I'd planned. We stumbled upstairs and had hungry, clumsy sex, as if we had only freshly discovered each other's bodies, but were losing faith in our own.

I wasn't in bad shape back then, but I knew I couldn't match that lithe hardness I had seen in Johnny Copeland. And I could sometimes sense Amber's disappointment in my body. It was something she could get past, not embrace. Her body, I wanted every piece of that.

I slept in very late the next day. I was shattered and only just letting myself acknowledge that. I had been in Afghanistan for weeks. Shells and IEDs were still going off in my dreams. I woke and came downstairs to find Amber padding around in my slippers and one of my shirts.

'Fetching.'

'This floor is cold.'

I kissed her and ran my hands up under her shirt. She let them stay there for a little while, then slipped away from me.

I remembered then the first thing she had said to me that had crossed the line, that had confirmed that we were going to be more than friends. *I love your hands,* she had said, watching them move as I spoke. It was late and we were drunk. Nothing else happened that night. Nothing happened for weeks after that night. But I knew then that it would.

'I should get dressed.' She trotted upstairs, and I went to the window, watching the ripple of the water caress the sand.

It was a cold, still day, the air hazy and damp. We stayed in the cottage till it started to clear, then drove along the coast to where my face was a little less familiar. Amber decked herself out in one of those furry-hooded parkas, so her face was buried in there whenever we were outside. It was a shame, I wanted to look at it more. We found a dreary little café and had tea and cake. I felt as if we were somewhere back in time, conducting a black-and-white affair from an old film.

We walked a little way inland and found the ruins of an old chapel. A young family was there, and a toddler ran up and down the mossy ground, her shadow flickering in and out of the pools of light cast by the sun streaming through the empty windows. I had started to wonder if I would ever have children. Gen had never really shown much interest in the idea. I could imagine having them with Amber.

We made our way across fields back to the beach. A pair of skeletal horses slouched away from us. It was cuttingly cold as we stomped down through the marram grass onto the beach, and Amber huddled into me. The hazy sun was setting in a grainy sky, but there seemed to be no colour to it. The afternoon existed in monochrome, the sands stretching out with intermittent stripes of the groynes reaching in from the sea.

I felt Amber pull away from me a little. She was craning her neck to look back in the direction we had come from. A couple of hundred yards back from us was the silhouette of a man, the dying sun over his shoulder. I felt Amber shudder, and she pressed into me again.

'You all right?'

'Dunno. I thought... nah, doesn't matter.'

'What?'

She looked back over her shoulder, and I did the same. The figure wasn't there anymore, just the long grey beach, the rippling dune grass, and a piece of stray plastic billowing in a gust of wind.

'Can we go back now?' said Amber.

We turned off the beach and walked back along a sandy path, looking for a different route back to the car park. The path ended in a track, which then opened up into the road. I suggested we retrace our steps rather than walking along a road in the gloaming. I started to turn back, but Amber slipped her hand out of mine and went on forwards.

'What is it?'

There was a car parked just at the end of the track where it met the road. A hatchback, one of those sporty ones with a spoiler at the back and double exhausts. It was quite beaten up. The front left panel had a big dent in the side, and there was a rust patch around the wheel and onto the bonnet.

Amber took another half dozen steps towards it and stopped, frozen to the spot.

'What is it?' I asked. But I knew already what she was going to say.

'It's the car. The one that was following us.'

12

AMABER

Questions ricochet around Amber's head. Why did Benny keep these negatives? What are they doing floating around in a box of pictures from 1978? What if someone has already seen them? Has Mika? Genevieve?

And where are the rest of them? She has found three images out of thirty-six that would be on the film. If Benny kept evidence of that evening, did he keep the rest? Did he keep the photo Amber took at three in the morning, her bare feet icy on the cold stone floor of the cottage? Did that picture even come out?

She finds she is scratching the light scar on the palm of her right hand, as if the wound is reawakening.

She tries to calm herself. Benny wouldn't have been so stupid. Maybe this is all there is. Just a scrap of images to remember that weekend, squirreled away where no one would think to look. She holds that thought and tries to let it give her a little comfort, but all she can think of is those shelves and shelves of hoarded images.

She scoots back to the scanner and pulls out the negatives. She almost tears them up, but stops herself. It's just a feeling, fallout from the unanswered questions going off like bombs in her head.

She takes an empty brown envelope from the table and puts the images inside. Then she goes to her handbag, rummages around and finds a pen drive. She takes it to the computer and saves the scans onto the drive. She puts the drive into the envelope with the negative and stuffs it away in her handbag.

She sits in silence and stillness, but her thoughts shout and contort.

The door of the studio rolls open. Amber jolts. A grunted breath escapes from her mouth.

'You okay, babe?'

'J, sorry, you made me jump.'

'I think we're needed for *supper.*' He puts on a posh voice for that last word, one he would never use.

She is looking at him, with the monitor a little to her right, facing at an angle to her. As he advances towards her, she glances to her right and sees what she has done. She's saved the pictures and stashed the envelope, but the images are still up on the screen, framed in the electronic tool panel of the scanning software.

She's over on the wheels of the chair as quickly as she can go. Minimising the program. Gone. Her body tingles.

'I'll be in. Just thirty seconds.'

'Really thirty seconds? Or one of your ten-minute thirty seconds?'

'Look, two minutes, tops. I just need to tidy up a bit and shut everything down. I'll be right with you.'

'Okay, okay.' Johnny backs away again towards the door. 'Grub looks amazing, by the way.'

He is gone, and she breathes.

She goes back to the monitor and closes all the programs down, double- and triple-checking there are no files left on the computer.

She hasn't been left any instructions about locking up, but she turns off all the lights and pulls the doors closed. Without the light from the studio, the clearing is now very dark. The only clear light is coming from the LEDs that glow along the path back to the house. She moves quickly across the clearing, but can't help glancing back at the studio, square and squat in the gloom. In the moment that she pauses there is a sound, then a flicker of movement, something dark wiping between two trees.

Just a deer, she says to herself, hurrying towards the lighted path. But as she reaches it, the LEDs blink out. She is blind for a moment, a hundred tiny globes floating on her retinas. She freezes, not even aware of where the path is under her feet.

She gives herself a few seconds for her eyes to adjust, stock-still, her heart thumping. Through the beat in her ears comes the sounds of the woods. Every crackle and breath. And something else now. Something moving. Is it footsteps? Very soft, as if trying not to be heard.

Amber tries to orient herself. The sound is behind her. She turns, facing the studio, which is visible only as a block of shadow. Now the sound — soft and steady — is to her right, as if it's picking its way around the edge of the clearing.

She fumbles for her phone, jabbing for the torch icon. She swings the light around the clearing — wanting to see and not wanting to see. The light strobes off the trees, catching and illuminating the silver birches around her. Her mouth is open to call into the darkness, but nothing comes out.

Then the sound is back. Not slow and steady anymore. It is the fast crack of human footsteps moving through the trees alongside her. Towards her? Parallel to her? She can't tell.

She doesn't wait to find out. She shines her phone torch at the path under her feet and runs.

13

mber takes a minute to catch her breath, and steps through the French doors to find a kitchen that is empty but for the smell of cooking. It makes her feel momentarily queasy, and she sits down at the table for a second just as the doors click again, and Johnny wanders in.

'Hi, babe.'

'Hi, J.' She forces calm into her voice. 'Did you come back to the studio?'

He frowns. 'No, the lady of the manor said she was just getting changed, so I nipped out for a cheeky vape.' He wiggles his e-cigarette at her and looks a little closer. 'You okay?'

'Yeah, sorry, fine. The lights on the path went off. I just got a little spooked. Dark woods at night, y'know.'

'Oh, I dunno, I like it.'

'Yeah, but you're weird,' she said, glad to find some humour, some normality between them. But it's just an inch deep. Inside, she still feels cold and shaky. 'You know what, think I might change too. Just be five.'

In the bedroom, she stows her handbag with the negatives and pen drive in it under her side of the bed, bundling a jumper next to it so it's not visible. She goes to the bathroom and splashes cold water on her face. It's not enough to make the feelings go, so she quickly showers and changes.

When she returns to the kitchen, Genevieve is holding a large glass of red wine, and Johnny is taking long sips from a beer. Yvey is there too, a little set back from everyone else. She has what looks like Coke in her glass, but there is a bottle of Jack Daniel's close to her on the sideboard.

'Sorry to be late.'

'It's fine,' says Genevieve soothingly. 'What can I get you?'

Amber wishes she could have a glass of wine. What she really wants is a cigarette. She hasn't smoked regularly in fifteen years, but she really wants one now. Just a drag.

'Something soft. Have you got fizzy water?' Amber feels she could ask for a specific brand and Sam would appear out of one of the cupboards and hand it to her on a tray with a straw. But Sam is nowhere in evidence. She wonders when he left, or whether he's still here somewhere in the house.

'I haven't thought to say congratulations,' says Genevieve. 'Do you have a due date? Johnny was telling me it's been difficult for you.'

Amber throws a glance at Johnny. He is very free with the way he talks about their personal life. She likes to keep things tighter to her.

'July,' she says simply. She has refused to allow herself to focus on the precision of a date that seems mythical. She lets Johnny jump in, content on this occasion to let him talk about their baby while her mind settles.

Genevieve serves the food. Amber is sure it is delicious, but her taste buds, heightened for months by pregnancy, now seem deadened to the flavours.

The four of them settle into conversation. Johnny is in ebullient form, full of opinions and jokes. Amber is glad — it allows him and Genevieve to dominate the discussion. Johnny talks about his music and how excited he is to be finally getting back into the recording studio at the end of the week with some old collaborators. It's in Manchester, so he plans to stay away for a couple of nights.

Their conversation drifts onto talk about travel, then what's happening in China and Italy, and whether the UK will go into lockdown. It feels both imminent and impossible. They seem to talk about everything but Benny. His absence is all around them.

Yvey eats mostly in silence. Every now and then she surreptitiously checks her phone until Genevieve scolds her. It elicits a roll of the eyes and a muttered complaint. She looks directly at her mother very little.

Amber remembers a similar period with her own mum, in the numbness of grief. They barely said a word to each other for days at a time. Later she realised the cruelty of what they were both unintentionally inflicting on each other. But it was a picnic compared to what came next.

Amber never understood why her mental unravelling was not immediate after the death of her father. It crept up on her. First came the refusal to eat enough, the anxiety and insomnia. Her concentration shot, she flunked her exams and had to resit and never regained the academic achievements of her early teens. Then came the nightmares and flashbacks to the day at the beach. And the outbursts of anger directed at her mother, throwing blame and unforgivable words at her. Their relationship never really recovered from that, and now Mum is locked away from her by dementia. She is unutterably sorry about that. She didn't have to lose two parents.

After dessert, Yvey slips off, and it isn't long before Johnny is yawning.

'Sorry, burning the candle and all that.' He stares at the empty wine bottle in front of him as if it is to blame for the number of times he refilled his own glass. 'I might turn in, let you two catch up, talk photos and stuff.' He goes towards the French doors, drawing his e-cigarette out of the side pocket of his jeans. 'Crafty vape before bed,' he says as if to himself and slips out into the back garden.

Amber fights the rising urge in her to join him, just calls, 'G'night, rockstar,' after him.

Genevieve gets up and puts the kettle on, and Amber feels the full weight of the knowledge that they cannot ignore Benny any longer.

14

When Genevieve comes back to the table and slumps in the chair, she looks suddenly tired. Failing to find the right words to say, Amber gets up to do the washing-up.

'No, please, don't worry about that.'

'But you've done so much. I'm so impressed by–'

'Just don't tell me how well I'm doing,' says Genevieve with a dry laugh. 'I think people always say *you're doing so well* to comfort themselves, not the bereaved.'

'Sorry, I didn't mean...'

'Not you, my dear.'

My dear. Those words crystallise a feeling Amber has about her relationship with Genevieve. She is only a decade or so older than Amber, but has always talked as if she is much more senior, and wiser with it. Perhaps it is the money, the semi-aristocratic lineage, the lifelong assumption of status.

'Thank you for coming, really,' says Genevieve, getting up just as the kettle comes to the boil. 'It's been so nice to hear Johnny play again. Such a talent. Hot drink?' Amber declines the offer, and Genevieve makes herself a herbal brew before coming back to the table. 'So, what do you make of the archive?'

'There's some really interesting material in there, particularly Benny's early work. You weren't kidding when you said he was a bit of a hoarder. But, can I say this now... I just want... I'm not sure if I can...'

Damnit, get the words out, she is thinking. *Just tell her you don't want the job. Run away from all this.* But then those negatives are back in her mind, and the rest of the roll of the film that is missing. *What if someone else finds the rest?*

'There's really no pressure, Amber. Take the job; don't take it. It's really up to you. But I did want you to see it. I did want you to come.' More of the certainty has gone out of Genevieve's voice. She looks down at the table, and Amber can see again through that crack in her shell at the current of loss underneath. 'Benny was just starting to slow down, to work less. I thought finally we'd be able to spend more time together. For a man who was so obsessed with capturing the right moment, his timing really was appalling.' She gives that dry laugh again.

'Yvey said he wasn't well.'

'That, my dear, is an understatement.'

'Was he...?'

'Yes, he was dying. Oesophageal cancer. They caught it very late. Stupid men — why are they so useless at going to a doctor? I think he might have had several months, but they would have been awful ones. And he was proud and vain. The prospect of all that suffering and indignity. But then...'

'Small mercies, I suppose,' says Amber, thinking of the bike crash, but immediately feels how callous she sounded. 'Sorry, it must still have been horrific when he had the accident.'

'Oh, I don't think it was an accident,' Genevieve cuts in

sharply. 'Though that does seem to be the line the coroner's going with. A dying man being reckless, yes? But...' She takes a mouthful of her tea. 'He loved that bike. Dreadful midlife-crisis nonsense. I think when he wasn't able to travel after his diagnosis, it became an adrenaline fix. He used to ride a lot at night. He wouldn't sleep. He'd be up all night in the studio or pacing round the garden, smoking. I still couldn't get him to quit. And he would go out in the early hours, tearing around the country lanes.' She tails off and stares into her cup. 'I hate that I wasn't here. I was visiting my mother. And poor Yvette, having the police turn up at the house the next morning.'

'I didn't realise. That must have been awful for her. What did the police say had happened?'

'He rode far too fast into a corner. Came off at high speed and got crushed under his bike. There didn't seem to be any other vehicle involved, and he was a good rider. He never went out if he'd been drinking, or pushed himself beyond his limits.'

As Genevieve speaks, Amber is back in the car with Benny, tearing through the village, rasping against the hedgerow, twisting and skidding to a halt. She is reminded of all the things Genevieve doesn't know about her late husband.

'I should have seen it coming,' Genevieve goes on. 'He used to talk about how he expected to die on the job. Shot or blown up, trampled to death by a mob. He once told me to push him off a bridge if he ever started getting senile. I just think he preferred the idea of a quick death over a slow one. I can see it being quite deliberate.'

'You think he killed himself? Did he give any warning? A note?'

'Wouldn't it be good if suicide worked like that? It probably only occurred to him when he was on the bike. Those decisive moments, you know. But looking back... I knew there was something pent up inside him. After he was diagnosed, he kept half-starting conversations. I never pushed him to talk, and maybe I should have. But perhaps you're right, Amber. Small mercies. I knew I was losing him. Maybe it was better this way.' There are fine tears running down Genevieve's cheeks, but she still has control of her voice. She wipes the tears away, and a silence settles between them.

It is Amber who speaks next. 'What time did it happen?'

'They didn't find him till the next morning, but they think it was sometime between one and three. Why do you ask?'

'Sorry, I don't know why. I'm never very good at knowing what to say. Which is stupid, because I should be an expert.'

'I understand. I suppose this must bring back memories for you.'

You have no idea, thinks Amber.

'Thank you for letting Yvette spend some time with you today. You must understand what she's going through even more keenly than I do.'

'Did you tell her about my father?'

'I did. I hope you don't mind. I just thought you and she could talk.'

'It's fine — it's just she told me she'd read about it in an interview, but I couldn't think where that would have been.'

'Funny girl. She seems so determined to cut me out of everything at the moment. If I'm honest, things have been difficult for a little while, and since she had to move school...' She lowers her eyes and doesn't go on.

'Well, you can tell her, whenever she wants to talk, she can.' Amber gives Genevieve a thin smile. She wants to reach across and hold her by the hands. But she also knows that as they have talked, she has told Genevieve a lie. Amber does, in fact, know why she asked what time Benny died. Because Amber is thinking about the time and sequence of what she did on that night.

She had gone to bed early, putting her phone on *do not disturb*. Johnny crawled in around midnight. Half asleep, she held onto him, buffeted by strange dreams. A little later she woke again, needing the toilet. In her usual way, she grabbed her phone to light the way to avoid turning the lights on.

There were two notifications on WhatsApp. A missed call and a message, both from the same number. It wasn't a number in her book, and the identity badge was just an anonymous white silhouette in a grey circle. She read the message:

I don't know if this is still your number. Can we talk?

She stared at the words for a long time, stranded in the dark on the toilet. She crept back to the bedroom, looking in on Johnny, dead to the world. She went to the kitchen and stood by the back door, as far from the bedroom as she could get in the house.

She called the number using WhatsApp, already thinking about encryption, about secrets to be kept from prying eyes. It rang and rang and finally died to nothing. It was two in the morning.

She deleted the message and cleared the record of the call from her phone. She went back to bed, blinking and awake till dawn. Already that night, she had a strong sense of who the message was from. It was a sense that surged when she found out about Benny's death.

Now, looking at Genevieve, sitting in the dead man's kitchen, Amber is certain. In her head, she can see Benny tearing up the road on his bike. She wonders if by the time she called him, he was on his bike, speeding to his end. Or was he already dead? And she wonders, if she had called earlier, what they might have said to each other.

What was it you wanted to tell me, Benny?

15

Amber is up with the sunrise. She opens the small window in the bathroom and looks across the stripes and patches of green beyond. She has long preferred mornings to evenings. The air is cleaner, the colours have more snap, and the light can only grow, not slip away.

Her mind feels a little reordered by sleep. She tries not to dwell on the things she and Benny might have said to each other. She also finds she is able to think more calmly about the negatives she found. Even if someone else has seen them, on their own they say very little. They could record a completely platonic moment. And she tells herself that Benny would not have kept the rest of the film. Those few frames were all he ever held onto, just a keepsake of a moment before it all fell apart, squirrelled away in a random box where no one would think to look.

It feels good to say these things to herself, even though she doesn't fully believe them.

Johnny is still sleeping, so rather than showering, she grabs her camera and goes out to walk the grounds. She lazily snaps a few photos, not really putting effort into the shots. In truth, she has always preferred photographing people. Objects and places might be beautiful, but for her they offer no real moment of connection. When you photograph people, you become part of the image. Even if you would rather not be.

After a light breakfast, she goes to the studio. She works quickly and more systematically than yesterday, taking strategic samples from the box files rather than trying to delve through them one at a time. She pretends to herself that this method has nothing to do with increasing the odds of stumbling across the rest of the negatives from the cottage.

All the thoughts she has this morning are in part an act of willpower. She is falling back on all the cognitive tricks she learned first from psychologists when she was a teenager, and then relearned from books when she was in her twenties. It is a little toolbox she can reach into when she needs to shut down the anxiety and catastrophic thinking.

But as she works, the good and bad thoughts come and go in waves: relief she has not found the rest of the film, and dread that this means it might still be in there somewhere.

TOWARDS THE END of the morning, Yvey saunters in and sits cross-legged on the floor, her headphones on. They smile at each other, but don't say much. Yvey just lets Amber work, and Amber can see her flicking through Instagram on her phone. Amber thinks about their interrupted conversation yesterday, and Genevieve's hope she might be someone Yvey can talk to.

Amber puts down the frame of slide film she has been holding against the lightbox and spins in her chair to face Yvey. She tries to ease in, asking her about some of her video art, but Yvey only half engages. So she holds her breath and dives in.

'Your mum told me about your dad's diagnosis. That must have been really hard. If you need to talk about what you're feeling...'

'Does it help? The talking.'

'Sometimes it can.'

'Doesn't stop him being dead though, does it?' Her voice is calm, but there is a low note of anger that breaks through more clearly in the next sentence. 'He should have had more time.'

'I know, it doesn't seem fair. Has your mum... has she said anything to you about...' Amber deliberately leaves the sentence hanging. She doesn't want to confront Yvey with Genevieve's ideas. But she does want to know what the girl is feeling, how much and what she is trying to process. Yvey's response is immediate.

'Yeah, Dad didn't kill himself, if that's what you mean.'

'I know it's hard to accept.' *And why should she accept it?* Amber never accepted it when people suggested that was what her own father had done. They were seldom direct about it, but they dropped their hints. They asked why such a knowledgeable sea swimmer would go out beyond those rocks in that tide.

'I know Mum thinks it was suicide. But he wouldn't do that.'

'I'm sorry, I shouldn't have...'

'It's okay,' she says, but she doesn't look it. She looks very sad and very lost. Amber wants to give her a hug, and has one of those moments where she realises how distant she has been from her close friends, how much she misses their physicality. She hopes this year will be different.

The glum look goes from Yvey's face, as if she is forcing herself to seem brighter. She stands up and comes over to the lightbox. The slide film on the box is a set from the early 2000s, right at the end of the film era: vivid Kodachrome of India, a deluge of reds and greens and rich browns.

Amber is about to start talking to Yvey about the images when a buzz from her right distracts her. It is her phone, glowing softly with a new notification. She picks it up. A WhatsApp message. She unlocks the phone with a press of her thumbprint. Probably Johnny being lazy, she is thinking.

It's not Johnny. It's an account she doesn't have in her phone. Just a mobile number and a white silhouette in a grey circle. She thinks back to the message and missed call the night Benny died. But it's not that number either. And it's not Sam. It's someone new.

The message is a picture. She has her WhatsApp set so it doesn't automatically download the images. There is just a blurred box on the screen, teasing a preview of the photo. But even in the blur she can see the frame within the frame. She can see there is a sitting figure. Even before she taps to download the full image, she has a tingling sense of what she is going to see.

It is a woman holding a wine glass, sitting in profile. She is framed in the rectangle of a sliding door, pushed open. It is Amber at the cottage beside the sea.

The phone buzzes again. Another message. Just words this time.

I see you.

Amber feels the floor go underneath her.

16

Friday, 31 January 2020, 2 a.m.

The road ahead is a tunnel of black. Just the small rolling cones of light from my car's headlamps and the weaving red dot of the motorbike's tail light. He is going fast, taking the curves in the middle of the road.

I accelerate to catch him. My lights flash off the pale trunks of the passing trees and glow in the patches where the rain hasn't dried. The vibrations of the uneven tarmac rise up through the car, into my hands wrapped tight around the steering wheel.

I'm closer at the next corner. I watch as the rider leans strongly into it. When he straightens, he flicks his head back to see who is behind him.

We are on a straight. My foot is right down on the accelerator. My headlamps are on full. A few more seconds and I'm right behind him. He tries to move a little to the side to let me overtake, but I'm not interested in that. I ease off.

I think for a moment he is going to brake, pull out to the right and drop behind me. Or squeeze by on my inside. I give the wheel a flick back and forth, swerving in the road. He opens up the throttle again and pulls away.

We take the next curves more steadily, and it feels as much a race as a chase.

'Are you enjoying this, Benny?' I say to him in my head. 'I think a little bit of you is. Is there a void that's felt empty for a while? Have you missed this thrill? Isn't this how you would rather it happened?'

The road is open now, fields on either side, long and straight, rising up. Both of us are pushing our speed. He is getting away from me. But then we're back in the cover of trees, and the road starts to wind again.

I'm a bit too eager on a corner, and I nearly lose it, the side of my car fizzing as it scrapes along the undergrowth. But it gets me close, really close. I'm almost touching the bare back tyre of his bike with my bumper.

I know my lights must be blinding him now if he looks in the mirror, but he keeps his head down and forward, giving it all he dares on the next bend. Another brief straight and he's away. But I know the next corner. A zigzag warning sign in its red triangle zips past, then the black-and-white stripes of the chevrons are ahead.

He brakes at the last minute. I brake a moment later, slamming to a halt, but not before I've caught the back wheel of the bike as it turns. My car skids a little, and I steer into it, just on the edge of control. But Benny has lost his. I see the bike wobble, Benny struggling to hold it, then the front wheel goes the wrong way, and it almost flips. It is down, on top of him, still moving. It's ploughing forwards along the road and into the crash barriers. They bend and buckle with the impact.

I cut my engine, and the noise of the bike fades too. For a moment there's no sound at all other than my own breathing in my head like a hurricane.

I watch for a few moments. Then I see movement. A foot twitching and flapping, then a hand.

I grab a small pouch from the glove compartment and reach down into the passenger seat footwell, where my hand finds a motorcycle helmet. Just to be safe. Just so he can't see my face if anything doesn't go to plan.

Then I'm out of the car and round to the boot. I take out the petrol can, stick the pouch under my arm, and reach back in for the torch. It's one of those big powerful Maglites that could double as a cosh.

I get to him and am relieved to see he's completely trapped by the bike. Still moving, but fitfully, and with no sounds coming from under his helmet. I shine the torch at his leathers. They seem to be intact, and I can't see any blood, but I don't know what it looks like inside. Even so, it's hard to take. I almost throw up inside my helmet, but just manage to keep it down.

I go a little closer. 'I'm so sorry, Benny,' I say softly. 'But it's better this way. Better for everyone.'

I feel the weight of the petrol can in my hand and put it on the ground next to me. I take the pouch from under my arm, feeling the shape of the syringe full of the potassium chloride I've cooked up. Lots of low-sodium salt and a bit of bleach. Enough to stop his heart.

Using either is a risk. But leaving him alive is a bigger one now.

I lean over and see the petrol cap on the bike is still intact, and there is no petrol leaking from the tank.

No, that won't do.

I take out the syringe.

I feel sick again. This time I vomit in my mouth and have to swallow it.

I'm weak. I can't do it. I can't breathe.

I go back to the car, pulling off the helmet, gasping. I look at the dashboard clock. Quarter past two in the morning. How long can I wait? How long before someone else comes down this road?

I give it ten minutes, then twenty, then half an hour. Each minute passes like a year.

I get out and go back to the bike. Benny's body is still. Carefully, I pick my way around the wreckage and pull the edge of a glove down. No response. I take his pulse. Nothing. I step back. It is over.

Benedict Raine is dead.

17

Amber is aware of Yvey speaking to her, but her words are white noise. Amber presses the side of the phone, and the photo disappears. She needs air. She goes to the door of the glass box and slides it open. Breathing slowly, she looks out into the clearing and the woods beyond.

I see you.

Yvey has come to her side. 'You okay? What's up?'

'Sorry, I just... I just got some bad news about a friend.' She reaches inside for a memory, something to embellish a story, but she lets the feeling go. Never elaborate on your lies until you have to. Buy time to think. She's learned that.

'Oh... sorry.'

'Think I might just take a bit of a walk.'

She steps outside, but doesn't know where to go. She doesn't want to leave the studio, gripped by a wave of agoraphobia. And she doesn't want to be where anyone will see her — especially not Johnny, not Genevieve. But she's committed now and goes on out, walking around the studio and into the woods away from the house. The wind plays in the trees around her as she imagines walking on and on, never turning back.

She compels herself to look at her phone again, opening WhatsApp. But the image is gone. The message is gone. In front of her is written, twice over:

This message was deleted.

It takes a moment to remember that you can delete a message for everyone in a WhatsApp chat. Does it delete the image from your phone? Amber can't remember. She searches through her image gallery, through all the folders, but the photo is gone, as if it never existed, as if she imagined it. She has to look back at the thread once more.

This message was deleted.
This message was deleted.

She takes a couple of slow breaths, reaching for her mental toolbox, trying to repeat to herself the calm thoughts she had this morning about what she found in the archive. The thoughts feel even emptier now.

She thinks about the negatives and images in her handbag. Where is the bag? Where did she leave it? She is gripped by a need to destroy the negatives and the photos, before being overwhelmed by a sense of hopelessness. What's the point? Someone already has them.

She goes back to WhatsApp and types:

Who is this?

But she can't bring herself to send it. A tiny, childlike part of her brain is pretending that if she ignores it, then it's not real. She starts to bargain in her head.

Someone knows a secret about you, Amber. That's okay. You've lived with this secret before. You've always lived with this secret. It did send you mad, though.

A tiny laugh escapes from her mouth. Like a lunatic. She is allowed to think like that. She is allowed to call it *crazy* and *lunatic* and *mental*, because it is what *she* went through. It is hers. Hers like her secrets.

She walks slowly back to the studio. Yvey is gone, and there is nothing more from her phone. It does not buzz, and the screen does not glow.

AT LUNCHTIME, Amber steps through the French doors into the kitchen and feels as if her thoughts must be written all over her face. Johnny is at the table with his MacBook open and his headphones on, fiddling with tracks in mixing software. Genevieve is setting cold cuts out, and Yvey is dancing hot baked potatoes in her hands from the oven to the table. Mother and daughter appear to be in conversation, as if the force field that was there between them last night has broken down. The radio is on, lilting out classical music.

The scene is so calm and convivial. It is as if they are all in cahoots. As if this is all some sort of sick practical joke, and someone is about to shout *Surprise!* and project the rest of the pictures from the roll of film on the wall.

Amber sits down next to Johnny. He unplugs his headphones, leans over and kisses her on the cheek. She feels hot. He must notice her reddened skin.

'You okay?' he says very quietly, almost just mouthing it. She nods and forces a smile. 'I came to see you,' he says a little louder, but still under the hubbub of family conversation and music. 'But Yvey said you got some bad news and went for a walk.'

'Uh... yeah.' Her mind scrambles. It fixes without premeditation on her old friend Grace, thousands of miles away. Someone Johnny knew, but only fleetingly. A keeper of secrets. 'Yeah, it was Grace.' Amber lets herself pause, thinking Johnny might take a few moments to catch up. He is narrowing his eyes.

'You know, Grace Hughes. I was at school with her. Doctor, moved to New Zealand. Anyway, her... her husband, Dave...' She reaches for just enough detail. 'He had a nasty accident.'

'What happened?'

Her mind goes blank. She nearly says skiing, but quickly catches herself, remembering it is early autumn in New Zealand. *Shit shit shit.* 'Dave's into all sorts of extreme sports. It sounds like his quad bike rolled on him.' She feels a breath of relief leave her, convinced at her own plausibility. 'They think he's going to be okay. I found myself thinking about their kids... and I just had a moment. I needed a bit of air.'

Johnny reaches across and squeezes her hand, then places it on her stomach. And she hates herself.

IT IS a long time before she can think calmly and rationally about the message on her phone. It has helped to return to the studio, where she doesn't need to look at anyone. With all the windows switched to opaque, she feels almost protected by the isolation of the place. She is pacing. The movement is helping her think.

The names and intentions of the people who could have sent the message bounce around in her head. The actions of a jealous grieving widow tormenting her dead husband's love? What is there to gain in that? It doesn't square with Genevieve's kindness and generosity. Nor does Genevieve seem like a woman who has time for games.

And what might that picture of Amber mean to Yvey? It's from a time before she even existed.

She tries to think about Mika and Sam. She can see them less clearly and knows nothing of their history, their feelings, their real identities under the briefly glimpsed exteriors.

She even thinks about Johnny. She can construct an idea of him finding the pen drive and sending the message — but it bears no relation to the person she knows. He couldn't do this. He's too much on the surface, too easy to read. At least that's how he's always seemed to her. Maybe that's her blindness.

She feels almost dizzy and stops pacing, trying to stay for a moment in one place. She thinks about the rest of the negatives: the pictures she knows about, and the ones she doesn't. There are only two other photos on that roll she knows about for sure. Benny took one, and she took the other. Even though she's never seen it, it's the second of these, the one she took, that makes her feel cold to her core.

But what else was on that roll? What other pictures did Benny take that she didn't witness? There are still blanks, like spots of amnesia on her memory of that weekend all those years ago.

Amber presses the switches on the smart glass. It all goes from opaque to transparent in an instant. She looks into the stripes of the trees, overlapping in layers till less and less becomes visible. There is something she cannot see. Something or someone who is here.

Then she is moving again, through the door at the back of the room, and up the stairs to the archive. She looks at the rows of shelves, boxes and negatives, packed dense and

unknown. The feeling at the funeral comes back to her —
that illogical desire to be there to know that Benny has died.
To see that coffin resting in the church. To know that he has
gone and his secrets have gone with him.

She knows that he is dead, but it does not feel anymore
that he is gone.

18

BENNY

Saturday, 10 November 2001

I tried to reason with Amber as we retraced our steps back along the beach. She was adamant it was the same car she'd seen before. There was no point trying to argue her out of that, because I recognised the car too. But I told her she had to get out of her head the idea it meant someone was following us. She needed to stop building something sinister out of a coincidence.

'So it's the same car. That's not very surprising. He was going in the same direction as us.'

'Back there on the beach as well. I wasn't imagining it.'

'Imagining what?'

'I'm sure there was someone...'

'Someone what?'

'Someone watching us.'

'You sound... honestly you're sounding a bit...' I was going to say *crazy*, but I censored myself. It was too late, though. She knew where my thought pattern was going.

'Don't you dare. Don't you dare use what I went through against me. I shouldn't ever have told you.'

'I'm sorry. I just want us to try to enjoy this time we've got together.'

'Okay. Sorry.' But she didn't sound it.

'What is it you're worried about?'

'Honestly, it's not just the car. I'm worried about everything about this. About your wife, about Johnny. I'm sorry I'm jumping at shadows. I'm sorry I'm so stressed. I don't think I'm very good at this.'

'At what?'

'At having affairs with married men.'

'Men? There's someone else you're fooling around with? Why didn't you tell me?' I cracked a smile, and she mirrored it, but without meaning. I reached out for her hand and held it. She let me, but didn't really hold it back, just let it hang in my palm.

The sun had set by the time we got back to the car park. There were only half a dozen cars still in the big dirt square. In the far corner, the dancing shadows of a couple and their large energetic dog played in the gloom. My car was in the middle of the car park, with no others around it. But it wasn't entirely on its own. There was someone next to it, half stooping to look casually through the window. It was something I'd seen enough times before. People liked to have a nose around the old thing.

I didn't break my stride, and I didn't look at Amber. I just kept on towards the car. The man saw us and straightened. With a twist on his heel he was walking away. He was in shadow, at a distance, and wearing a thick coat. Even so, I got a sense of him: tall, broad across the shoulders. He moved with a slight roll to his walk.

We went to the car and got in in silence. Amber didn't even look at me. It was as if she already knew what I was going to say if she said anything about the man. I didn't speak to her either. I didn't tell her about the small dark worm of a thought that had started to wriggle at the back of my mind.

19

On the surface things appear normal for the rest of the Saturday, but Amber feels a heaviness in the air like a thunderstorm coming.

She makes a point of leaving the studio before it gets dark. The only thing she hears as she moves quickly back to the house is the voice inside her head repeating over and over:

I see you.

No demand, no threat. No indication of how much more they know, or which of the other pictures on the roll of film they have seen. She expects something else — another message, a signal from someone — but there is nothing.

Almost nothing. When she gets back into the house, Sam is there, and she wonders why he would be working on a Saturday evening. He and Genevieve stop their discussion abruptly as she comes into the kitchen. Sam has a folder in his hands, and he slowly closes it. He is dressed down, but still immaculate and fashionable.

Amber looks at him and can't place his age. When she met him the previous day, he struck her as someone in his mid-thirties, but now she isn't sure. In different aspects, he seems to flash an older face, like a trick of the light.

Amber manages to make small talk for a few minutes before the pair leave. They move upstairs to Genevieve's office, and Amber is the one left feeling shifty, loitering on the curve of the stairs like a furtive teenager spying on her parents. The door opens, and Amber scampers down and attempts to look casual, leafing through the catalogues on the front desk.

'Be seeing you,' Sam says as he leaves, a polite smile without much warmth.

Genevieve stays in her office, and the quiet calm of the house sits heavily. Amber wants to leave, but knows she can't do anything to raise suspicion or show alarm. She must retain the smallest amount of control that she can.

For dinner, on Yvey's request, they order pizza and all eat in front of a fire, even though it's a mild evening. Genevieve and her daughter seem less distant from each other, at one point remembering Benny to each other.

'You know it was here, this very spot, that I told your father I was expecting you?'

'Too much information,' says Yvey, her voice all teenager. But she is almost smiling.

Amber feels overwhelmed by the crushing conviviality of it. She makes an excuse and goes to bed early. Johnny, taking the wrong cue, follows her up. He takes a shower and comes out of the bathroom naked, his brown body shining, standing proud. He slides in next to her, his hands playing across her stomach.

She feels distant as they make love. Not disembodied, but rather the opposite, shrunk right down within her physical body, like hiding in a box in a small room of an echoing mansion.

When she finally sleeps, she has the same uneasy dream she has had sporadically for years. She is in an empty open space — a vast flat expanse with no colour or texture. She is being followed. Sometimes she can see her follower; sometimes she just knows she must keep going or the relentless dread will be upon her. Sometimes she can run, sometimes she is stuck, held by invisible hands or ropes. There is never any resolution to the dream. She does not get away and is not caught. It plays like a looped piece of music: again, again, again.

ON SUNDAY, Amber is glad to be leaving. At breakfast she asks Genevieve to come to the studio. As they walk down the path through the woods, she is convinced she is going to tell Benny's widow she cannot take the job. But as the two women stand in front of the rows of boxes, she knows she has no choice but to. She cannot leave this place — its photographs, its people — unexplored.

'I need a week to tidy up a couple of projects, but I can start the following Monday.'

'So soon? Are you sure? There's no real hurry. I thought you might need–'

'The money would be welcome,' she replies quickly, telegraphing to Genevieve the sense of this being a practical decision. It feels like enough cover to ask what she asks next. She has been looking at the scanner, thinking about the errors Mika made with its setting. She sees his face in her head — the bright blueness of his eyes and his lighthouse hair. 'Shame Mika isn't sticking around.'

Genevieve doesn't respond, and Amber works hard on the casualness of the next question.

'How did he come to assist for Benny?'

'Oh, through an agency. Benny arranged it.' Genevieve

flicks her hand as if swatting off a fly, and there is a finality to her voice. It is not something she wants to talk about.

'He's no Sam, clearly,' Amber says, trying to find a way to probe indirectly about the other man in this house.

'Well, quite. I don't know what I'd do without Sam.'

'Where did you find him?'

'Oh, he's been with us forever. Very loyal.' Again there is a sense of closure in the voice, as if this is a topic Genevieve doesn't want to explore.

Amber isn't sure what she was expecting to learn about these two men's identities, their histories or how much they could be trusted. She has half a question in her head about the other people who work on the property and with the Foundation, but it dies on her tongue. Because as she looks at Genevieve, the thought that has been worming its way around her head since she woke crawls back to the top. It's that it wasn't Mika or Sam who brought her here. Or anyone else. It's that the only person who had the power to pull Amber back into Benny's afterlife is the woman standing in front of her.

20

AMBER

There has been no sign of Yvey all morning, but as Amber is loading her bag into her car, she comes skipping out of the house, childlike again, dressed in her giant onesie.

'Do you mind if I give you my number, Amber?' she asks, like a shy girl asking a boy on a date. 'I'd like to.' She looks down at the ground.

'I'd like that as well,' says Amber, smiling. 'You can have mine too.' They exchange numbers, Yvey's thumbs flashing over the keys on her phone like lightning. Again Amber wants to hug her, but feels forbidden. Suddenly, Yvey is hugging her. Not a lingering hold, just arms thrown around her neck and a tight, fast squeeze.

'Sorry, I...'

'Don't apologise.'

Yvey looks at her feet, a little lost, and runs inside.

Amber and Johnny leave the house in their separate cars: his rental, hers the dull little hatchback that used to belong to her mum. They never needed a car when they lived in London, and here they are, absurdly, with two. The eight-year-old Amber — full of dreams about saving the planet — would not be impressed.

The empty-eyed and twisting sculptures follow Amber's retreat from the farmhouse. As she leaves the drive, there is a man standing there dressed in green overalls. She makes eye contact with him as she slows to turn out into the road. He doesn't smile, doesn't look away, stares straight into the car, expressionless. Perhaps she is imagining it. Perhaps he doesn't see her at all through the strong light reflected on the glass. But she cannot suppress a physical shudder, and she is glad that Johnny is not with her.

Half a mile later, she wishes he was. Driving home separately makes her feel uneasy, and dark thoughts crowd her mind about accidents, and illogical ones about reaching home and finding that Johnny has vanished en route. So she accelerates to catch up with him, and tails him closely along the country roads, not wanting to let him out of her sight.

THEY REACH HOME and park in the large gravel layby at the end of their potholed lane. Because, although they live right on the edge of the country, they don't even have space outside their house to park a car. Their front garden is tiny, with no room for a drive, and the surrounding land belongs mostly to the big house next door. Until recently, there was a large, noisy family living there. Now it is empty, shrouded in scaffolding and plastic awnings.

Their own house doesn't have space for a large family. Amber sometimes wonders if it even has space for a small one. It's not so much an objective lack of rooms, more the way that her and Johnny have spread out to fill every corner since they moved here from their rented London flat eighteen months ago.

It was Amber's mum's sudden deterioration that

prompted the move, and they hadn't really planned to stay. They both miss London and their friends, but the prospect of moving back to the city to have their baby didn't appeal. Amber likes being surrounded by so much green and open space. It makes her feel she might survive maternity leave — such that it is for a freelancer. And she likes being twenty minutes from a big teaching hospital. She has the route well mapped in her mind. The thought of being anywhere remote or clogged with traffic scares her. Even at the Raine farmhouse, she took a few moments to calculate the journey straight to the hospital. She knows if things go wrong, a few precious minutes could make all the difference.

Over lunch, Amber watches the news twitchily: the drumbeat rumours of lockdown, the fear that it is only a matter of time before the health service becomes overwhelmed and unable to care for her and her baby.

She thumbs through emails on her phone, distracting herself by reading a long and excited pitch for a new project with her frequent collaborator Ed Kapoor. Ed is a journalist with a great nose for a good feature and an uncanny knack of finding interesting people to photograph. He's the one who introduced her to Luiz and his friends, and she's always felt a little guilty he got none of the credit. But Ed doesn't mind. It's all about the story for Ed.

She can't muster the focus or enthusiasm to reply and, seeing the time, gets ready to go out again. This afternoon, she has arranged to visit her mum in the care home.

When she gets there, the home feels different since her last visit. It is more like a hospital: an increased disinfectant regime, more staff behind masks, and the communal rooms half-deserted.

Her mum seems far too young for what is happening to her. She is only in her early seventies. She lived on her own for so long, in her little rut of existence, that the early signs went unnoticed by others, and were wilfully ignored by her mum. Then came the sudden deterioration: the kitchen accidents, the furious outbursts, being found wandering in her nightdress across Port Meadow, looking for Amber's father.

Today, in the home, she seems calmer than she has been. The dramatic decline has levelled out into a slower process of wastage, like the fading of an old photograph left too long in direct sunlight.

Amber sits down by her bed and can see that her mum knows her and doesn't know her, the awareness flickering in and out like a radio scanning for stations. Amber tries to tell her again about the baby, but she doesn't think it registers. She is glad her brother already made her mum a grandmother three times over, when she was still able to experience and remember the joy.

So they sit in silence with each other, one mind lost, the other wandering. Amber finds herself thinking about Genevieve's elderly mother, and how Genevieve was visiting her the night Benny died. Her thoughts wrap round again to how awful it must have been for Yvey to receive that morning knock from the police. And, if Genevieve is right about it being suicide, she wonders what sort of man Benny was to kill himself on a night he knew his daughter would be alone. She shouldn't have to wonder this. She knows exactly the sort of man he was. But still. She thinks about Genevieve's absence and hears Yvey's words about Benny in her head. *He wouldn't do that.*

Amber gets up to leave. Her mum smiles at her and tells her that her daughter is coming to visit. There is nothing pleasant about the way her mum is falling away from awareness and from life, but sometimes, when she is peaceful like this, Amber feels a strange pang of envy. She wishes that many of her own memories were not always with her, bearing down on her.

And now, since she found the negatives, since she received the strange WhatsApp message, it feels as if the memories themselves have escaped from her head and are threatening her.

Her phone buzzes. It makes her skin tingle. She hardly dares look. She pulls it quickly out of her pocket, like plunging her hand into cold water.

It's a number she knows, and she relaxes.

You still alive? Coffee tomorrow? K.

Kay Hamilton. Amber knows she can't put her off any longer.

21

'C'mon, what's up?'

Kay leans a little towards Amber as she speaks. They are sitting on a bench in the shadow of what used to be Oxford's prison, but is now a posh hotel. Amber pulls her takeaway coffee close to her, feeling its heat radiate towards her chest.

Sitting with her mum, Amber really wanted to see one of her closest friends. But Hal is in London, Ryo is in Cambridge, and they've both got troubles of their own. The person Amber most wants to talk to is Grace, but she is in New Zealand. Grace, the keeper of secrets, and Amber's only confidante during her affair with Benny. One of only two people who knows about the affair at all.

The other person who knows about Benny — at least that Amber is aware of — is Kay Hamilton.

Amber stands up. 'Can we walk for a bit?'

Kay springs to her feet, the way she always does. She has one of those straight-up-and-down, athletic bodies, and there is never any slowness to her.

They walk out of the hotel complex onto the main road.

The city is still and quiet, its usual tourist hordes thinned out by a world that is closing.

'So?'

'I'm fine, really. Just been a strange few weeks.'

Kay and Amber have been meeting for coffee on and off since Kay stopped working a year ago. She calls it early retirement, but Amber knows she was laid off in one of the periodic decimations that have swept through newsrooms in recent years. Kay sold her London flat and moved out to a little village east of Oxford.

Amber and Kay's last coffee meetup was supposed to be just after Benny's funeral, but Amber made an excuse. She didn't want to hear Kay's opinion on whether she should take the job — or whether she should visit the Raine farmhouse at all. But Kay is a terrier, and there are only so many times you can put her off without making her nose twitch.

'It's about Benedict Raine, right?' says Kay.

'Am I that transparent?' This is no small fear for Amber.

'Freddie MacRory said she saw you at the funeral. Said she was sorry she didn't get to talk to you.'

'You're still in touch?'

'On and off,' Kay says with a shrug. Kay and Amber were at the same college, although a decade apart. The two women didn't in fact meet till much later when Kay was a reporter at *The Sentinel*, and Amber did a stint at the paper on a series of features. 'But I didn't know you were still in with the Raines.'

'I'm not, really, but Genevieve invited me. And I felt... well... I don't know what I felt.'

'What did she want with you? Freddie said she saw you and her in a deep-and-meaningful chat.'

Amber doesn't answer, just frowns at her friend.

'Oh, you know how the old girl likes to gossip.'

'And you don't?' says Amber a little sharply.

'What can I say? Old habits. Ear to the ground and all that.'

'Sure, sorry.' Amber isn't really annoyed with Kay. It's Freddie she's thinking about.

I see you.

She wonders again if Freddie ever put two and two together about her and Benny. She was often at the Raine London house parties back in the day. Did she ever see what was just below the surface? Could she detect what Johnny and Genevieve couldn't? These thoughts have always troubled Amber, but they have a darker hue now.

Amber tries to think what to say to Kay, but can't find the words. She is caught between silence and lies, between the knowledge that to say nothing will only intrigue her friend, and that any inventions will likely unravel. She decides to plot a middle course — to tell Kay a little without revealing all. Just the things other people know. So she describes Genevieve's proposal at the funeral and the invitation to the farmhouse.

'Returning to the scene of the crime, is it?' Kay says with a conspiratorial half smile.

'I never actually went to the farmhouse when we were...' Amber tails off.

Kay is looking expectant, but Amber has always been guarded about sharing details of her affair with Benny. It wasn't even something she told Kay about voluntarily. It was something Kay guessed, right at the time the two women got to know each other.

Amber remembers the occasion in strange patches of vagueness and absolute clarity. They were at the pub after work. Kay was monopolising Amber, talking a lot, asking plenty of questions. Amber had a strong sense Kay might be chatting her up. It wasn't an unpleasant sensation. They had located their mutual connection in Freddie, so Amber wasn't surprised or perturbed when Benedict Raine turned up in their conversation. Amber was on an even keel in those days, and Benny was years gone from her life.

She can't remember how she gave the game away. Was it how she spoke about him? Was it the way she tried to wriggle away from honest answers to Kay's questions about their relationship? What Amber does remember clearly is Kay giving a hard laugh, shaking her head and saying: *'Don't tell me you were one of those silly young things who let themselves get fucked by Benny Raine.'* Then Kay looked momentarily disappointed, and the sense that there had been something flirtatious to the conversation solidified.

But the truth was that Kay was right to say what she did. Amber had been a silly young thing. Benny had taken advantage of her. He had used his celebrity and renown. She might not have been the first woman he had done this to, but he had still made her feel special at a time when Johnny had seemed distant.

It is so hard to see through the shattered glass of what followed, but she really did want Benny back then. She didn't love him. At the time, she wasn't sure she loved Johnny either, and she allowed herself to believe he was sleeping around to assuage her guilt. She didn't really understand what it was to love Johnny till later, till afterwards.

What she felt for Benny was infatuation. His insouciant charm that never felt sleazy because it carried with it the hint of disinterest. The way his hands made her feel when they touched her. His goddamn talent. Because she was as guilty as millions of others of swallowing the idea of the difficult genius, the moral grey zone of the powerful artist.

But none of this was an adequate excuse. So yes, she got fucked by Benedict Raine, in ways Kay doesn't even begin to know. Even Grace never knew how the affair ended. Kay knows even less.

'Did you know Benny was really ill?' Amber asks Kay as they walk through Oxford, trying to move the conversation away from herself and towards Benny. She relates the talk she had with Genevieve about Benny's illness and the idea that he killed himself.

Kay is quiet for a moment, then shrugs. 'I suppose that makes a grim kind of sense. And this is what's got you out of sorts?'

'I'm not out of sorts. I have lots of sorts. Nothing but sorts.' She smiles weakly. 'It's just...'

'It's just what?' Kay makes a winding motion with her hand.

Amber is thinking about the things Yvey said to her, about how the girl was on her own the night Benny died.

'Oh, I don't know, I'm just not sure he killed himself. Doesn't seem right somehow.'

'I guess if he didn't kill himself, it was an accident.' Kay is frowning, as if failing to keep up with Amber's reasoning.

But it's no good, because there is the reasoning Amber is saying out loud, and there is the real reasoning going on inside, hidden from Kay. And this internal reasoning isn't logical. It's just a turmoil of thoughts about Benny's death, his final phone call to her, her invitation to his house, the negatives, the WhatsApp message. There is something in the corner of her vision, a flicker in the viewfinder that will only be revealed when the film is developed.

Amber finally recognises the tension she is feeling. She doesn't want to tell Kay the truth, but at the same time she is disappointed that her friend cannot shed any light on the situation. Kay has only ever known Benny at one remove — as a friend of Freddie, as a famous photographer, perhaps with a glancing professional acquaintance at one time or another.

They keep walking, turning right to head into town, but

are blocked by a burst water main spreading a pool of water into the road. A pedestrian, running to dodge a bus, jumps over the huge puddle. For a second, his reflection is caught in the water, the stride of his legs forming a perfect diamond.

Kay finally speaks again. 'You want to know what this tough old bird thinks?'

Amber manages a laugh. Kay is only in her early fifties, and on the occasion they've gone jogging together, has left Amber in the dust. Even so, she likes to play the wise old aunt to Amber. She is always the one giving the advice, rarely taking it.

'I think you have more important things in life to be worrying about than what Benedict Raine did to himself,' Kay says. 'What is it you owe him, anyway?'

It's a throwaway question, but it reaches right into Amber. Yes, she resented Benny for years. But they were also tied together by their shared guilt, by what she did, and what they did together to protect themselves from the consequences. It would be easy just to hate Benedict Raine, but to hate him meant hating herself as well.

Kay keeps going. 'Honestly, I think you've got more inter-esting work to be doing than looking after his old holiday snaps–'

'They're not...'

'Whatever they all are. Besides, you've got enough other things to be thinking about right now.'

Amber knows Kay is about to start talking about the baby. Sure enough, the next moment she is going on about the *little wee one.* Kay of all people, without a sentimental bone in her body. Sometimes Amber thinks Kay is overcompensating for her initial reaction when Amber admitted she was pregnant. It was almost as if Amber had betrayed the sisterhood in succumbing to the banality of parenthood. The moment solidified the asymmetry in their friendship and seemed to shine a spotlight on Kay's loneliness. And it did nothing to dent Amber's sense of what Kay might really feel for her.

But at least this talk of babies enables Amber to leave the conversation about Benny behind. They find their way to the centre of town and walk past the big art store on Broad Street. There is a window display of Benedict Raine prints for sale. At its centre, the Lebanese boy stares out at them: those fearful, vengeful eyes.

Kay finishes a question, but Amber doesn't reply. Because she has nothing to say all of a sudden. Something else is crowding into her brain. She has felt the soft buzz of her phone in the back pocket of her jeans.

22

AMBER

Amber doesn't take the phone out of her pocket. *It's nothing*, she tells herself, trying to dampen the dual desires to look at it right away and never look at her phone ever again.

She becomes aware Kay has asked her a question and is waiting for a reply. 'Sorry, what?' But she doesn't even hear the words the second time, because she has given in to the urge and pulled out her phone.

It's a message on WhatsApp. She is about to look at it, but notices Kay glancing over. She slides the phone away, the message unread. Her skin is tingling coldly as if someone is passing a low, steady electric current through her.

'You good?'

'Yeah, fine,' she lies. 'Look, I might head home.' Amber steers them down a side street, away from all the shoppers, feeling as if all their eyes are on her.

'I was hoping we could do a bit of shopping, maybe even get some lunch.'

'Sorry, I've got a lot on. Got to finish up some projects this week so I can start working on...' She doesn't continue, not wanting to mention Benny again. She feels the depth of the scepticism in the look Kay is giving her.

'How about we try again later in the week? Thursday, maybe?'

'Sure, okay, yeah, Thursday,' says Amber without thinking, desperate to break free so she can look at her phone.

'Grand, but you're all fine, sweetie? Really?' Kay gives one of her kind smiles. The sharp lines dissolve, and it becomes the kind of face you might tell all of your secrets to by mistake.

In truth, part of Amber does want to be able to tell Kay everything, to have someone she can completely confide in. She's never had that, not once in her life. But she knows what she does have. She has Johnny, and she cannot imagine her life without him. And she has begun to imagine a life with him and with their child. She has to protect that at all costs.

'Thank you, Kay. You're too good to me. I'm just having to adjust to a lot at the moment.'

'That's why I'm here to talk to, you silly wee girl. Whatever you need to say, I'll listen.'

'I know, and thank you. But talking doesn't always help, you know. Sometimes it's better not to.'

Kay gives her another sceptical look, but that's too bad. There can't be any more truth to Kay. There must only be lies and omissions. Amber should be able to do this. She has lied before. She has lied for years. But her capacity for lying feels as if it has worn off. Maybe it's the pregnancy, that lazy excuse of *the hormones*. In front of Kay, who has that kind smile on her face again, Amber feels exposed and transparent, a sense she is wearing all her thoughts and feelings just beneath the surface.

Before Kay can say anything else, Amber gives Kay the briefest of hugs and walks away. She goes along the lane, the old stone of two Oxford colleges rising above her. She is round the corner before she takes her phone out of her pocket and brings up WhatsApp. It's that anonymous number again. There is another photo, again a blurred box waiting to be downloaded. This time she can't see the outline of the image in the blur: it's just darkness with patches of light coming in from the right of the image.

She opens it. It takes a few moments for her to see what it is. It is slightly out of focus, underexposed, a woman standing next to a window, a towel around her.

Amber sees herself in the picture and remembers this photo being taken. She hears Benny's voice like it was yesterday, telling her she is beautiful. The light is moonlight, she recalls now, strangely strong. A clear cold night in a warm house.

Quickly, her fingers shaking, she takes a screenshot on her phone, determined to preserve the message before the sender deletes it. Then she saves the image to a separate folder on her phone, double-checking it is there, that it is real. And she doesn't hesitate with the reply this time.

Who is this? What do you want?

She glances round, half expecting to see Kay trotting nosily after her. But there is no one there, just the high walls reaching up either side of her. She stares at the picture she has just received, thinking too about the photos Benny took of her outside the cottage. There is only one other photo she knows that was on this roll of film. It was a picture Amber took.

She looks at her phone and keeps on looking at it, waiting for something else. A message, a reply, another image.

But nothing.

She tries to breathe regularly and walks on towards her home as if everything is fine, as if everything in her world is not about to fall apart. Her body feels strange and mechanical, as if she is having to instruct her lungs and limbs how to do their jobs. And in these quiet side alleys, she feels very alone.

She finds her way back to one of the main roads running to the north of the city, and is at first relieved by the presence of other people. But soon, all the faces start to push in on her. They are watching her. They know what she did. It is not true — she knows it cannot be true — but the feeling surges in her.

Then the vibration of her phone again against her hip, and she snatches it out of her pocket. Another image. She opens it and at first there is a sense of relief that it's not the photo she knows about. Then she sees what it is.

It is a dark image round the edges, with a soft splash of light in the middle. It is without blur, and the exposure is well judged. That same moonlight is coming in from the edge of the picture. It is falling on Amber, who is lying on a bed, just barely under a sheet.

Amber looks at her face in the photo. She is sleeping, oblivious to the photo being taken.

Underneath this image is a message:

What happens next, Amber?

She stares at the words. She is asking herself the same question.

23

Saturday, 10 November 2001

For an old cottage, it was warm. The heat from the wood burner downstairs filled the house, and steam wafted out from the open bathroom door. Amber stood by the window in only her towel.

'Do you think Genevieve suspects?' she asked. This was new, a spontaneous mention of my wife. I didn't want to engage with the question, so I pretended not to hear, rummaging around in my bag. She didn't let it go. 'You must have thought about it?'

I stuck my head up. 'Honestly, no. I would love to say she trusts me completely, but that's not true. But she likes you too much. You two get along. Even if she doesn't trust me, she trusts you.'

'That doesn't make me feel very much better about myself.'

'I think that's standard fare for this type of enterprise.'

'You make us sound like we're drilling for oil.'

'Why do you ask now, anyway?'

'I've been thinking about that car and that man,' she said.

'Please, not that again.'

'You don't think your wife would have us followed?'

I didn't answer.

'Well, do you?'

'Not by a piece of muscle in a Ford Capri. Please, let's not talk about her. And stop being paranoid.'

She didn't reply, just picked at the curtain, peering out into the night. It was a clear one, a moon just past full peering back at her. She opened the curtains a little wider, and her mood seemed to soften with her next words.

'Turn the light off, would you?'

I obeyed, and the only light now was from the moon, falling on her like a street lamp in its brightness.

My camera was on the chest of drawers next to where I was standing. I couldn't resist. I didn't have time to think much about the exposure, just twisted the lens to fully open and tried to keep my hands steady and nail the focus in a single movement.

She caught the snap of the shutter and flicked her head back to me.

'I told you, Benny, don't be a creep.'

'You looked so beautiful.'

'You're so corny.'

'I mean it. You do.'

'Just don't leave the film lying around for your wife to find.'

'I'm not a fool.'

'No, I don't expect you are,' she said with a smile.

I put my camera down and crawled across the bed to her. I reached out and gave the towel a firm tug, and it slipped from her.

What followed couldn't have been more different from the previous night. The clumsiness was replaced by slow care, the newness by a deep sense of familiarity with every curve, every taste and smell. The hunger was still there — I felt it at least — but it was steady and patient, pacing itself.

My hands ran all over her skin, finding their way inside her till her breathing tightened and shortened as if all the air had rushed out of the room and every breath was a desperate gasp for oxygen. Then, for the first time really, she explored my body with her lips and tongue, and took me in her mouth. She crawled back up me, took one wrist and pushed my hand hard down onto the bed. Then she was climbing on top of me, utterly confident in her body, perhaps ignorant of its power over me, perhaps knowing entirely. She arched her back, leaning away from me, putting her hands back and grabbing my legs. She didn't look at me as we fucked.

I thought about the way she had been with me that weekend. Emotionally distant, but physically available. Nervous, spooked by the car, talking about my wife. Then this *display*. That was the only word I could think of it as. I remember these thoughts coming together into a searing sense that this was the end of us. This was sex as a farewell gift and a reminder of what I was never going to get again. The next day, we would drive back to London, she would go back to Johnny, and I would go back to Gen.

Afterwards, we lay feet apart in the bed. There didn't seem anything left to say. I played the day in my head. Amber's words before we'd had sex crept in, and her suspicion about Gen. I tried to push the intruding thoughts away, but they nagged at me. I wouldn't put it past Gen to send someone to spy on me. But they would be someone discreet, and I'd never know about it until I got the divorce letter from her solicitors.

That thought itched from time to time. When I scratched

it, it showed me the financial hole I'd be in without my wife's money to keep me afloat. It reminded me how tightly I was tied to her.

But that wasn't what was really bothering me about the man we had seen. I tried to put the thought out of my mind. The world was silent and dark. I was alone with Amber. Alone for possibly the last time.

I looked over at her. She had fallen asleep, the sheet pulled lazily across her. So much of her was in shadow, but the white of the sheet over her torso glowed in the moonlight through the window.

That desire to capture her came back, to possess a part of her forever. Tonight I could do what I was too drunk to do last night.

I said her name gently, but she didn't stir. I got very slowly up off the bed and eased towards where I had left my camera on the chest of drawers.

I took more care with the settings this time, thinking about a shutter speed that wouldn't shake, an aperture that would capture all of her laid out there on the bed. As I took the first picture of her, her body became in my mind a corpse laid out under a shroud. I shook the thought away and inched towards her.

I took an edge of the sheet in my hand and pulled it very gently towards me. It crept off her, showing her to me and my camera. She gave the tiniest twitch, and I stopped, heart in my throat, the sheet as far down as the bottom of her thighs. Then she was still again, fast asleep, oblivious.

I took another photograph. I moved in closer. Another photograph, and another, possessing each part of her in turn. I stepped back to take in all of her again, and in that moment, she was only mine.

I took another. And another. And another.

A wind is winding up across the meadow, and the horses are running again. A low black cloud crawls along the horizon. Amber walks back home the way she was walking when she read the news about Benny.

She stops for a moment and looks again at the photos on her phone. She's never liked looking at pictures of herself and has never been a good photographer's subject. It is impossible to spend so much time scrutinising other people's faces through a lens and not feel an unbearable pressure when it is turned on you. These images are especially disconcerting. She looks at herself from outside and across all the years and feels disassociated from her own body and perception.

Her memories of that night in the cottage do not quite fit the pictures. But it has always been hard to pull apart what she felt during the evening, and what she felt after what happened later that night. The whole trip is stained with how it ended.

She remembers telling Benny off when he took the picture of her by the window, but it felt more like an annoyance — Benny's camera as a buzzing insect to be swatted away — than any sort of threat. And her mind was muddled, still caught between her desire for Benny and her worries about the man, the car, the near-miss.

The pictures look different now. They only conjure a single feeling. Now, when she looks at herself, standing by the window and fast asleep, she feels violated. Violated then by Benny, and violated now by the person sending these photos to her.

She feels a rising sickness. She looks at the words in the message again.

What happens next?

The next thing she remembers is waking, the room cold around her. Benny was passed out on the bed next to her. She got up and pulled on a jumper that lay on one of the chairs and went straight back to bed. Then the next memory, being woken by the noise downstairs in the cottage, and everything that followed from that.

But what about those sleep-dark times in between? What happened then? She feels tendrils of discomfort, like cold hands on her naked skin.

She wants to be inside, warm and with Johnny. At the same time, she doesn't want to be near him. She doesn't feel she can look at him and keep the truth inside her anymore. Over the years, the lies she has told him have settled and been covered by all the layers of time and their memories together. But now, they are scratching their way to the surface and crawling towards her.

She leaves the meadow over the bridge and follows the towpath past the boatyard and sailing club. Then left, along a wide track and past the pub, and she is on their lane. She walks past the sporadically placed houses until she gets to the large one clad in scaffolding next to theirs. A piece of sheeting is loose, flapping like the wing of a giant, injured bird. She hurries to her front door, almost tripping on a small pothole, and lets herself in.

The house is full of music — the hurried syncopation and blaring brass of Buddy Rich. Maybe Johnny doesn't hear her enter, because she finds him standing in the front room, his hand in his back pocket, as if he has hurriedly got up from the sofa and put his phone away.

'Didn't expect you back so soon, babe,' Johnny says. Amber thinks she catches something forced about the easy cheer in his voice, but she shoos the feeling away. 'How was Kay?'

'Same as ever.' She doesn't want to dwell on the conversation she has had. 'I should get some work done.'

'Yeah, me too. Don't really feel ready for the session. You're still cool if I go up to Manchester?'

'Of course I am. Why would you not go?'

Johnny comes towards her and wraps his arms around her. She feels strangely suffocated by his embrace.

'You sure?' he asks.

'Yes, I'm sure.'

'Just checking. You seem a bit...'

She should smile and brush this off, but she reacts with automatic annoyance. 'A bit what?'

'Honestly, babe, you seem a bit stressed out.'

'I'm fine, J, I've just got a lot to finish up this week so I can get started on the Raine job.'

His embrace loosens. 'I thought you said you weren't going to do it?'

'Yeah, I...' She has been meaning to tell Johnny about her decision — or a version of it — but couldn't find the words or the moment. She is glad it's out in the open now, but at the same time she feels transparent again. 'Talking to Genevieve before we left, I just... I felt I owed it to her, y'know.'

'You shouldn't do things because it makes other people feel better,' he says severely.

'Better give up on the music, then.'

'You know what I mean.'

'Do I? Look, I won't stay at it long. There's a lot of donkey work they can hire someone else to do. I just want to get a decent first look at the collection. There's some really powerful stuff in there.' She feels the weight of the double meaning in her own words.

'You said you'd rather be taking your own photos.'

A wave of annoyance washes over her. 'I know what I said,' she snaps before she can think about it. She recognises this feeling — a hyperarousal of her anxiety, the internal fight or flight struggle escaping as anger. 'But I know what I want to do, okay?'

'Sure thing.' He smiles kindly, but he backs away and holds his hands up.

'J, please, I'm sorry, I didn't mean to–'

'It's fine, babe.' He kisses her on the forehead and, changing the subject, asks what she wants for dinner. He steers her towards takeaway because he knows it's his turn to cook.

This sort of diversion is his mechanism to deal with moments like this. He's always hated confrontation, that's who he's always been by nature. He's relaxed, he's warm, he can find the humour in anything. There were times, early on when they were together, when she wished he would lean into an argument, not slip away from it. But later, it might have been part of what saved them — and saved her from the sort of arguments that end in confessions. Arguments that end in endings.

Amber realises she is scratching the scar on the palm of her hand again.

25

AMBER

The paperwork sits on the desk, full of bureaucratic malevolence. Amber is catching up on admin, trying to sort through her receipts and accounts. She thought it might provide a mundane distraction from the messages on her phone, but she can't focus on it. She gets that same feeling she did when she was sat in school exams, knowing she was failing, the numbers chaotic on the page in front of her. She hears Johnny moving around in the house, metres from her and a hundred miles away.

She gives up on the admin and attempts to return to her photographic work, but quickly feels oppressed by the obligation she has to deliver. The benefit of the small amount of work she does for the press agency is that it's quick. There is no time to dwell on an image. Take the shots, pick the best ones, send them in. And when she's working on features, there is the guiding pressure of collaborating journalists and editors to bring it all together. But her longer-term projects have a habit of festering while her feelings about the images wax and wane.

She looks through a portrait series she's in the middle of,

for one of the grander Oxford colleges. They're not portraits of the Master and the dons, or even the students. They are the porters, the cleaners, the gardeners, and all the other people who keep the college ticking over. It's been a really scrappy year for work, and she was glad of the commission, but looking at some of the photos now, she feels there's a dishonesty about them. They grant these people a status that their employer doesn't give them in their day-to-day lives. A PR job. But who is she to criticise anyone for the gap between what they are and what they seem?

She reads Ed Kapoor's email again and thinks about calling him, but maybe not to talk about his feature idea. Ed the journalistic bloodhound, Ed who has never met the Raines and doesn't know anything about Amber's history with them. Ed and Amber don't even really socialise, and he has only met Johnny twice. Ed is all work. It's one of the reasons she likes collaborating with him. He lives in a tidy corner of her world insulated from the messy rest of her life. That and the professional trust they share, the understanding that sometimes you don't need to ask questions, just follow the other's lead.

Amber's phone buzzes. She jumps like she's been electrified. She sets it to silent before she even checks who's messaged.

It's just Kay:

Nice seeing you today. Hope you're ok. You can talk to me whenever, hope you know that. xx.

Amber doesn't reply, and puts the phone down. Then she moves it out of her eyeline. She listens to the house for a moment, making sure she cannot hear Johnny approaching, then fishes her keys out from her bag. She unlocks a sturdy drawer in her desk. It was the drawer she went to the day they came back from the farmhouse. It still doesn't feel the safest place to hide something, but the lock is strong, and Johnny would never have any reason to look in there. But there is still a moment of anxiety, before she opens the drawer, that the brown envelope with the negatives and pen drive will be gone.

It is still there, stuffed under various poorly ordered bits of paperwork. She pulls out the pen drive, shoves it quickly into her computer and reformats it, erasing the scanned copy of the images. She is about to take a cigarette lighter to the negatives themselves, but she has the same feeling she had in Benny's studio, and stops.

She examines the negatives against the light, feeling that if she looks closely enough, they might be able to tell her a secret. That something in them might betray the person who left them in that box, who copied them, who sent them to Amber.

But, of course, there are no clues. They just preserve a moment that, if unphotographed, would have disappeared forever. Nothing that has happened since they were taken and developed can help her.

She shoves them roughly back into the envelope, and the envelope into the drawer. Then she reaches for her phone and stuffs that in there too, so she won't even catch it out of the corner of her eye.

It means she doesn't see the messages from Yvey until a couple of hours later, when she gingerly fishes the phone out again. It's a short string of single lines — hitting send after every thought in that unexamined way. Not like the slow, overanalytical manner in which Amber approaches every communication.

She can hear Yvey's voice in the girl's thread, saying how much she enjoyed meeting Amber, and could they hang out the next time she is in Oxford? It makes her smile initially, but then gives rise to an uneasiness she cannot quite pin down. Perhaps it is the teenaged gush of the messages, the eagerness to be liked and approved of, and the slightest hint of infatuation with an older mentor. But she is projecting again.

Amber is glad she didn't have text messages as a teenager. She is glad, in fact, that there weren't mobile phones or social media at all when she was growing up, with that indelible mark left on the internet from every bad opinion and misjudged joke. Even 2001 was a different age for that, her life not yet a trail of digital footprints. She wonders if these days she'd be able to conduct an affair like she did back then, or whether technology would betray her.

Amber looks again at Yvey's messages, and the girl's uncertainty about Genevieve's theory of Benny's death comes back to her.

She messages Yvey back, thinking hard about what words to use. She is friendly, but a little formal, and non-committal. Then she turns off the phone. As the screen goes black, she can imagine for a moment that if she never turns it on again, she can be protected from all this. Her secrets will stay hidden. The sender of the messages will just disappear.

Before long, she gives up on her work, closes everything down and goes to drink tea in the kitchen in silence. Time slides by underneath her until Johnny comes into the kitchen carrying bags of takeaway triumphantly, as if they are the heads of vanquished foes, shouting, 'Tonight we feast!'

Silly, irrepressible, cheerful Johnny. She sometimes thinks she has married a permanent teenager, but wouldn't have it any other way.

I don't deserve you, my love, she says silently to herself. *I don't think I ever have.*

She persuades him they should eat in front of Netflix so she doesn't have to try to make conversation, then crawls to bed early. She pretends to be asleep when he comes in, but she feels a million miles from it. She is just lying there, rigid, hyper-aware of her heartbeat, her breathing and the strange popcorn of the baby's movements inside her. When unconsciousness finally creeps across her, she dreams, and when the dream ends, it throws her into the strongest sleep paralysis she has had in years. Awake, but unable to move, her whole body crushed and bound. She wrenches herself from it and blinks at the dark room.

She plays the familiar dream back to herself. She is in the open, empty, colourless space. She is alone apart from the other figure in the distance. But there is something different. The figure is not following her. She is following them. And she feels something in the dream very strongly. She knows that the person she is following is in danger. She is certain that, even against her own intention, she is going to cause them harm.

For a moment when she wakes, everything is fine. Her mind is blank of all the fears of the previous days. She is cosy in her duvet and can hear music. A warm, familiar smell is wafting up from the kitchen.

Then it all comes rushing at her. She feels her heart jump and run. Her neck is hot as the blood surges, and she feels queasy. Even the smell in her nostrils doesn't feel right — as if it's something burning.

Disoriented, she reaches for her phone. Where is it? And where is Johnny? She lurches out of bed and runs down the stairs. He is in the kitchen, calmly flipping bacon in the pan, peering into a saucepan where eggs are poaching. And her phone is just where she left it before she went to bed. Switched off on the kitchen counter.

'Morning, babe. Good timing. Thought I'd make us a proper breakfast.'

'It's Tuesday.' Amber's mind is flipping between the sick panic of what she felt upstairs and the comfort of everything she can see in front of her.

'I can't make my wonderful wife her favourite breakfast on a Tuesday?'

He is right. It is her favourite. It's perfect. Bacon with the fat trimmed off and left to crisp up in the pan, slightly hard poached eggs with bread so fresh he must have snuck out early to go and get it, slices of avocado and tomato. And she clocks now what the music is — it's a Spotify playlist that they've each added tracks to over the years in a game of musical Consequences.

For a few moments, as they sit and eat in companionable silence, everything is okay again. But she feels queasy soon after finishing. She manages to wait until Johnny is playing his keyboard loudly in his foam-soundproofed studio to rush into the bathroom and vomit.

She brushes her teeth furiously to take the taste out of her mouth and cover any hint on her breath that Johnny might detect. But she knows he will have already noticed something is wrong. And before long, he will ask her again about it. He will dig deeper, not just try to patch over the spaces it is leaving between them. And she will have to lie to him again.

The hardest lies to tell are pure invention. The easiest ones are malleable on the outside but with a hard centre of truth. They are not paintings; they are doctored photographs. They work because you can half-believe them yourself.

What happened to Amber after her father's death was so real, and remains so vivid, that she has never had to invent a syllable of it. When she went to college, she tried to hide it, wipe the slate clean. She wasn't going to tell anyone about the blind panic of that day on the beach, or the sweat-soaked, dream-harassed nights that followed, or the explosions of anger and despair. She told herself — and almost believed — that she had beaten it. It was the past. The future was blank and new.

But when she first met Johnny, there was something about him that made her want to tell him everything. Maybe it was the way he didn't pry, didn't want to *understand her trauma*, wasn't like those people who tilted their head on one side and spoke in a soft therapy voice as if she were a bit simple. No, Johnny was just unflappably *cool* about it, as if what she had been through was something of the least consequence about her, like her bad teenage taste in music.

'All the best people are a bit cracked,' was how he put it, reeling off a list of tormented musicians.

In a way, it was easy in the months after she came back from the cottage, to blame her behaviour on a recurrence of her teenage mental health problems brought on by the stresses of starting out in a competitive career. She could talk about the situations she had to face as a photojournalist, the aggressive macho culture of the newsroom, the precariousness of her contract. It didn't matter that in reality, none of this on its own accounted for her mood swings, her panic attacks and nightmares, her flaring temper. Because she always had that first true horror to hang it all on, that primal past.

Johnny had no reason to disbelieve her, but with that came a gnawing, compound guilt. It was not just that she was lying to Johnny, but that she was sullying the memory of her dad to use him as cover for what she had done. These two smoking black holes in her life were connected, but not in the way Johnny thought. Not in the way that anybody knew.

It was only slowly that she learned to lock the guilt away. Both the guilt about the act, and the guilt about the lie she told to cover for it. Like boxes inside boxes, secrets within secrets.

And now, that old lie is ready to be taken out again.

Amber finishes brushing. Reaching automatically for her pregnancy multivitamins, she finds the bottle is almost empty. She still suspects they just give her expensive wee, but she can't leave anything to chance, not this time. So she forces herself to get dressed and go out of the house, across the meadow and to the pharmacy in Jericho.

She felt imprisoned in the house, and outside feels like a fugitive. She glances around and walks quickly. Past the pub she's not been out to in months, past the slightly ropey curry house that's been a fixture here since she was a teenager, past the café where she and Kay sometimes get their coffees.

It's then she sees the man in a long blue coat, his hands in his pockets, looking into the window of a small art gallery, oddly static. It's only a small sense of familiarity, a little glitch in her brain, but she thinks he looks like Sam. She wrestles with herself to stop from going back to the art gallery to check.

But she loses the fight and goes on over, all manner of thoughts going round her head about spotting him so close to her house. Then her phone starts ringing. It's a withheld number. She lets it go on ringing. Maybe it's one of those spam calls. She keeps going towards the art gallery, but can't help but answer it.

'Hi, Amber, Sam here.'

Her brain misfires. She is staring in through the gallery window at someone who must be a complete stranger. And the more she looks, the more the resemblance to Sam falls away. The odd coincidence gives her a cold feeling, as if she is slipping between a real and a dream world. She realises she hasn't spoken for several seconds, and Sam's insistent voice on the phone pulls her back into reality.

Sam says he is calling to talk about arrangements and contracts, but he peppers his talk about rates and invoicing with questions about her work and recent past, as if he is trying to build a fuller picture of her in his mind. It feels like a subtle sort of interrogation, comparing her answers against what he might already have found out about her online or through Genevieve. Due diligence for his boss.

Because she can suspect Sam all she wants, hallucinate his presence in the high street, worry about is inquisitiveness, but he is only a cog in a machine. All of Amber's thoughts again lead back only to Benny's widow. That is the cold logic of this spiral of threat. All the things that have been happening have started not since Benny's death, but since she was invited to the funeral and then to the farmhouse.

On the surface, Genevieve has been as she always was: professional, deliberate, unemotional. But underneath? Never present when those WhatsApp messages buzzed on Amber's phone. Not there in the kitchen on that night Amber fled through the trees. Not at home the night Benny died.

At the same time, Genevieve is almost too visible in all this. Why bring Amber to the farmhouse at all? Why not simply send the images and messages? Because the person sending them seems almost to be willing a confrontation. A confrontation like the one that happened almost two decades ago.

Amber starts to feel as if she has been looking at this from the wrong perspective. She has been thinking about this from where she stands, not from where Benny did, not from where the people around him stood. The same scene can look very different from an alternate angle. She is gripped by the need to talk to someone who knows Genevieve now and knew her all those years ago.

She looks in her phone, scrolling down to see if she still has a number in her contacts. There's nothing there, but it only takes a moment on Google to find what she needs. Sometimes it seems nothing is hidden about anyone anymore. She looks at the number — a landline at Amber's old London college. Before she can stop herself, she dials, almost hoping for no answer or a machine to pick up. But after a few seconds, there is a click, the rustle of paper, and a short cough. Then a voice, out of breath.

'Hi... sorry... just a sec...'

'Is that Florence MacRory?' She doesn't know why she uses her full, formal name. 'It's Amber Ridley.'

27

The new campus building near Paddington station is bright and cavernous, half modern art museum, half corporate headquarters. It ranges up over several open-sided floors that intersect over one another, and wide wooden staircases flow up the centre from the foyer. The place mills with fashionable young students and hums with excited chatter, oblivious to talk of social distancing or lockdowns. It's a world away from the grubby brutalist buildings that Amber remembers from when she was a student.

When she sees Freddie, her old tutor stands out, but not in the way she had at Benny's funeral. While her bright attire had contrasted with the sombre mourners, in this sea of youth she looks like someone stranded from another time. Her slightly hippyish clothes are poorly matched, and her hair looks messy rather than extravagant. Even her striking features seem a little diminished. She looks tired and irritated.

Freddie was nothing but light on the phone. She was sorry she'd not caught up with Amber at the funeral, and had been hoping she might make contact. Freddie seemed to have no idea Amber had moved out of London, so when she suggested a coffee the next day, Amber didn't protest. It was only an hour on the train, and the gaps in Freddie's knowledge put Amber at ease for their meeting. It said to her that Freddie had not been keeping tabs on her, not watching her.

Amber was still not entirely sure what she was hoping to gain from seeing Freddie. She felt half in need of an ally — someone who might have information from inside the Raine household — and still half-suspicious about what Benny might have told his closest friends.

Trapped between these urges, Amber is at a loss for what to say as they sit down with their coffees. So she is glad, at first, that Freddie has always been someone who will fill any silence. It seems she has something she wants to get off her chest. Before any attempt to catch up on the years since they've seen each other, Freddie is ranting about the university administrators and their petty demands. Her voice is usually a pleasant one to listen to — still full of the Ulster lilt of her youth. But now it sharpens up around the invective and gallops through a list of grievances. It's not entirely out of character for Freddie to run off on a tangent, but Amber finds the barely pent-up rage disconcerting.

'Not tempted by retirement?' she interjects when Freddie draws a breath, hoping to get her off the topic of work.

Freddie throws a conspiratorial look around her. 'I think they'd like me to retire. But they can't get rid of me. Like a bad smell. Though I'm only teaching two days a week now, not always in the big smoke...' And she goes on, telling Amber about how she thinks the department heads have been trying to force her out, and how she got sick of London anyway, so commutes in now from High Wycombe.

Amber can instantly see the geography, as if looking at a satellite image in her mind. High Wycombe: a large market town surrounded by the Chiltern Hills.

'So you're near the farmhouse?'

'The farmhouse?'

'Benny's place.'

'I suppose so.' Freddie sounds annoyed, but Amber cannot tell if it is in reaction to the question, or just residual bad temper from her tirade against the university administrators.

'Did you go there a lot? I mean... did you see much of Benny... towards the end?'

Then Freddie's shoulders drop, and she is uncharacteristically silent for a moment. The irritation that has been seething around in her seems to lift, leaving her frowning and uncertain.

'Did you know he was ill?'

'It made sense afterwards, I suppose.'

'What do you mean?'

Freddie doesn't seem to want to answer. The gaps in her speech become long and considered. 'I only saw him once or twice in the last year. But the last time... He seemed, I don't know, preoccupied. He kept asking me about my regrets.'

'*Your* regrets?'

'Oh yes, but I knew he was talking about himself. He was never the most emotionally literate person, was he now?' Freddie shrugs and looks up at the high atrium above them. 'But all of us have things we regret, don't we?'

Amber is glad Freddie isn't looking at her when she says that, because the words set up a small twitch that runs across her shoulder blades. She shakes out the feeling. When Freddie does make eye contact again, her old tutor is smiling, but as if to cover sadness.

'But how are you?' she says to Amber, forcing the words out.

It is enough to pull the conversation into a different space, and they begin to catch up on the missing years. Amber tells

Freddie about the pregnancy, her career, Johnny's music, their move out to Oxford. She doesn't mention anything more about the Raines, and for a few minutes it is as if she has forgotten what has propelled her to this meeting.

It's only when she takes the plunge and tells Freddie about the archive job that her old tutor's manner flickers. It is the specific mention of Genevieve that provokes the reaction — a sense that Freddie is fighting to suppress something she wants to say. It isn't much, but it's a tell. Freddie always wore her emotions on the outside, bright and loud like her clothes.

'What?'

'Ach, nothing.'

'No, really. The way you looked when I mentioned Genevieve.'

Freddie adopts her slightly faraway look, as if searching for someone in the sea of faces around them. 'Just make sure you get paid and keep your receipts,' she says curtly.

'What's that supposed to mean?' Amber leans forward, forgetting her fear. She feels almost excitement, as if she has landed on something here that might begin to explain what is happening to her.

Freddie shakes her head. 'Did you know that over that marriage, Benny lost control of everything? He was never any good at hanging onto money, always spending, never saving. That's who he was. Everyone said Gen was the kind of person he needed to add a bit of sense into his life. Someone with a bit of acumen. I thought that too for a while. But it's not right. Benny was a free spirit. He needed someone to be free with. And you know what I found out? By the end, all his rights and royalties, even his income, everything... it all ended up being controlled by that Bayard Foundation.' Freddie lets out a snort and repeats the word *foundation*. 'I think it's why that woman married him, not that stockbroker — I don't think she could have controlled him in the same way.'

'Which stockbroker?'

'You know that, surely? Hardly a secret. Yeah, Gen was engaged to some Swiss stockbroker when she met Benny.'

Amber wants to ask more, but Freddie doesn't let her. She seems almost annoyed about the interruption and swings back round to the Bayard Foundation. It's clear it is this that Freddie wants to talk about, and it's not long before she's adopted that same manner she used to talk about the university administrators.

She tells Amber that the Foundation is linked to the Panama Papers — that international scandal of offshore finances. She talks about money laundering, dodgy deals, even investments in the arms trade. Then she goes steadily off-piste, drifting towards talk about international finance, bankers and political control, as if she has forgotten completely what prompted the diatribe.

The more Freddie talks, the more Amber recognises a familiar language and mindset. Freddie wants her to know how things aren't reported in the mainstream media, and about a nebulous *them* who are controlling things behind the scenes. She leans into Amber as she speaks, as if she is in possession of privileged information.

The phrase *Deep State* falls out of Freddie's mouth, and then the coronavirus somehow makes its way into her ranting. That threat that is heading inexorably towards them, waiting to infect these crowded spaces.

'You think any of it is *real*?' Freddie declares loudly as if she wants everyone around them to hear. 'You don't think it's just about fear, about another way to control us?'

A cold feeling runs through Amber. She has the sense of not fully recognising the person in front of her. The woman whose anti-establishment takes Amber used to enjoy — used to agree with — has been replaced by an altered version. Amber knows she should argue with what Freddie is saying, but it feels futile. Driven by her own fear, she has come here hoping for facts. But she has found only someone gripped by their own paranoia.

Amber finishes her coffee quickly while Freddie continues to talk. Then she makes her excuses and leaves. As she walks away, she glances back. She sees Freddie reaching around and gathering up her belongings, which have become scattered around her. She looks small and old and a little lost.

28

AMBER

On the way back to Oxford, Freddie's words rattle around inside Amber's head in time with the motion of the carriage. She is feeling sad and a little bemused by the state of her old tutor. Still, she can't help herself from going over and over everything Freddie said, trying to pick apart the facts from the delusion, examining every phrase and gesture for unstated meaning.

She thinks about Freddie's talk of regret — Benny's, and perhaps her own. And when Freddie said Benny needed a free spirit, was she talking about herself? Did she hold a flame for him for a long time?

She thinks about Genevieve and her jilted Swiss stock-broker— how she must be no stranger to infidelity herself. And she thinks about Freddie's accusations of Genevieve's control over Benny.

By the time the train pulls into Oxford, Amber even finds herself mulling on Freddie's lurid accusations about the Bayard Foundation, as if somehow international webs of financial corruption might hold the key to all this. Amber feels no saner, no more able to grip the truth, than Freddie was.

She sits on a bench at the station and gets out her phone, diving into Google to pick through the bones of Genevieve's life. But she finds little else. Genevieve Bayard-Raine's presence on the internet is like everything else about her — professional. Notes on her family's business dealings, her education at the Sorbonne and Oxford, her early career in auction houses without a real need for an income, and the work of the Bayard Foundation. Not a hint of scandal, and no mention of her stockbroker.

These disjointed facts tumble around as Amber walks home. At one moment they feel significant, the next worthless internet flotsam. The tumble in her head doesn't stop as she turns the key in the front door, preparing a normal face for her husband, gripped again by the feeling that soon she will have to lie to him again.

Soon turns out to be *now*. The moment is waiting for her with him in the hallway.

'Where have you been?' His voice is worried.

'I told you I was having coffee with a friend.'

'You've been gone hours, and you know I have to get going to Manchester this afternoon.'

She looks at her watch. It is later than she thought. Her fraught mind has become unfocused on how much of the day has gone. It makes her want to look at her phone again. Too much time has gone without another message. She fears it, and she wants it to come.

'Sorry, it was in London.'

'London?' He says the word as if it is an exotic, far-off place.

'Yeah, you know London, J, the place we lived for most of our adult life before ending up in...' She throws her arm around their small and peeling hallway.

'Jeez, babe, I hope you didn't go anywhere crowded.'

'What do you mean?'

'Coronavirus, that's what. You know it's worse in London.'

'There's been like a couple of hundred cases there. It's a big city. Chill out.'

It's a weaponised phrase to use against Johnny, given the knot of fear in her own stomach. And she hears in her voice the echo of Freddie's dismissal of what's happening in China, in Italy, what will inevitably happen here soon. Her own fear feels compounded. But she doesn't back down.

'Besides, you're about to bugger off to Manchester for the rest of the week, so don't tell me I can't go and have a coffee with a friend in London.'

The strength seems to go out of Johnny. His broad shoulders droop a little, and he looks contrite, like a child caught stealing. He reaches out his hands and takes hers.

'I'm sorry, you're right. I shouldn't go.'

'Don't be ridiculous. Of course you should go.'

'I think maybe I should stay with you.'

Amber takes her hands back and walks on into the house, not wanting to engage with where this is going. But she senses this time that Johnny wants to lean into this argument. He has been storing up that feeling whilst he waited for her to come home.

He isn't aggressive in what he says next, but there is a firmness and directness. He is no longer the eternal kid, but the man in his late forties who he really is.

'You're stressed, you're crabby, you seem really distracted. I know you're not sleeping well. You're talking to your friends, which is fine, I have no problem with that. But it also means you're not talking to me. All since we've come back from the Raine place. I do notice these things. I'm not stupid, you know.' He pauses. There is a new look on his face. 'And it got me thinking. You and Raine.'

Amber flinches inwardly. It's finally coming, but worse than she thought it would be. He has finally seen, finally realised.

'I remember how it was with you two back in the day. I know he meant a lot to you, maybe more than you...' He stops, shaking his head. Amber can't stay silent any longer.

'What, J? What are you trying to say?'

'I'm not going to psychoanalyse you, babe. You know I think that shit is mostly bollocks anyway. But when we knew him... you and him, it was like...'

'Like what?'

'Look, I never met your dad, and maybe Raine was nothing like him, but–'

'My *dad*?'

'Okay, babe, I'll say it. Raine was such an obvious daddy substitute. And I think his death has hit you harder than you think, and you haven't acknowledged your grief. And all the other grief it brings back for you. But this job, it's not going to bring Raine back. It's not going to bring anyone back. There, I've said it.'

Amber almost laughs, a strange rush of relief and embarrassment at the misreading of her relationship with Benny. The second part of the feeling squirms inside her. Johnny has seen but not seen. He has looked at the picture of her and Benny in his head and missed an object clearly in view. She lets it sit there in his head without disturbance.

'I'm sorry, J.' She holds her hands out in front of her belly. 'You're probably right.' She leans into his analysis, wrapping more truths into her lie. 'And with Mum... God, I wish I didn't have to go and see her the way she is. And I wish you and me didn't seem so far from all our friends... and I know we said this year would be different, but sometimes I wish we'd never moved here. And I wish I didn't have this broken part of me that just... just for no bloody good reason malfunctions.'

Johnny is silent for a moment, then comes towards her and wraps his arms around her.

'How many times do I have to tell you you're not broken, babe? And like I told you, if the Raine job isn't helping, don't do it. You don't need any extra things messing with your head. You should be taking it easy. And if you're doing extra stuff, you should be doing it for yourself, not puffing up some dead posh dude.' He realises his misstep and holds up his hand. 'I'm sorry, I know what he meant to you. Even if I remember him being a bit of a jerk sometimes.'

'It's not about him, it's about his work,' she says weakly, feeling the weight of the lie.

Johnny exhales sharply, and Amber feels a flash of anger.

'Oh, c'mon, you're always making excuses for all the brilliant arseholes in the music industry.'

He steps back and holds up his hands. 'All I'm saying is that if you want me to stay, I will.'

'Really, you should go. I mean, who knows, we'll all be under house arrest in a week.' She smiles weakly and hugs him again, but he's a little stiff in response.

He goes into his studio, no more words between them. Then he packs the hire car, and he is gone, their goodbyes full of unsaid things. The moment he walks out of the door, Amber wishes he had stayed.

She takes out her phone and stares at it. No new messages.

She replays the aborted conversation with Johnny. These half-arguments are always left unfinished by the things she cannot reveal. It makes her think about Genevieve again, and why she might be willing Amber towards a confrontation.

Her suspicion that Genevieve was having Benny and her followed evaporated with the events of the final night at the cottage. And nothing that followed in the years after said to

Amber that Genevieve had anything to do with what happened there.

But now, all these years later: these photographs and messages with uncertain motives behind them. It all leaves Amber with a heavy sense of unfinished business.

Then her thoughts loop back round to Johnny and his naive misreading of her and Benny. She doesn't believe he can be so close to the truth but fail to see it. It doesn't feel quite right. She does not doubt her own guilt, but she no longer trusts Johnny's belief in her innocence.

29

BENNY

Sunday, 11 November 2001

I stopped as the counter on my camera showed 34. There seemed no part of her body left to explore.

I pulled the sheet over her and put my camera back on the chest of drawers. I lay down on the bed a good distance away from her, but couldn't sleep. I looked at the clock as it wound itself towards one in the morning.

I felt all the shame that I should in the moment. But I knew the feeling would wear off. She would never know. These photographs could never hurt her. Only I would ever look at them. I would see only what I had seen before, what I had touched before, what had been mine for a short while.

But I kept looking over at my camera, its lens shining a little in the moonlight slinking away from the window. I pulled on some pyjama bottoms and a T-shirt, suddenly aware of my own nakedness. I left the bedroom, taking my camera with me, not wanting it in the room with us. The human conscience is strange and irrational like that.

I went downstairs and dumped the camera on the sofa in the living room. I moved through into the kitchen and drank a glass of water while I kept catching my own reflection in the glass. I turned off the lights so I didn't have to see myself anymore, and looked out on the undulating shadows of the sea.

Eventually I felt exhaustion wash over me, and I climbed the stairs. The temperature in the room had dropped, and Amber had turned on her side, pulling the sheet in bunches over herself against the cold. I lay down on the bed and passed out.

The crack of glass from downstairs must have materialised as a gunshot in the war raging in my dream, because the first waking memory I have is Amber sitting bolt upright in bed, shaking me. She was dressed in a cashmere jumper and huddled under the duvet that before we had thrown on the floor.

The discrepancy from how I had last seen her made me feel as if I was still playing out a strange half-dream in my head. Then I felt the deep cold in the room, and my brain caught up with the time that must have passed. I was gripped by a panic that she knew what I had done. I glanced around for my camera before remembering it was downstairs. Then I read the look on her face. It wasn't anger in her eyes. It was fear.

'There's someone downstairs,' she hissed at me.

30

The knowledge that someone loves you has an extraordinarily protective power. It's like a force field. Amber has always felt that. In a crowd, at a party when she felt the pressure to socialise, or just sitting quietly on her own. She can't find that feeling anymore.

She couldn't feel it as she came back from her afternoon walk across Port Meadow, the sun setting, a low mist forming over the sweep of the grass. She couldn't feel it as she cooked her dinner on her own in the kitchen, the turned-down radio mumbling in the background. She couldn't feel it as she tried to read as she ate, unable to finish a sentence or hold a thought in her head.

And every time she tried to fill her mind with anything calm or peaceful, it would be crowded out by the thoughts of the messages, the cottage, all the lies she has told. They settled on her like crows picking at carrion.

She is sitting in the living room now with the TV on, hoping for distraction, but the Netflix algorithms, fed by Johnny's watching habits, keep serving up grim and violent titles. Even the auto-play trailers put her on edge.

It's a strange mismatch about Johnny. Laid-back, never angry, but he binges on violent movies. Perhaps that is the knack: to outsource the need for violence to the screen, not store it up inside you until it comes out unbidden and unexpected. Perhaps. After all, few people would meet Amber and think her capable of what she did.

She finally finds something soothing to watch — a mindless makeover show — but still keeps the volume down low. She is listening to the house so she can know what every creak and crack is, so her mind does not invent things. Her phone is on vibrate. She wants to be able to hear from Johnny, but dreads the notifications. Her heart still surges a little in her chest whenever it buzzes.

Johnny messaged when he arrived in Manchester — conciliatory and attentive — but has been quiet for a while. There are a few notifications from group chats, and there is one message from Kay. She's trying to sound casual, but Amber can detect the concern in Kay's text at Amber's failure to respond to her messages since they had coffee. Amber is touched by her concern, but she can't bring herself to reply. Part of her still believes that nothing good can come of confiding any more in Kay, but another part is creeping towards the idea of letting her in. Amber needs at least one ally in this world.

As she sits, Amber's growing belly has a dull ache, its tissues and ligaments stretching and rearranging. It is like the feeling after too big a meal, even though she could only pick her way through half of her dinner.

She starts to feel drowsy. Although it's not late, only just gone nine, she is exhausted by the days of sleeplessness piling up inside her. But she doesn't want to leave the warmth of this room and venture up the cold stairs to her bed and lie there without her husband. She curls up on the sofa and closes her eyes, the soft flicker of the TV still on as company.

The next thing she knows she is wide awake and standing in the middle of Port Meadow. She knows immediately she is dreaming — a strange lucid state she has encountered before. There is a low mist across the grass, and she knows her father is with her, although he is not visible. She also knows she is being followed again. Then the grass becomes the Norfolk sands, which become the sands where her father died, and everything in her life is crashing together. The waves are pounding great rocks that have risen from nowhere, a strangely metallic sound.

Then she is awake, and she knows that the sound has come from the old knocker on her front door, clanging three sharp raps.

She is up on her feet like a cat sprayed with cold water. She inches towards the windows and with twitching slowness pulls up a corner of the heavy curtains. She can't see. It's not clear. It's too dark outside.

Get a grip on yourself, Amber. She pulls herself straight and marches out into the hallway. She is clutching her phone. She has already selected Johnny's number and has her thumb ready to dial it.

'Who is it?'

The voice from the other side of the door comes back, thin and uncertain. 'It's Yvey.'

A mber doesn't open the door immediately. A flurry of words seeps through the old wood that she cannot decipher. Eventually, she unchains and unlocks the door. A light drizzle has set in, and Yvey stands in the dark, damp and small. She has a hood up, but the points of her face are picked out by the light from the doorway.

Amber ushers her in and on through into the living room. Yvey takes off a trendy little satchel bag and shrugs off her jacket — a dark red leather thing worn over a hoodie. She paces around the room a bit before sitting in an armchair. Her hair is pulled back, with just a little of her fringe falling across her face.

Amber can now see even more of Yvey's resemblance to Benny, the way these things bleed through with familiarity. But it isn't the Benny she knew. Yvey is like the old photos of the young Benny — dashing and foppish.

Yvey starts to apologise.

'It's fine. Just tell me what happened.' Amber finds the uneasiness she has been feeling has flowed away, displaced by Yvey's evident distress. It is easy to be calm in a crisis, if it's someone else's crisis.

'I was in Oxford, hanging out with mates. I came in on my scooter.'

That perfect little Vespa Amber had seen at the farmhouse pops into her head.

'I left it near the station, and my friends all went home, and I went back, and it's gone. I'm sorry, Amber... I got a cab here. I was a bit freaked out and just wanted to talk to someone I knew.' She looks away again and half mutters: 'Mum's gonna kill me.'

'Have you called the police?'

'They won't care about a stolen bike. Anyway...' Yvey tails off. Amber waits for the completion of her thought, but it never comes, leaving the weight of something unsaid heavy in the room.

Amber is full of different reactions: surprise, uncertainty, even a slight sense of gladness that Yvey has come to her and thrown her out of her own anxiety. Yvey sits forward on her chair, her hands cupped together, and Amber recognises a girl still caught in grief and fear.

'Let me get you a drink. What would you like?'

'Do you have any hot chocolate?'

'I'm sure there's some lurking at the back of a cupboard somewhere. Make yourself comfy, get warm.'

Amber goes off towards the kitchen and puts on the kettle. The white noise of its boiling stops her being able to think, and she finds she's grateful for the moment of blankness. But as she comes back in with the drinks, a question nags at her.

'Do you mind me asking how you know where I live?'

Yvey looks down, embarrassed. 'Yeah, sorry. Got your address off Mum because I wanted... ah, it sounds dorky... I wanted to write to you.' She shakes her head as if to underline the foolishness of her idea. Amber wonders for a second if she ever shared her home address with Genevieve, before remembering it is in the footer of some of her emails.

'It's not dorky,' says Amber, and the two sit in an awkward silence for a moment. 'Look, you should at least call the police. Let them know about the theft — for the insurance. But I'm not surprised your mum doesn't like you riding that thing. Were you really planning on heading home at this time of night?'

'Don't lecture me, please. I feel bad enough as it is. Dad bought it for me, for my birthday. It's vintage. He had it restored specially. Mum hates me riding it. Especially since Dad...' She looks away from Amber.

'I'm sorry. Have you called your mum?'

Yvey grinds a noise in her throat in response, her body language signalling its reluctance, her feet curling up tight under her.

'She'll understand. She won't be angry. She'll just want you to be safe.' The incipient maternal instinct surges in Amber, a feeling that still only comes and goes. She puts a hand to her stomach, feeling a deep truth: she will care about this person inside her more than she cares about anyone. She will always want them to be safe, even if she is angry or disappointed. Whatever else she suspects about Genevieve, she has to believe this is true for her too. 'Maybe you could just tell her the scooter broke down for now. Tell her the rest when you're ready.'

'I'll text her,' says Yvey sulkily, as if resigned to the inevitable. She gets out her phone, and her thumbs skid across its surface at speed. 'She'll be way too drunk to drive, though.'

Yvey falls back in her chair, and Amber thinks back to the weekend at the farmhouse. Genevieve drank steadily, but not excessively, never seeming the slightest bit drunk. That was how she remembered her from before as well. She didn't ever seem like someone willing to lose control. But is she always like that? Does she ever let her grip loosen? What does it look like if she does?

Amber wants to ask Yvey these questions, but knows she shouldn't. All the same, she can't shift the feeling that Yvey is sitting on something about her mother. She remembers their standoffishness with each other at the farmhouse, how they rarely seemed to make eye contact. Maybe it means nothing, just the usual dynamics of a mother and her teenage daughter. But she can't put away the feeling that something is off. She tries to find a way to get under the skin of their relationship.

'Do you mind if I say something, Yvey, from experience?'

Yvey cocks her head a little.

'You shouldn't forget how hard this has been on your mum. I know it can feel at the moment that you're alone in what you feel, but you're not. I just hope you find a way to talk about it all with her.'

'I've tried.'

'She said she felt you were cutting her out.'

'We had... we had an argument. A big one. I said some mean things... but... You know she never even told me about Dad killing himself — about her *thinking* that. I had to overhear her talking to friends about it. Didn't even treat me like enough of an adult to tell me what she was thinking.'

'She was probably trying to protect you.'

'I don't need fucking protecting.' There is a sudden anger in her voice, a defiance.

'You might not feel that, but–'

'She's just so set on this idea that Dad killed himself. But he wouldn't, he *wouldn't*.' She sniffs up her frustration. 'Mum wouldn't listen to me, though. They never bloody listen, do they? So, yeah, I stopped trying to talk to her about it.'

'But you do believe it was an accident?'

Yvey looks away now. She says nothing. Amber wants to ask her more. She wants to ask her what she thinks really happened, what she knows but isn't letting on. She wants to know all the things unsaid, all the things unsayable about her mother. But she bites her tongue, telling herself there is just a scared teenager in front of her. She is looking for shapes in the clouds, faces in the shadows.

Amber changes the subject, asking her about school, but draws little out. Trying for a bit of a girly chat, she asks if Yvey has a boyfriend.

Yvey shakes her head. 'Why d'you assume boyfriend?'

'Sorry, I... You're right, I shouldn't presume.' Amber flushes, feeling foolish.

'Nah, s'alright. It's chill. I kinda go with the flow. There was someone at my old school, before I...' She tails off. 'Didn't really work out, if you have to know. We weren't *right together.*' She puts big air quotes round those last words and gives a sneer. Then she adds, in half a whisper: 'Better off without the gaslighting bitch.'

A graceless silence sits between them. Ambers stands up, patting her legs. 'Has your mum replied?'

Yvey fishes out her phone, looking at it for no more than a couple of seconds. She shakes her head and makes an action with her free hand like someone downing a bottle.

'I tell you what, why don't I run you home? We can explain to your mum together.'

Yvey gives a big sigh, halfway between relief and resignation. 'Okay.'

THE DRIZZLE CUTS into the house the moment Amber opens the door. She hates how dark their lane is. She pulls her coat tight around her and leads Yvey out along the lane.

No one has seen to the loose sheeting on the next-door house, and it has worked its way further free. It's now flowing away from the section of roof and attic window it had covered. There is no glass in the window, just a black hole filled only with the dark recesses of imagination.

They make their way down the lane towards the layby where Amber's car is parked. Even in the dark, within a few feet Amber can see something is wrong. The car is lopsided, sloping towards its rear right wheel. She finds herself running towards it. The tyre is flat, half airless and distorted, the rubber squeezing out from under the weight of the unsupported wheel rim.

Amber hears Yvey's voice from behind her: 'What's wrong?'

'Flat tyre.' The anxiety breaks back over Amber, and she lets out a curse into the night. She looks back at Yvey, who is hugging herself against the rain, glancing around her.

'Can we go back inside, please?'

'It's fine,' says Amber, but she doesn't feel fine. She crouches down and fishes her phone out of her pocket, shining the torch at the tyre. There's nothing to see, just bulging rubber. When she looks up, Yvey is backing away towards the house, still looking about twitchily.

Amber stands quickly and almost has to crouch right back down again. A shooting pain runs up from the nook of her right hip across her belly. Then, just as quickly, it is gone. She feels dizzy and a little sick. She reaches out a hand and leans on the car.

'Amber, what's wrong?'

'Nothing... just... just a cramp.' She takes a breath, then two. Then a few more, counting between them, letting the sense of panic flow away. There is no more pain, just a satisfying ripple across her innards that feels like movement.

'You're right,' she says, 'let's go back inside.'

Yvey is off at a clip back to the house, but Amber goes a bit slower, allowing herself to feel her movements, her muscles, her baby inside her, who is now moving as energetically as she's ever felt.

Yvey is waiting impatiently at the door, and Amber lets her in. Before she follows on inside, she looks back down the lane towards her car. It's silent apart from the *flap-flap-flap* of that loose sheeting and the hiss of the rain on the road. In the other direction, it's just fields and the dark, dirty grey of clouds. But opposite her house, on the far side of the lane, is a small knot of trees in front of a line of a dense bank of foliage. The space between the trunks of the trees is almost total darkness. Then the darkness moves.

32

I see you, Amber, but do you see me? You're looking right towards me, but I've shifted back into the gloom of the undergrowth.

I've been watching you. I shouldn't, but I couldn't leave it alone. I should be more direct with you, just have it out. But it's not that simple. I can't take the risk. So I'll just keep on watching for a while, see what you do next.

But what is Yvey doing here? What's brought her to your house at this time of night? The look on your face when you opened the door — you weren't expecting her, were you? What were you talking about in there? What is it she wants?

She's always been a bit of a loose end, has Yvey. Another loose end. That's the trouble with loose ends. When you think you're tying one up, it always seems to create another somewhere else. I didn't really think I had much to worry about from her, but sometimes a nasty little thought nags at me.

That night, that last night of Benny's. Could she have walked down the drive and seen me parked in the lane? Could she have seen me follow Benny off on his bike? Could she identify the car?

No, not in the dark. I can't start to think like that. I just need to watch and wait a little longer.

It feels like a long time that you stand there, framed in the glow of your doorway, looking right at me, but not seeing.

Finally, you go inside. I breathe again, and the wind in the foliage replies around me. I am alone again in the darkness.

33

BENNY

Sunday, 11 November 2001

I held Amber's hand. It was cold. She was sitting very still, canting her head to listen. Her fear seemed to have subsided and been replaced by a state of hyper-readiness, as if her flight was turning to fight.

'Are you sure there's someone downstairs?' I asked her.

'Of course I'm bloody sure. Someone just smashed a window.'

I looked around the room for anything useful to defend myself with, but there was nothing. I was relieved in a way. Never bring a weapon to a fight unless you intend to use it. Confrontation went with my job, but mainly I was used to defusing it. Even if it meant handing over everything of value you had to hand. I've never pretended to be a hero or a hard man.

'Stay here,' I told Amber and got out of bed. I turned on the lights as I walked down the stairs. I wasn't creeping or trying to disguise my presence. I wanted the intruder to know I was here and I wasn't afraid to meet them face to face. I was afraid. Of course I was afraid. But I was also full of a different kind of uncertainty. I tried to quell my earlier thoughts and void my mind of the questions that had been running round it.

The staircase led straight into the downstairs living room, and I hesitated as I rounded the final corner. But there was no one there. I crossed the living room, pausing at the door that led to the kitchen. I took a breath, pulled down the handle and gave the door a quick kick.

I could see into the kitchen and on to the extension. That was where the man was standing, in front of the sliding doors. The glass behind him lay shattered into a thousand pieces, and a rock the size of a human head lay behind him on the floor.

My first thought was that this man must have assumed the cottage to be empty on a freezing November weekend, but as I stepped through into the kitchen, that idea cleared from my head. He didn't run when he saw me. He barely moved. He just rolled the weight of his body from foot to foot and shifted his wide shoulders around as if limbering up.

'What do you want?' I asked him as calmly as I could, fearing he might answer me. But he didn't reply.

I tried to take him in quickly. He wore a big scrappy green canvas coat and baggy black trousers that looked like they came from an army surplus store. He had a poorly kept dirty-blond beard and a beany hat pulled right down to his eyebrows.

'I don't want any trouble. I don't have much cash, but you can have what I've got.'

He still didn't reply. It felt as if he was waiting for something, or unsure what he was supposed to do next.

Then I saw his face change, his eyes flicking behind me.

The next moments moved very fast. I turned my head for just a moment. Amber was standing behind me in the kitchen. She was holding my camera at hip level. I'm sure I heard the click of the shutter, but there wasn't any time to consider what the hell she was doing, because immediately in my periphery I could detect the intruder rushing towards me. My head snapped back towards him just a moment before his fist connected with my jaw.

34

There has always been a slim dark space between perception and paranoia for Amber, a place where her fears lurk. Movements in the corner of her eye, a face in a viewfinder that isn't the one she sees with her own eyes, flashes of images and double takes that hurtle her back through time. So she doesn't trust what she sees in the shadow of the trees, but doesn't want to linger any longer in the darkness to test that feeling.

She locks the door behind her and takes a moment to breathe.

The flat tyre is real, though. That isn't a figment of her imagination. But it could have happened any time. She could have picked up a slow puncture coming back from the farmhouse. She's not driven the car since then. Not everything has to mean something.

She tries the breathing again, glad that Yvey has gone on into the house and can't see her face. She rubs her hand across her stomach. The pain she felt as she stood up by the car has gone, but the memory of it is still running through her. She imagines herself telling Johnny off for worrying at every little cramp.

She gets out her phone, but there's nothing on it, and she finds herself opening WhatsApp and tapping on Johnny's avatar. She waits for it to update his status.

Last seen today at 19:17.

She is gripped by a desire to know exactly where he is, what he is doing, who he's with. A weird dark thought flickers through her mind, her automatic trust for Johnny suddenly infected by the virus of suspicion coursing through her.

The image of him hurriedly standing and pushing his phone away as she returned to the house two days ago springs into her mind. Has he been honest with her? Is he where he says he is? She knows a couple of the musicians he's recording with: should she call one of them just to make sure?

She wants to shout out loud at these thoughts as if she could scare them off.

She goes into the living room. Yvey is sitting where she was before, curled up in a ball, looking vulnerable and small again. Amber has so many more questions for her: about her mother and father, about why the girl seems so scared. It can't just be a reaction to a stolen scooter and the flat tyre. That doesn't seem enough. There is something else, she is convinced of it.

She tells herself things will seem clearer in the morning, and tries to watch a bit of TV with Yvey just to bring something else into the room other than their fears. But soon she can feel her mind crashing, pulling her towards sleep.

'I think I need to go to bed. Look, you can get a cab home, I'll pay.'

Yvey gives her answer to this suggestion with just her expression and her body language. She keeps her feet tucked up under her and pulls her shoulders closer in, as if anchoring herself to the sofa.

'Or that thing pulls out, so you can crash here. We can call your mum in the morning.'

Once Amber has set up the sofa bed and found a duvet, the wave of exhaustion has passed, but it has left a dull ache behind her eyes. She goes to the hallway and kitchen one more time to check she has locked all the doors and windows, and climbs the stairs. She takes out her phone and texts Johnny. Not really saying anything: just that she is going to bed, just that she loves him.

He replies as she is collapsing into bed: a badly spelled message full of drunken declarations of love. She tries to picture him with the other musicians, knocking back drinks, laughing and maybe still lazily jamming.

The protective force field of being loved returns momentarily, and despite the hyper-vigilance state of her mind, she is unconscious within moments of lying down, falling straight into her recurring dream.

She is woken by a strong need to pee. Then the sensation changes. It is in all the same places she felt as she stood up by the car, but duller, more persistent. She is used to hip pain when she wakes — it's been there for weeks, since she started sleeping more on her side. But this is something new, a strange grip across her abdomen. She tries to push the worst thoughts away as she limps a little to the bathroom, stretching the discomfort out of her hips. Then that ripple again, followed by what feels like energetic movement.

She closes her eyes for a moment, trying to focus all of her perception down into the centre of her body, trying to feel the life inside her.

Bang, bang, bang.

For a moment, it is as if the noise is coming from inside her own head.

Bang, bang, bang.

No, it's from the house. It's the front door. Someone is pounding on it.

Memories hurtle around inside her like jagged bits of metal. She is back in the cottage all those years ago, following Benny down the stairs towards the intruder. She didn't hesitate. She was scared, but also gripped with that sense of needing to see for herself. Almost a journalistic rush. The urge to pick up Benny's camera must have come from the same instinct: to make a record of this stranger — a man who wanted something or meant them harm. That couldn't be stopped now, but she could claim a piece of evidence. Never miss the moment. Never flinch from the shot.

The things she did after that — she is less clear where they came from. Some primal, limbic space within her, inaccessible before or since. But she knows what she did, and she cannot get away from that.

The pounding comes again: *Bang, bang, bang.*

Then a change to the sound — a deadened rattle. Someone is shaking the door of her house. Someone is trying to get in.

35

Sunday, 11 November 2001

I fell sprawling backwards, as much as anything out of surprise and loss of balance. The punch was well landed and hard, but I'd been hit worse. Looking up at the man as I lay on the floor, I thought he could hit a lot harder if he needed to.

He met my gaze. I thought he was going to pile in on me or start kicking me, but he didn't. He gave me a very deliberate look.

I saw Amber now. She was rooted to the spot, staring down at the camera at her hip, as if strangely dissociated from what was going on around her. Like a sleepwalker, still trapped in a nightmare. Then her eyes met mine for a moment, bewildered and frightened.

My attention was swiftly back on the intruder. He was moving the hand he'd hit me with behind him into his back trouser pocket. When he brought it back out, there was something new in it. He squeezed it, and it clicked, a shining blade flicking out. He pointed it right at me, his eyeline following the point of the knife. It seemed to be telling me to stay where I was, to not try anything.

He took half a step back, paused, then started moving towards Amber.

I just moved on instinct now, scrambling to my feet. I shouted as I barrelled into him, and he half twisted towards me. It put him off balance, caught in the twist, and we crashed to the floor together. The hand with the knife reached away from me as he fell, and I grabbed his wrist, pinning it to the ground.

Amber was down on the floor next to me. I didn't understand why at first. Then her hand was with mine, pinning the intruder's wrist, trying to prise the knife out.

The man gave a jerk with his arm, and the blade slashed across Amber's palm. She fell back, clasping her hand under her arm, then scrambling to her feet. She was looking around desperately. Of all the things to grab, she reached for the large chrome coffee pot. She held it up and brought it smashing down on the intruder's hand, again and again until the knife was out, and she kicked it away from him.

I felt his other fist connect with my face, but without much power. I was holding tightly onto him, not giving him any space to swing. But he managed to use his body weight to flip us both over, and he was on top of me, pinning me down.

I'd seen plenty of fights in my life, but been in very few. And they'd just been brief tussles — someone trying to grab my camera, or a cop barging me away from the front line of a protest. I'd never fought like this, with the feeling that my opponent might kill me.

It's hard to describe what I saw next because everything was moving so quickly. I glanced towards Amber, but couldn't see her face because of the man on top of me, just her fast movement. First she was moving away from me, crouching on the floor. Then she was coming back.

There was hardly any blood as the knife went into the side of the intruder's neck. Precisely, quickly. Then Amber staggered back.

The intruder lurched off me, his hands up to his neck. He didn't cry out in pain. He just looked astonished, as if everything he had ever known and believed had been pulled away from him. Then — it must have been an automatic reaction — he pulled the knife out of his neck.

The blood flowed almost instantly, chasing the blade away from the wound. Again, nothing more than a look of lost astonishment. Then he crumpled, blood pouring from him onto the stone floor of the kitchen.

I expected Amber to start shouting or screaming. But she was dumbstruck, muttering something over and over. Her hand was bleeding badly, and she held it against her chest.

'Towels, get towels!' I shouted. 'Or sheets.'

I was in one of those situations I had seen before. A knife wound, a gunshot, the trauma from an explosion. I knew what we should do. I looked at the intruder and knew it was probably futile, but we should do it anyway. Amber didn't move. I pulled myself up and ran to find whatever I could to stop the bleeding.

By the time I came down, it was already too late. Amber was sitting on the floor, the intruder's head propped in her lap, his blood pooling around her bare legs. His eyes were open, staring up at her still with that look of bewilderment. But it was an illusion. The man was not feeling surprise or pain or fear. He wasn't feeling anything at all. He was gone.

36

Amber is frozen on the landing of her house, the memory of those blood-drowned moments pulsing in her mind. She's safe here, she tells herself. She's not going to be attacked in her own home. Then she thinks about that empty house next door, and that her next neighbours are a hundred yards away. Far enough not to hear.

She wrenches herself out of her paralysis and runs back into her bedroom. She pulls on her dressing gown and grabs her phone. She doesn't even check for notifications or messages, just presses the keypad and taps in 999. She doesn't dial, not yet. The sounds from outside have stopped.

Treading softly down the stairs, she is aware she has nothing in her hand to defend herself with. The only things she can think of are the knives in the kitchen, and that thought makes her feel sick. Yvey is standing in the doorway of the living room, still dressed, but blinking and rubbing her eyes.

They both stand in the darkness, just listening. Nothing, silence. Amber moves into the room, listening to every breath, every creak. She turns on the light. Then she hears the sound.

Tap, tap, tap.

She can't place its source at first.

Tap, tap, tap.

The window.

She brings her phone up in front of her, ready to press the call button. That moment, a message comes through on it. WhatsApp. That same number, that same blank white silhouette.

Look out your window.

She is rooted to the spot. She doesn't want to look and has to look all at the same time. She inches towards the curtains and grips them. She needs to know who is on the other side. One swift yank and a curtain is open, like tearing off a sticking plaster.

All she sees at first in the glass is her own reflection, the light in the room too bright. Then she sees there is something on the window. It's a photo, a small piece of sticky tape attaching it to the glass. She can't make it out for a moment. Then she sees. It is Amber, asleep in the cottage, that same soft splash of moonlight on her in the dark of the room. But this time the sheet has been pulled back to show her nakedness.

Looking at it, she doesn't feel shame or fear anymore. She feels rage. She runs out of the living room, barging past Yvey, and fumbles the keys from the hook in the hall. They fall, and she scrabbles on the floor for them. She's unlocking the door on her knees, then she is up again, and the door is open.

She looks out but can't see anything — it's pitch black, and her eyes have lost all their night vision. Her feet are fast into a pair of sandals by the front door, and she is outside, running to the end of the path. She can barely make anything out for a second. Then she sees the movement of a shadow in the road. Someone is running, fast, short and slim. The rage fills her again. She shouts at the night.

'Come back, you coward!' But now she feels afraid again and retreats towards the house. Yvey has come out and is peeling the photo off the outside of the front window.

'Don't!' Amber shouts at her. 'Leave it, please.'

But Yvey is already looking at it, a frown creasing across her face. Then she holds out the photo.

Amber snatches it from her. 'Go inside.'

Yvey meekly complies, and Amber follows. They stand in the hallway, looking at each other, their silent questions thrumming in the air between them. Eventually, Yvey speaks.

'What is this, Amber?'

'I think you should go home now. I'll get you a cab.'

Yvey does something that surprises Amber. She steps forward and takes the photo from her hand. Amber should take it back, but she is transfixed by the new forcefulness Yvey is projecting. She is studying the photo, her face creased in a frown: confused, sympathetic.

'Please, the photo,' Amber says.

'What's going on? Who was that?'

'You think I fucking know?' The words are full of Amber's rage, and Yvey flinches.

'I saw how you were at home. Something was going on then, and something's going on now. What is it, Amber?' There is a slight whine in her voice.

'Please give it to me.' Amber's voice matches Yvey, both caught in their different confusions. Yvey finally proffers it back, and Amber walks away from her into the living room, ashamed to be looked at. She sits down on the sofa and forces herself to look again at the photo of her exposed body. She turns it over for the first time. There is a message written on the back in crude block capitals.

WHAT WOULD JONNY SAY?

It makes her skin crawl, and she turns the message away from her, faced only with the photograph. This young, foolish, violated girl, naked on a bed.

When Yvey sits down next to her, she doesn't move away. It seems futile to keep this from her.

'My dad took this, didn't he?' Yvey says very gently.

'How do you know that?' But the question is unnecessary. Both women must know there is only one man at the centre of all this.

'What happened between you and him?'

'It was a long time ago. I didn't even know he took this photo.'

'And now someone's trying to get at you because of it? Why?'

'I don't know, Yvey, I don't know. I wish I did.'

A new look comes over Yvey's face — a look of deep seriousness that Amber hasn't seen before. 'Do you think... it sounds crazy... do you think this is something to do... something to do with my dad's death?'

Amber doesn't say anything, because she cannot avoid the fact that the two must be connected.

'D'you believe my mum? D'you really think Dad killed himself?'

Amber can't answer. She closes her eyes and is back in the cottage. She is thinking about the photo she took of the intruder, about how she killed him, about the secret she has hidden from everyone in the world for all these years. Everyone except Benny. And now he is gone, but these images are not. She is being punished. Someone is punishing her for everything she did.

She opens her eyes and looks at Yvey.

'What do you believe? You don't think it was suicide, and I don't think you believe it was an accident either. Why is that?' She reaches across to Yvey and grips one of her shoulders. 'What is it you know? What is it you're not telling me? Why is it you came here tonight?'

The girl pulls away out of her grasp, standing up and stumbling back.

'I told you, I had my scooter stolen.'

'Then why not just get a cab home? Why not call your mother? Did you come here to try to tell me something? You've been acting like you're terrified since you got here. What is it you're scared of?'

'What happened to my dad?' says Yvey starkly, boring a look into Amber. 'You would tell me if you knew.'

'Of course I would.' Amber hesitates before asking the next question, but then throws herself into it. 'Do you think your mum knows something? Do you think she's not telling you the truth?'

Yvey's eyes go down again.

'I don't know if anyone's telling the truth,' she says forlornly. 'Mum said she was visiting Granny, but when I talked to Granny about it at Dad's funeral, she didn't know what I was talking about.'

A cold feeling rises in Amber. 'Have you spoken to anyone else about this?'

Yvey is looking at the floor, chewing on her lip. 'I think you're right. I think I should go.' Without saying anything else, she picks up her coat from where it was draped over a chair and pulls it quickly on.

'Wait. Stay.' But Yvey is heading towards the door. 'You have to tell me what you know.'

Yvey has opened the door and is halfway down the path.

'At least let me get you an Uber.'

Yvey turns back, hesitating. Amber brandishes the photograph at her.

'And you don't know anything about this?'

'Of course I don't.'

'Nothing about the messages I've been getting?'

'What messages?'

'Someone's been...' But Amber doesn't go on, frightened of how even the smallest thread might unravel everything.

'I'm sorry, Amber,' says Yvey, and she is walking quickly now, away from the house. She breaks into a little trot, scampering off into the darkness.

'Please wait,' Amber calls out after her. But Yvey doesn't stop, and Amber finds herself following to the end of the path, then beyond it, chasing down the road after Yvey, possessed by her unanswered questions. Her feet slap and slip on the wet ground, so dark beneath her that she can't judge its distance and surface. She's not going fast, but her foot catches on the edge of a pothole. She feels a wet splash on her bare skin, and her balance is thrown.

She is falling. She gets an arm out before she hits, but is surprised by the force through her body, by the shock wave that travels through her limbs and into her torso. And in that last bit of the fall, she came down hard on her stomach.

She rolls away instinctively, feeling the cold tarmac sharply through her dressing gown. She looks at her hands, the blood already beginning to seep through the grazes. She looks up for some sign of Yvey, but there is nothing. She shouts for help, trying to stand up, but is dizzy and disoriented.

Then Yvey is at her side, materialised out of the night, helping her up, asking her if she is okay.

'I'm fine,' Amber says, but she doesn't believe her own words. She runs her hands over her belly as if she can somehow sense the true effects of the fall. How hard did she fall on it? Has she hurt the baby? She is cold and numb. Her whole body feels strange. She is holding her breath, trying to detect some movement. Any movement. But there is nothing. No strange pains, no reassuring ripples, no popcorn sensation. None of the feelings she was having all evening. A screaming silence from within.

She grabs Yvey's wrist, hard. 'I think I need to go to the hospital. Right now.'

37

BENNY

Sunday, 11 November 2001

Amber had gone very quiet. She had crawled away from the body and sat on the floor in the glass extension. Her legs were crossed, and her head was bowed into her hands as if in deep prayer. I recognised the shock she was in. I was shocked too, but I knew more about what to do with the feeling.

I had been thinking very quickly: as the man attacked us, as I ran up to get towels, as I came down to find him dead. The suspicion I had come to wasn't one I could ignore anymore. I looked towards where the dead man lay, covered now in a sheet, and the idea wouldn't leave me. I knew what I did and said next was crucial. I had to take control of this situation. I knew what the right thing to do was, but I also knew what I was going to do. They weren't the same thing.

'You should have a shower,' I said to Amber as matter-offactly as I could manage. 'Take that jumper off now and leave it there on the floor. I'll deal with our clothes later.'

Amber finally looked up. She didn't turn to me, but we faced each other's reflections in the darkened glass.

'What? We shouldn't touch anything. Benny, we have to call the police.'

'You realise we can't do that.'

'We just killed a man.'

'*You* just killed a man.' It was cruel for me to do this, but I had to use her fear.

She dropped her eyes towards her lap. 'He was... I was defending you. It was self-defence.' But I could already feel the weakness in her words.

'Everything is over if we go to the police.'

'You think I really care about us right now?'

'I'm not talking about *us*. I'm talking about me, and I'm talking about you. We'll both be finished by this.'

'It was self-defence,' she says again, finally twisting round to look at me.

'Don't you see, it's not about that. This will all play out in public. Do you really want that?'

'You're worried about our affair being discovered? Is that it? Christ.'

'And you're not?'

'You're a piece of shit, Benny.' She re-engaged with my reflection in the window. 'Who was he, anyway?'

'How the hell should I know?'

'Maybe it's connected to... you never told me who owns this place. What if it's to do with them? Maybe we should call them.'

'Are you out of your mind?' I threw at her. 'Look, he was probably just a homeless guy, or some burglar taking a chance, or someone off his face.'

'Someone who's been following us all weekend? Why are you lying to me, Benny?'

I went silent, thinking for a moment about how much to say.

'Okay, honestly? You think someone like me doesn't make enemies in my work? I've spent my life taking photos of people who don't want their photos taken. You know how many times I've had someone want to kill me?'

'Enough to track you down later and... What aren't you telling me?'

I had to shut this down. 'You have to trust me when I tell you this. At the moment, no one knows you're here. No one knows you're a part of what just happened. And I can tell you, you want to keep it that way. If there are people who want me dead, there's no need for them to want you dead as well. Now, just do exactly what I say, and we'll be fine. I promise you.'

I looked at her reflection. It helped that she wouldn't face me. It was like two shadow versions of our true selves were having the argument. But now, I walked across the room and crouched in front of her.

'Kiddo, look.' I took her hands. One was wrapped tightly in a tea towel, dark with blood. 'Please look at me.' She raised her eyes to me, full of tears. 'If you really want to call the police. If you really want to have this dragged out in public. If you really think you can take all the damage that this is going to do to us. If you want this to follow you round for the rest of your life–'

'Stop it, Benny, stop it!'

But I wasn't going to stop. There was only one way this could end.

38

A mber is hunting in the eyes of the on-call obstetrician for a sign, any sign. But he is doing his inscrutable routine as he moves the ultrasound probe around her belly. The cold gel sends tingles around her middle and a shiver up her back. She closes her eyes, unable to look at the doctor or at the strange moving negative forming in waves on the screen.

She is waiting for the steady *whoosh-whoosh* of her baby's heartbeat. But she knows, even if she hears it, that it won't be enough to reassure her. She has done the reading and knows about the risks of a fall in pregnancy: the placenta separating early from the uterus, or a skull injury to the baby. Then there are all the things she has not read about but can imagine.

She had stumbled back into the house with Yvey and gone into a dissociated autopilot, calling the urgent contact number printed on her big plastic pregnancy folder. She ordered two cabs. One was taking Yvey home, the other taking her to the hospital.

A process of compartmentalisation was happening in her

brain as she sat and waited, shutting away all thoughts of Benny and the photos. All she could think about was the child inside her. She didn't even have enough attention to speak to Yvey. She just asked her to wait in the kitchen while Amber sat in her living room, wrapping her arms around herself. She closed her eyes, directing her attention down into her body. *Come on, come on, move!*

She didn't feel any guilt when her car arrived first, and she left Yvey waiting outside her house in the darkness. But as she drove towards the hospital, she felt negligent and unmaternal, as if it was her own daughter she had left there. She sent Yvey a text, asking her to message when she got home safe.

The person she wanted to call more than anyone was Johnny, but she couldn't. She got his number up but couldn't dial. She couldn't construct another lie; couldn't hear his voice and tell him she had done something reckless and stupid to endanger their child. Not with all the other explanation it would involve. She had to face this alone. If the news was bad, then she would tell him. She would tell him everything. There would be no more secrets between them. That thought kept her thumb hovering over the green dial icon.

Besides, right now he would be drunk. He wouldn't be able to do anything or come back to see her till the morning. She didn't want him to do something rash. She had visions of him rushing down, a crash on the motorway, leaving her alone, completely alone.

The decision solidified for her, and she put her phone away. She rode out the rest of the journey to the hospital in cold stillness, watching the stretching glow from the passing street lamps moving on the inside of the cab.

The hospital was still and empty. Her voice was choked with tears as she tried to speak to the midwife who greeted her at the clinic. She did not trust anymore the small feelings of movement she thought she had detected on the journey. She just knew that her whole world was on the edge of collapse, and she would do anything to protect this small part of it.

And now she is sitting, waiting for the obstetrician to speak, imagining all the worst things.

Finally, he breaks his impenetrable frown and gives a light smile. Not much goes in after Amber hears him say: 'Well, everything seems fine.' Just a wave of relief like the hit of a drug. She tunes back in to hear him talking about her blood pressure being a bit high. 'We should keep an eye on that. Has it been high generally?'

'No, fine, normal. It's all been normal.' *Normal.* Nothing feels normal anymore.

'And is everything else all right? At home, work and so on?' She can see the squint in the doctor's eyes, as if he has been able to read a piece of her mind with his ultrasound probe. 'Can I ask where Dad is tonight? Your notes said–'

She cuts him off. 'He's away for work.'

But she feels again that the doctor doesn't fully believe the story she has concocted about the fall — putting out the bins and tripping in the dark. And why would he? She feels that lunatic edge to her thought again. 'Look, it's all fine. I'm sorry if I overreacted.'

'No, you did the right thing.'

Amber tries to tell him again about the strange pains and vigorous movement she'd been feeling before the fall, and how she took the lack of pain afterwards as a bad omen. She gets muddled in her words and feels foolish.

'The sensations you're describing sound very normal.' He gives a small frown. 'But perhaps it's worth booking you in for a routine follow-up. And in the meantime, perhaps keeping a diary of movement and any pains might be helpful. But the main thing now is that...' He starts to make a *sh* shape with his mouth, but stops himself. 'Baby's fine.'

But she's already heard it. She's already heard him say *She's fine.* A daughter. And she doesn't mind that she knows. She is glad. She clings onto this new thought, and another wave of relief floods over her. It makes her start talking at speed about how long it has taken for her to get to this point, how frightened she is of losing the baby.

The doctor listens, giving reassuring nods, but she can tell his attention is already elsewhere, that he has other emergencies that require him. She feels small and alone again, her own crisis just a tiny wave in a great storm of humanity.

As SHE WALKS out of the hospital, a blurred line of sunrise is showing at the edge of the sky, like light that has bled through the cracks of an old camera onto a roll of film. She checks her phone, hoping to see some signal from Yvey that she has got home safely, but there is nothing. In the cab she sends her a brief message:

> *Everything fine here. Thank you for waiting with me. Hope you got home. A.*

The words feel heavy with everything unsaid.

The reply doesn't come through until she is letting herself into her house. It feels even more perfunctory and evasive than her own message.

> *thanks am home please don't tell mum*

Amber goes to bed and wraps her duvet around herself, thinking of Johnny's arms enfolding her like great branches. She sobs and does not sleep.

. . .

AFTER A RAIN-SOAKED NIGHT, it is a clear morning. The sun comes up and strikes her window, pushing shards of light through the gap in the curtains. She goes down to the kitchen and makes strong, real coffee. The pot feels heavy in her hand.

She sits looking out of the kitchen window. She knows it is early, and Johnny will be sleeping off his hangover, but she calls him anyway. He answers groggily at first, but realising it is Amber, a note of bewildered alarm comes into his voice.

'It's fine, J, everything's fine. I just didn't sleep well. I missed you. I wanted to hear your voice.'

'Missed you too, babe,' he says automatically.

'And I've been thinking about what you said, what we both said. About my dad, about this job and Benny, and... I just want... we're going to have a baby, J, and I want it to be a new start for us. I want to forget about the past. The only thing that matters is what happens next. And whatever happens, however hard it gets, we'll be okay, won't we?'

There is silence on the line, and she feels Johnny is very far away from her, further than she will ever be able to reach. What she has said to him is the truth. Behind all the lies and secrets, she has tried to find the truest sentiment she can express to him.

'Babe, of course we will. What's happened?'

'Nothing. I've just been trying to clear the nonsense in my head.' The return of the lie cuts into her. She cannot tell him everything she is thinking — that the fate of the child inside her is just a piece of the great puzzle of all her fears — but she still needs to hear his reassurance. She still needs to know that if all her nightmares follow her into her waking world, that he will not abandon her. 'It's just nice to be reminded that there will always be us. Promise me that.'

'Babe, from the moment I met you, there was only ever going to be us.'

She closes her eyes and imagines his arms around her again. All the strange dark doubts she felt the previous day evaporate for a moment. She doesn't doubt his words. She has never doubted any of his promises, but she also knows the emptiness at the heart of them. He might have meant his words, but they weren't real if they weren't made in the presence of the truth. All the times he's stuck by her, he's been protecting a lie without even knowing it. His devotion and her betrayal burn in her core.

39

BENNY

Sunday, 11 November 2001

Neither of us really spoke as we carried out the task — just my instructions to Amber, who silently complied. I knew I was taking advantage of her state of shock, but I didn't have a choice.

I had already bound the dead man's neck tightly to keep as much blood inside him as I could. After that, all I could find to wrap him in was the large roll of bubble wrap from the cottage attic. He crackled and squeaked as we rolled him into it. I placed some large stones from the beach into the last layer before binding the package up with parcel tape. I knew I would have to replace all these things, along with the sheet, the towels, the mop, the dented coffee pot. Cover every trace.

I was glad of the modern flooring in the kitchen and extension. There is a lot of blood in a human, and it would have stained stone or wood. We would have had no chance. But as we dragged the body out onto the decking, I looked back at the remaining bloodstains and thought we might just have a chance.

The moon had set now. It was just the stars and the angry hiss of the sea. After we dragged the body to the small boat tied to the post near the groyne, I walked back, scuffing up the sand.

I thought I'd need to row out on my own, so I was surprised that once we'd hauled in the body, Amber joined me in the boat. Perhaps it was a sense in her that she had to see it through. I held onto that thought. It felt like a guarantee of her future silence.

The sea was bigger than it had seemed from the shore, and the boat pitched and rolled queasily. Amber sat white and trembling as I rowed, watching the dim light from the cottage disappear. I had a vision of not stopping, of rowing us all out to our ends in the middle of the North Sea.

Amber interrupted my thoughts: 'Isn't this far enough?'

So we heaved the body over the side. It sank immediately down into the darkness. We looked at each other, sharing the knowledge that this moment would lock us together forever.

40

After speaking to Johnny, Amber crashes out and sleeps until late morning, her phone switched off. The sound of a far-off siren disturbs her sleep. She has the sense of someone next to her, but she wakes with a start to an empty bed and a burning appetite.

She heaps leftovers onto a plate and flops down in front of the news. It thumps its drum of impending pandemic doom louder now: images of shoppers hoarding food and toilet paper. She shovels the food into her mouth as if consumed by a need to fatten herself up. She thinks of her half-empty food cupboard, how Johnny and she have always lived day-to-day, week-to-week. Her brain still cannot process what is rolling inexorably towards everyone. It gives her a momentary sense of calm that it will be everyone's crisis, not simply her own.

For years she has wanted to block away completely what happened to her — what she did. To forget, to imagine that it didn't happen at all. Sometimes she has managed to feel that it happened to someone else. Or to an earlier version of her, an Amber from a parallel life, a shadow, a fleeting reflection caught in a moving mirror. But she just needs to look at that scar on her hand to know it was real.

The intruder was already moving towards Benny as she pressed the shutter on his camera. Then she saw Benny crumple from the punch, and the man was advancing towards her.

After that, it is a series of stuttering blanks in her memory, images interspersed with black frames. She remembers being down on her knees, trying to grab the intruder's knife, then the pain in her hand. Then she had the big chrome coffee pot, and she was smashing down on the man's hand. The knife was free.

She could have acted differently. She could have taken the coffee pot to the back of the man's head. Or slashed the knife at his back, or stabbed his legs. But she didn't. She saw the knife, saw Benny, and saw the soft vulnerable flesh of the intruder's neck.

The next moment that is completely clear to her is sitting on the floor, holding the dying man's head in her lap, the life draining from him, a look of lost confusion on his face.

She doesn't know why she can remember the man's expression but not the face itself. She has played and replayed to herself that night over and over until she stopped trusting her memory of it. Because memory isn't burned with the precision of a photograph. It is soft, it changes, it rebuilds itself again and again. And all that has really stayed with her, all that she really trusts, is the look of those strong blue eyes.

She felt hollowed out as Benny dropped her off at Norwich train station the morning after. It was partly to avoid any risk of being seen together, but it was also that they couldn't be in each other's company any longer. There was a repelling force between them: at the same moment that they both realised they were tied together forever, they knew also that they had been splintered apart.

She let herself into Johnny's flat, where she'd been living since she graduated, feeling deeply grateful that he was away on tour. As she fell onto her bed, she did not feel panicked, just exhausted, empty and numb. And in the familiar confines of the cosy space she shared with her boyfriend, already the sense of it all having happened to someone else was forming. She realised starkly in that moment that this was how she had maintained her affair with Benny. She hadn't been unfaithful; she had merely partitioned one part of her life away from the other. And now, rather than letting the lie collapse, rather than letting all the guilt flow in, she felt she had to keep it separate forever.

She found herself drifting into a thick, blank sleep, as if in a drugged state. When she woke, she ventured towards her bag and slowly unpacked it as if it was full of toxic material.

At the cottage, they had put all the clothes, sheets and towels through the washing machine to get the worst off. Then Benny had put most of them in his car to dispose of elsewhere and replace later. He had asked Amber to get rid of her jumper. He said it reduced the risk for him not to have anything of hers in the car. The jumper still had a great dark stain across its middle. She had wrapped it carefully in a plastic bag and put it at the bottom of her luggage.

She finally got to it now and was gripped by an illogical feeling that she should hold onto it. It was a sense that she needed proof about what had happened, even though that proof was dangerous.

In the end, without removing it from its bag, she simply stuffed it deep down in the black plastic rubbish bag that filled the kitchen bin. She put the bag in the wheelie bin, and the next morning watched the dustmen flip the contents into the rubbish truck. Landfill seemed as sensible a place as any, just a tiny speck of rubbish among the millions of tonnes of London waste.

It was another two weeks before Johnny came home from his tour. In the meantime, Amber took a few days sick off work and avoided seeing anyone. It gave her enough space to construct what she thought was a secure place in her mind to store what had just happened to her — what she had just done.

'What did you do to your hand?' Johnny asked, almost the first question after he'd come in through the door. The wound was getting better, but she still had to wear a dressing, because every time she moved her hand, the skin would reopen. She should have got stitches. If she had, she might not have that light scar still there.

'I got bored and went ice skating,' she said, having decided on something prosaic. 'That open-air one at Somerset House.' A small embellishment to make it ring true. 'Got a bit run over.'

He took her hands and kissed her fingers the way Benny had at the cottage. She did her best to repress a shudder, but some of it came through. He didn't really pick up on it, just hugged her as if she might be cold.

'You should be more careful, babe,' he said, and that was all the lie she needed to tell that day. It was only in the months that followed that she had to steadily construct her latticework of deception. And as the flashbacks worsened, the nightmares became more frequent, so the need to isolate herself from Johnny grew. It was then she fell back on that primal trauma of her father's death.

'I'm sorry I'm broken,' she would say, until it became a refrain.

'You're not broken,' he would reply. 'No more than anyone else.'

Even so, there were times she believed he was on the verge of leaving her. There were even times she told him he should. There were times she nearly left herself. Times she disappeared for a day or two just to be on her own.

And, just as when she saw Genevieve after the cottage, each time she didn't tell Johnny the truth, it became harder to break down that wall. Each lie compounded and reinforced the one before it. But just as the burden of the lie became bigger, so did her love for Johnny. The fact he was determined to stay with her despite all this bound her to him.

Eventually, in a way she did not fully understand or want to examine too closely, it all began to recede. The memories of the cottage became less fierce, the physical symptoms less debilitating. There was a hardening that formed within her centre, and a shell that grew around her.

There were still questions to be asked: about what really happened that night, about who that intruder was, and why he had been there. But as much as Amber wanted to know the truth, she also needed to bury the event completely. Those two feelings fought in her each time she turned a paranoid eye to the news and police reports from the local area.

It was months after the weekend that she saw the short news report on the primitive website of the local Norfolk paper. Remains washed up on a beach near Cromer, fifty miles or more north of the cottage. Badly decomposed, said the report, and not yet identified. Police were making enquiries.

The only other thing Amber wished she could know was who owned the cottage. The Land Registry would have the information, but an anonymous enquiry was impossible. So after finding the news of the remains, she stopped searching. But for a year or more, each time the doorbell sounded, she had a flash of the police at the door. But they never came.

And now, it isn't the police who have come for her. It is someone unseen, unknown.

She finishes her food and turns the television off. She

showers for a long time, feeling for those moments protected by the water cascading over her body, curving its way round her changing shape. That maternal instinct swells again, stronger this time, more certain. Less dominated by fear, more by determination. A desire to protect. A desire that she will not let what is happening destroy everything she has.

She repeats to herself the words she said to Johnny: the only thing that matters is what happens next. She cannot run from the past, always following her across the great empty space of her life, and she cannot let it catch her. She must catch it and stop it. There can be only the future now.

41

AMBER

Showered and dressed and sitting at her desk, Amber turns on her phone almost more in expectation than fear. But she finds nothing new from that grey, unfeatured face. Silent, waiting.

As she is holding it, her phone starts to buzz, and she answers it like a reflex. She wishes she hadn't. It's Kay. Amber doesn't want to speak to her now.

'Hello, sweetie. Weren't we supposed to meet this morning?'

'Were we?'

'Yes, you said you could do Thursday?'

'Did I? Sorry, I... Look, Kay, I'm sorry I'm a bit flaky right now. I'm just going through a rough patch.'

'I understand. You just let me know if there's anything old Kay can help with.'

'Thank you, I will.' For a moment she contemplates again bringing Kay into her confidence, but once again draws back, settling on a weak promise to catch up.

Amber hangs up and tries to refocus, knowing she must keep going or the relentless dread will be upon her.

Before she got in the cab to the hospital, she had the presence of mind to do one thing. She took the picture that had been stuck to her window, and locked it in the drawer where she had stowed the negatives.

Now she retrieves the photo and forces herself to look at her unconscious, naked form laid out on the bed. Her sense of violation feels oddly deadened. As much as she is repulsed by the photograph, she is also fascinated by it. It is a window into a moment she does not remember, and might hold a key to things she cannot see.

A feeling she had before about the negatives comes back to her. It is the sense that if she looks closely enough, they might be able to tell her a secret.

It's then she sees it. This photo, scanned and printed, has something those negatives did not. And it is something that was too small to recognise in the pictures on her phone. But it is clear now, an artefact in the image where the white of the moonlight bleeds against the shadow of the room. There is a slight banding where the brightness ends, and a halo that extends beyond it into the darkness. She has seen that effect before. It is the error Mika made on the scanner.

She gets a quick spasm of muscles across her body, reflexively putting a hand to her belly. She checks the suspicion. This doesn't feel like proof: any number of people might be able to use that scanner imperfectly. But that figure running away from her house — she is sure it was a man. Someone short and slim, moving with the speed and energy of a young person.

What would Mika want from her, though? Who the hell even is he? Just a cocky kid, hired through an agency. And now he's off somewhere else, absenting himself from the scene of all this.

He is a blank in her mind. No, not quite a blank. His face is there. Boyish, handsome, tanned. Those piercing blue eyes.

Lots of people have blue eyes, she says to herself, pushing away the ideas of that connection. *Be logical about this.*

As she fishes out the business card Mika gave to her at the farmhouse, she remembers she gave him hers too. Which means he has her mobile number.

She looks at his card. Mika Vilander. What is that name? Scandinavian? His accent wasn't anything other than English. But what does that tell her?

She opens a browser and tries a few searches. There's nothing obvious on social media, but then who uses their real name anymore? He must have a portfolio. You don't get to be Benedict Raine's assistant from nothing. Finally she finds it, a white, sparse website, with a few galleries of grungy images. Aggressive, lenses right up in people's faces. Bright, distorted colours. Almost a violence to them. Nothing about their aesthetic has any kindred spirit with Benny's work. But aesthetics isn't an assistant's job. It is to fetch and carry, sort and organise, and find your way round an archive. To know where everything is. Even the images that have stayed hidden for years.

She pictures Mika and Genevieve and the hostility that lay between them. Was that a front, a deliberate show put on for Amber's benefit? A bluff to cover their true allegiance?

And what about Yvey and Mika? What was that cold suspicion she seemed to have for him? She trusts Yvey's reaction more, as much as she trusts anything. She is still troubled by the convenience of Yvey being at her house when her tormenter came for her. But Amber believes the fear she saw in her face, and the sense that she too is looking for the truth about Benny. And anyway, Amber was looking right at the girl when the first WhatsApp message arrived. Unless a co-conspirator sent it.

This last thought conjures a twisted image of everyone in it together, each suspect taking a turn at plunging the knife.

Mika, the son of the murdered intruder; Genevieve, the betrayed wife; Sam, the dark fixer; Yvey, the innocent foil. A cabal intent on dismantling her.

But why stop there? Perhaps she is looking too closely at the people she can see, not imagining all those she cannot. Who else is lurking just out of view? Beyond the opaque glass, in amongst the trees. The man in the green overalls, his expressionless stare as she left the farmhouse.

She shuts her eyes, trying to stop chasing her thoughts in circles, trying to pull herself out of the mire of supposition and paranoia.

She takes another look at that picture of her asleep, exposed. Then she is on YouTube, digging out that last interview of Benny's, the one she watched on the day she learned of his death. She watches it again, inspecting and measuring each of his words.

I think it's time to tell it all. Let it all out into the open.

She hears in her head Benny's words at the cottage about all the people who wanted him dead, and is certain now she believes Yvey's unstated suspicion of murder much more than Genevieve's theory of suicide.

What was it Benny wanted to tell? Was it just what happened at the cottage, or something else? And who might have wanted to stop him from saying it? A man tried to kill Benny years ago, and someone has now succeeded.

That man at the cottage also tried to kill me. Did someone want me dead then? Does someone want it now?

Amber knows there is a key to this, locked in her memory. Those strong blue eyes and the forgotten face. She tries to remember the intruder again, but nothing new comes. Because her memory won't simply submit to willpower. It cannot be cajoled and blackmailed into giving up its secrets. But the face is not just locked in her memory. It was also captured on film. Her only hope of understanding all this is the same thing she fears seeing.

She picks up her phone again and stares at the little empty white box in the messaging app, the smiley emoji button gloating at her.

Why has her tormenter not sent the photograph of the intruder? Why, for that matter, have the photos not all come at once? She still cannot fully grasp the psychological calculus of the campaign against her. Perhaps the torment itself is simply the point.

Unless they don't have the photo. Does it even exist? Did it come out?

She types:

Do you have it?

She deletes the words. No, she can't show any doubt or allow any ambiguity. There is a sequence to the photos she has been receiving, and she knows how it ends. At its core, her persecution by this faceless stranger cannot be about her infidelity, or about her naked body, violated by Benny's camera. This must be about the man who bled to death on the cottage floor, and the photo she took of him. A photo not only of a moment, but one that holds in it all the things that led to it and everything that followed.

This game has to end.

I know you have the photo of the intruder. What is it you want from me?

She hits send, and she waits.

42

AMBER

The brightness of the morning is short-lived, a veil of cloud swallowing the blue sky. Out of the window above her desk, Amber can see nothing but an expanse of fields. The view is textureless and almost monochrome in the flat grey light.

When her phone gives its short buzz of a new message, and she sees it is from that blank grey face, she almost feels relief. It is a sense, at least, that she is getting closer to something and is exerting the smallest touch of control on the situation.

It is just an image, no words.

The first thing she sees is that the photo is overexposed, a whiteness bleeding from the kitchen lights, giving the image an almost ethereal quality.

In her instinct to take it, she hadn't thought to play with the settings on the camera, just glanced down where it sat against her hip, and squeezed the shutter button.

Now she knows the camera had been set to take pictures in the moonlight — those pictures of her. But the overexposure has an advantage here. It means the shadowed face of the intruder is perfectly visible. The hat is down to his eyebrows, but the rest of the face is clear.

There is no colour in the photo, so she cannot see those blue eyes the way she saw them back then. But she can see a well-structured jaw and cheekbones, a mouth puckered in uncertainty. Perhaps he looks a little fearful too, realising the weight of what he is there to do.

The full extent of the picture is also different from her memory. In her mind, this photo has always been a close-up of the intruder. In fact, from where she was standing, it is a wider shot. Benny is there, right at the edge of the frame. He is looking back towards Amber. What does his face say? It shows surprise, a little confusion, and something else perhaps. A hint of anger?

After a few minutes, a text message follows.

What do I want? I want you to stop lying. It's time to tell the truth. All of it.

She looks at the words and tries to hear a voice behind them. She feels like responding: *I don't know the truth. I wish I did.*

She looks again at the face of the man in the picture. Not just a fragmented memory, but a staging post on the way towards the truth. She has to have the courage she didn't have before to find out who he was.

She starts with what she knows, finding the local paper that reported the body found near Cromer. But there is nothing to see — no online archive beyond the last few years. Following the links around the edges of the page, the paper seems to have been bought recently by a large news network. She can imagine the newsroom now as a shadow of its former self, decimated by cut after cut. Perhaps she is glad of that, glad there are no longer banks of eager local journalists chasing stories about mysterious bodies.

Looking beyond the paper, the online trail appears at first cold. Rather than narrowing down towards her target, the search spreads out in front of her on the screen. The web is full of stories of bodies washed up on the Norfolk shores. Most have been identified, and most weren't treated as suspicious by the police. Suicides and accidents. Perhaps men in their prime, going for a swim, their daughters waiting for them on the shore.

Then she is in the official Police Missing Persons website, with its pages and pages of unidentified bodies, full of stark details of fatal injuries and states of decay. Severed limbs washed ashore, burned torsos in derelict houses, decomposed remains dredged up in fishing nets. There are lists of distinguishing features, hair and eye colour, clothing, possessions, false teeth, jewellery, tattoos. Some have photos, others police sketches, some just blank silhouettes. The records go back to the 1960s, body after body after body.

People who died, and no one has claimed them, no one has mourned them. Amber finds herself gently crying, all her own losses welling up inside her and pouring silently out. She blinks away the tears and tries to find a way to narrow her search to the Norfolk area, but the website won't let her do that. So she arranges all the cases by date and slowly zeros in on the months after that weekend at the cottage.

She props her phone up next to the computer and pinches in on the photo of the intruder so she can see it as she flicks through the entries.

There are no faces that match, but there is something. There is a case with the right dates for the body found at Cromer. As she starts to read the entry, it looks like so many of the bodies that have washed up on beaches over the years.

There is no photo or sketch, and the description talks of remains rather than a body.

As she reads, Amber feels cold and sick. She wonders about the knife wound in the intruder's neck. But there is nothing that suggests the police know how this man was killed. Nor have they obtained a DNA match with any records, or any other distinguishing features. But the estimated age, height and weight of the man match Amber's memories and the photograph.

There is a link at the bottom of the page:

I may know this person: Click here to contact the Missing Persons Unit with details about this person.

She backs away from the computer, her breath beating up and down as if she has been exercising. She tries another tack — in part to pull herself away from that glowering police contact link — and finds the main missing persons charity website. Even filtering by gender and when they went missing, she still has to scroll through pages and pages of entries. People's sons, fathers, brothers. Lost and troubled faces. The face of a toddler, clear-eyed and innocent. She thinks of the people who reported their relatives and friends missing, and wonders who the important people in the intruder's life were.

Then, there he is. She looks to her phone and back to the screen, back and forth, again and again. But she can't avoid it. It's him. She clicks on the face, and his page appears.

Finn Gallagher.

A colour passport photo, almost like a police mugshot. A hard unhappy frown on his face.

Age at disappearance: 32

Missing from: Peckham, London

Missing since: 08 Nov 2001

There's a reference number and white writing on a magenta square:

*Finn, we are here for you whenever you are ready. We can
listen, talk you through what help you need, pass a
message for you and help you to be safe. Call. Text.
Anytime. Free. Confidential.*

And that's all it says. A link sits underneath:

Report a sighting.

Amber flicks back to the tab with the police website.
I may know this person.

She finds herself clicking the link. A form appears in
front of her. She could do it. She could tell the police everything and send them the photograph of Finn that sits on her
phone. She could bring it all crashing down around her.

It feels like the times she would stare at her stockpiled
sleeping pills, wondering if she had the courage to down
them all with an old bottle of brandy. Courage or cowardice?
Or the times she thought about disappearing herself.
Walking out through the door and never coming back.

She says his name out loud: 'Finn Gallagher. Who were
you?'

But the way towards the answer is a vast empty darkness,
like the night and the sea stretching out in front of her.

43

The only results for Finn Gallagher lead back to the missing persons page Amber has just been looking at. She thinks again about the time before we all left our footprints everywhere we went online. But the web only goes so deep. She needs help.

It's time to take a risk. It feels like a crazy thing to do, but there's nothing sane left. She knows she is hastening her own exposure by doing this, but that destination seems inevitable now. The car is hurtling towards the wall. She just wants to be in control of it.

But she will split her risk, place different parcels of trust with different allies. She makes a phone call. It's to Ed Kapoor. The bloodhound and people finder who lives in that insulated corner of her life. It is time to break the seal.

'Ed, hi.'

'Amber, long time no-speaky. You get my email?'

'Yeah, Ed, sorry, been hectic. Need to ask you a fave.' Her tone is matching his as she forces a casual air into it.

Before she called, then as the phone rang, and as they exchanged pleasantries, she has been constructing a fiction to couch her request in. It will be an idea for a retrospective, some research on a photographic subject from long ago. But as she opens her mouth, the pretence falls away.

'I need you to find out about someone for me.'

'Umm, what's this about?'

'Can we do this on a no-questions-asked basis?'

'Uh, sure. You okay?'

'Yeah. I'll tell you someday. There's a guy I photographed when I was just finishing college. And I recently came across him on a missing persons website. He disappeared not long after I snapped him.'

Ed cuts her off with his sharp, barking laugh. 'What, you want me to find him? You need a private dick, mate.'

'No, not that. I just want you to find out what you can about him. Anything.'

'Anything?'

'Yeah, background. Family? Any kids, say? And maybe any priors. Any trouble with the law?'

'Not a nice person, you're saying?'

'No questions asked, Ed. Please. Trust me.'

'But you're all right? Sorry, that was a question.'

'I'll allow it. I'm fine, really.' And for a brief moment, she feels it. She feels not entirely alone.

It doesn't last. She hands over Finn Gallagher's name and promises to send Ed a link to the missing persons page. It feels like handing over a loaded weapon, and for a second she feels Ed is going to sniff her out. She imagines him making a great and sudden deductive leap and accusing her of murder. But he just gives a grunt to say he's got the name written down.

'As soon as you get anything, can you let me know?'

'I'll do what I can.'

And he is gone. Amber wants to vomit.

She sucks the feeling down and moves on to the second

request for help she know she needs to make. This one is a much bigger ask, a bigger risk.

She bounces her phone in her hand, takes two slow breaths and dials Kay's number. The phone rings and rings. Finally, Kay's voice is there.

'Hello, sweetie. Still alive, then?'

'I'm sorry, I've been hopeless. Look, are you free?'

'For you, always.'

'Do you think you could pick me up? My car's out of action. I need a lift somewhere.'

'Sure. What's this about?'

'I'll explain when I see you.'

She hangs up, and a hot flush runs across her cold core.

44

The sky is crushing down now, a pall of dark grey cloud. Amber climbs into the passenger seat of Kay's car.

'So, where are we going? Road trip? Rob a bank?'

'I was hoping you could drive me to Benedict Raine's house.'

'Oookay. What happened to your car?'

Amber ignores the question. 'I thought maybe we could talk on the way.'

'What's this about?'

'I can trust you, can't I?'

'Of course you can.'

'I mean, I can tell you things, and you're not going to tell anyone?'

'We really are going to rob a bank, aren't we?'

There is something forced about Kay's jollity. It feels like compensation for Amber's mood — heavy, sombre, frightened. Kay reaches down for the handbrake, and the car moves off. Amber takes a breath.

'When I saw you last, and I wouldn't tell you what was

really up. That I'd been thinking about what happened to Benny and...' She pauses and weighs the words in her head before she says them. 'What if I told you I'm pretty sure he was murdered?'

Kay laughs, hard and staccato.

'This is serious.'

Kay rearranges her face into a frown.

'I know we never talk about Benny,' says Amber. 'I know this is my fault, because I've always been ashamed of the affair. But, can I ask you, how much did you really know about him?'

Kay just shrugs, driving a little too fast down the narrow lane.

'Ever since we first met, and you guessed about me and him... It's clear you didn't like him.'

Kay shrugs again. 'I didn't really know him. But his reputation was hardly a secret.'

'Sure, but from friends, gossip... what did you ever hear?'

'Look, the thing about Benny... He was only ever about himself.' The flippancy is finally gone from Kay's voice. She gives a fast, hard sigh. 'I only met him a few times. But, well, Freddie once said to me you could always have a mighty time with Benny, but that he never really cared so long as he was having one. Not sure he ever gave much thought to the people he hurt along the way.' She glances momentarily off the road and catches Amber's eye. 'But you know this already, don't you?'

Amber doesn't answer, just looks down.

'So, am I surprised that someone might have wanted to kill him at some point in his life? 'No, I'm not. But neither would I be surprised by the idea he killed himself rather than face a difficult end and dealing with the pain of the people who loved him. I'd guess he never changed, right up to the end.'

Kay stops, her lips pursed as if holding in an unexpressed emotion. When she speaks again, there is irritation in her voice.

'I'm not exactly sure what it is you think I can tell you about him, sweetie, but you do need to tell me what the hell is going on.'

'I don't know that I can. Not all of it. I don't *know* all of it. If I did tell you, you'd understand why I couldn't. But you said whatever I needed to say, you'd listen. And I need you to trust me, and I need to trust you. You're the only person who knows about me and Benny that I can talk to, and I need your help.'

'Then I'll help you,' Kay says solemnly.

It gives Amber a feeling that Kay might not judge her too harshly if she knew the whole truth. She might just be someone who would protect Amber's secret. But two decades of silence are hard to break. So Amber speaks slowly and carefully, weighing again which truths to tell, and which lies.

'During our affair, Benny told me he'd been attacked by a man and killed him in self-defence. And he kept it a secret — as far as I know, for the rest of his life. But after he discovered he was terminally ill, he also talked about a confession, about letting everything out into the open. But then he was killed. And, honestly, Kay, I know there are decades between those things, but I just can't help but think it's all connected.'

The car slows a little, as if Kay is having difficulty concentrating on the driving and listening to Amber. She lets out a slow whistle.

'That's a bold pitch, sweetie, I've got to say. Can I ask why you've not gone to the police with all this?'

'Because I don't have any proof. Because I'll seem like a crazy person. Because... I think Genevieve might be involved in this somehow.'

'Huh. Look, Amber. That Bayard woman, I wouldn't trust

her to look after my pint while I took a piss. But you really think she killed him?'

'I don't know. I only...' Amber's voice falls away, unable to find the words to express her fragmented suspicions. There doesn't seem any way of explaining everything without revealing her part in it all. 'What do you mean, you don't trust Genevieve?'

Kay waves a hand away from the steering wheel. 'Ah, nothing.' But her mouth is twitching like it isn't nothing.

Amber starts to think about Freddie. About her chaotic mind and strange fixations; about her dislike of Genevieve and her ideas about the Bayard Foundation. Amber tries to explain it to Kay, but becomes lost in the telling, unable to fit the pieces into the puzzle.

Kay shrugs. 'Freddie has her ideas, y'know. But I'll tell you, I've covered every crime you could imagine. People do foolish, terrible things. People get themselves in so deep that they can't see a way out. People do things because they *have* to. And it's those people that the law goes after, because they're easy to catch, and they have victims that are easy to see. But when was the last time you saw a banker go to jail, hmm?'

Kay has become increasingly animated as she talks, and she shakes her head as if clearing something from her mind. 'But, honestly, Amber, what's any of this got to do with you? I'm still not sure why you took the job doing the archive. Friend to friend, I think you need to take a break. Christ, why am I even driving you to his house?'

'Because I need to look through the archive some more. I think I can find something there. He kept *everything*. It was like he was obsessed with not throwing away a single image. There's got to be something. Maybe not something that will mean enough on its own, but if I can put it together with...'

She tapers off, aware she is pushing the limits of what she

is prepared to reveal about her own guilt. Kay has slowed the car. They have left the town and are on the country roads, heading towards their destination, but Kay has spotted a layby and pulls over into it.

'At what point do I get to say I'm worried about you, sweetie?'

'*I'm* worried about me.'

'Then you won't mind me telling you you're chasing shadows here. You're the one sounding like a conspiracy theorist. You're looking for evidence you don't know exists for a crime that you don't know happened.'

'I'm not crazy.' The words come out raw and angry. But she doesn't fully believe them. She does feel half-crazy. For all the things she knows are true, she can't help but admit that Kay is partly right. 'I'm sorry, I just needed to stop feeling so alone in all this. Can you drop me off, and maybe not go too far? Just be on the end of your phone if I need you. In case anything...'

Kay makes a throaty huffing noise. 'If you're worried for your safety, then I should come in with you.'

'No, I don't want to create suspicion. I'm still meant to be doing the job there. Just be at the end of the phone. Will you do that for me?'

Kay is shaking her head. She starts to drive off, looking sharply behind her, as if preparing to turn across the road.

'Don't you dare take me back to Oxford. If you do, I'm just going to get a cab. I thought you would be someone who would help me.'

Kay grits her teeth in displeasure, but keeps driving. 'Are you completely sure about this?'

'Yes, completely. Please.'

Another shake of the head. 'Okay.'

They move on through the winding roads in silence, their speed picking up again, Kay's aggressive driving giving away her frustration at Amber. They get close to the farmhouse, and Amber asks to stop at the top of the driveway. She starts to get out, and feels Kay's hand on her arm.

'Please don't try to stop me.'

'I just want you to think about what you're doing.'

'I've done too much thinking.'

Kay's eyes fall. 'Look, just be careful. You mean a lot to silly old Kay, you know.' Then she unclips her seatbelt and leans across to Amber and hugs her. The hug lingers, and Amber lets it, absorbing all the comfort she can get from it, thinking about her own isolation, about Kay's loneliness, about the first time they met, about how she is gripped by a sense that this might be the final time she sees Kay, how she feels if she steps past the threshold of the Raine farmhouse, she might never leave.

She uncouples and lets herself out of the car before she has the chance to change her mind.

45

BENNY

Sunday, 11 November 2001

The farmhouse was quiet the day I came back after the cottage. A dark Sunday afternoon, and all the builders' tools lay silent. A dead time.

I didn't expect Gen back till late, maybe not till Monday. She had been away on a last-minute trip she had to make to Paris to sort out some family business. The way she'd talked about it, it sounded as if someone might get murdered if she wasn't there to broker the peace.

I went to my study. My camera felt heavy as I took it out of my bag and placed it on my desk. There was no need to lock it away. I miss those days when you couldn't tell what was in the camera just by looking at its back, when you couldn't download and share the images at the click of a mouse.

If anyone looked at that camera that afternoon, all they would see would be all its marks of age and wear, a technology coming to the end of its life. And if anyone opened the camera's back, the images would be gone forever in a second.

I nearly did it myself. I nearly flipped open the back and let the light from my desk lamp burn it all up.

The house was freezing. I lit a fire and sat cross-legged on the floor right up close to it and smoked cigarette after cigarette. I could still sit cross-legged then and get up without using my hands.

I liked this place when it was quiet. I was reminded why we had bought it — well, Gen had bought it. But when we first moved into it that summer, nothing was finished, everything was chaos. Builders and noise were everywhere. I had just wanted to take some time off. I had been working non-stop, and I was exhausted. It was a summer when I didn't want to do anything, or talk to anyone, or think about anything. Just sit in the sun and drink. But I couldn't get a moment's peace.

I know I can't blame the building. I can't blame Gen or Amber. I knew who was responsible for what had just happened.

Gen came home earlier than I expected. She sat down beside me by the fire and kissed me. I was all ready to give my invented excuse for the archipelago of bruises spreading down the side of my face from my forehead, but strangely she said nothing about them till much later that evening. Even so, I felt the events of the weekend radiating off me, as if they might penetrate Gen's mind if she stayed too close for too long. Eventually, she said:

'You should stop smoking, my darling.'

'Yeah, I know, I know.'

'What if I gave you a reason to?' She reached over to her handbag that had been lying on the floor next to her, and slid out a small plastic wand with a blue tip and a frosted oval window in its middle. There were two bars in the window.

At the time, I barely remember feeling anything. I made all the right noises, but I was numb, angry, confused. The conversation I'd had after leaving Amber at Norwich was still running round and round my head.

The full sensation came later. A child coming into our life was like a loud noise waking me from a bad dream. With it came a growing hope that I could put everything behind me, that somehow our daughter could be a shield against everything that had happened before she arrived.

Over the years, though, that feeling has left me too. At times, I have loved her so much that it hurt, and we've had immense fun. But I don't think I've been a decent father any more than I've been a decent husband.

Yvey and I are too alike, too wilful, too hard to tie down, too stubborn. I think Gen did her best, but I don't know. There have been so many times I just wasn't there to see.

So I can't blame Yvey for all the money we've spent on child psychologists. And I would be a hypocrite to lament all her lying. The varied, creative and compulsive lying. Maybe part of me admires her for how adept she is at it. She will make a wonderful novelist perhaps. Or a politician. I can't even hold too much against her what happened at her last school. Perhaps the relationship she developed with that teacher was something about the absent parent in her life. Perhaps the lurid stories she told her about Gen and me to gain her sympathy had, for her at least, a nugget of truth in there.

The violence in her, though, I can't account for that. To attack that teacher in her street in broad daylight. I'm guilty of a lot in my life, but violence isn't one of them. No, I'm not sure that's true, not if I'm honest with myself. I can see now that to wish violence into being is itself part of the act. It's just violence coated in cowardice. I've seen the faces of soldiers, and there's more honesty in them than in the people who send them into battle.

We were grateful at the time that Yvey's teacher could be persuaded not to press charges, but now I wonder if the teacher wasn't as innocent as she liked to claim. Perhaps violence was all Yvey felt she had access to. Sometimes I think we should listen more to her lies. I think sometimes, in a funny kind of way, they've been her attempt to tell us the truth.

Sure, the boy cried wolf, but in the end there really was a wolf.

'Oh, hello, Amber. Hadn't expected to see you till Monday at the earliest.' Sam is a little prim in his greeting, as if she has upset his precise plans for the day. Then he sucks his teeth. 'Unless we're all confined to quarters by then, I suppose.'

'Yeah, sorry to descend on you.' Amber is willing a casualness into her voice, but it sounds fake and scratchy in her head. 'I got a bit ahead with my other projects. Thought I'd pop over and get a head start. That's okay, isn't it? And I was hoping I could spend a bit more time handing over with Mika before he's off.'

'Yuh, Mika, he called in sick yesterday.' There is a slight wither to the way Sam says Mika's name, and the word *sick* hangs with scepticism. 'Not heard from him today.'

'That's a shame. Nothing serious, I hope.' Amber's voice is blank, but the thought going through her head is the figure running away from her house into the darkness, and now Mika's sudden, convenient absence. 'Is Genevieve here?'

'Not currently.' The curt answer is all Sam has to say.

'And Yvey? Does she have classes this afternoon, or is she around?'

'Yvey?' There is the flicker of a frown on Sam's face, as if the question has been inappropriate. 'I'm afraid keeping tabs on her is rather above my pay grade.'

Sam smiles weakly, and in the silence that follows, Amber can just detect a sub-bass vibration in the house, like muffled music through doors. She has a momentary instinct to go past Sam up the stairs to find Yvey's bedroom, but she pushes the idea away.

'Well, if you don't mind, I'll be out at the studio,' she says to Sam, trying to match his tone.

'I'll have to unlock it for you.'

'Would you mind?'

'Not at all,' he says, in a way that suggests he does.

They walk together through the house and along the woodland path. It is already mid-afternoon, and the light is low, slanting through the branches, pulling out long shadows from the trees across the path. When they get to the clearing and the studio, Sam stops and looks at Amber.

'I'm sure it's none of my business, but can I ask, are you all right? You seem a little...' He waves his hand non-specifically.

'I'm fine, thank you.' And she doesn't say anything else, turning Sam's brevity against him.

He gives a thin smile and lets her into the studio. She watches him as he retreats towards the house, not moving from the glass until she is sure he is gone. But then she finds herself filled with an urge to follow him, as if she might somehow be able to spy on him without being seen.

She presses the button on the windows to turn off the world outside, goes through the door at the back of the room, and climbs the stairs to the archive.

When she first came here, she discovered there was no easy system for the contents of this room. It has not been neatly organised by date or by subject or theme. But she did get a sense of the pockets of chronology here and there — rows of boxes and files that grouped around certain years.

She looks first for anything from the months and years immediately before that weekend in the cottage, telling herself over and over that there must be something to find. At the same time, she is filled with a deep sense of desperation, of the creeping acceptance that Kay is right, that there is nothing to see, that she is inventing imaginary evidence.

She cannot find the energy to take boxes up and down between here and the lightbox in the studio, so she sits on the floor, holding the negatives up to the angled light from her phone, hoping to illuminate their subjects. But she cannot see enough. She has not been able to see enough this whole time. There are huge vistas inaccessible to her.

She goes on searching, rifling and reordering, spreading files across the floor in between the shelves. Benny's words at the cottage echo in her mind, about all the enemies he could have made in his life.

She pictures his visceral despatches from Northern Ireland in the late seventies. The years he spent in Central and South America in the eighties with the drug gangs and paramilitary warlords, sometimes dodging their bullets, sometimes insinuating himself into their circle. She thinks of his part in shining a light on the war crimes in the Balkans in the nineties, of the searing images of concentration camps and mass graves.

There could be a dozen, scores, hundreds of people on Benny's list of enemies. Unless she can find the man she killed, a photograph of any of these other people will not help her.

She opens a box and finds it full of personal films from the late nineties, this time prints, not negatives. It's portraits of family and friends in punchy Kodak colours. At first, it's of people she doesn't know and has never seen before. Then she finds one of Genevieve, her head thrown back in laughter in a way that feels at odds with the persona that Amber knows. And there is one of Freddie in the heyday of her strange beauty. Her hands are piling up her red hair on her head, and her face is a little dipped, her eyes burning into the camera. What is that look? A sort of defiant sultriness. Freddie the woman who introduced her to Benny. Freddie at the funeral. Freddie still close to the family, but with strange unresolved feelings for Benny and against his wife.

And in amongst all these, Amber is surprised to find one of Kay leaning against a green door, a sardonic half-smile on her face, a cigarette in her hand. Like Genevieve, she looks different. Facial features that are sharp on the woman Amber knows look fine, almost delicate. Her eyes, which are now ringed with crow's feet, are clear and bright in the photo. Amber hears Kay's voice in her head from their conversation in the car, and wonders if there was an edge of pain when she spoke about Benny that didn't quite match with a glancing acquaintance.

A guttural sound comes out of Amber's throat, desperate at the suspicion she now has for everything and everyone. She is grasping, helpless. She lies back on the floor, surrounded by everything and by nothing, close to tears, her energy sapped.

Her phone buzzes on the floor next to her, and she jerks upright.

'Ed, that was quick.' Seeing Ed Kapoor's name on the caller ID, Amber has tried to flip her voice into her professional mode, but it sounds fake and weak in her own ears.

'Yeah, well, I started with the easy stuff. You want to know what I got?'

'Uh-huh.'

'Your man Gallagher. Born 1969 near Belfast. Seemed to spend a lot of his youth in trouble with the law, as far as I can tell — fairly minor stuff, but a bit of time inside.'

Benny's photos flash in Amber's mind — angry young men, hard eyes staring out from under balaclavas.

'Any links to paramilitaries?' But as she asks the question, the maths catches up with her — Finn would have been only a kid when Benny was taking those shots.

'Well, you know, these things are all tied up together there, aren't they? But anyway, he moves to London in his mid-twenties. Again, seems to have a few minor scuffs with the law, but stays out of jail this time. Keeps some interesting company from what I can tell, but seems to keep his nose clean enough.'

Ed clicks his tongue on the back of his teeth. 'But here's the thing I find interesting: he wasn't actually from the wrong side of the tracks to start with. His parents were well off. His dad owned a fair bit of land, and his mum was a history prof at Queen's Belfast. So, for whatever reason, Finn is a bit of an outcast. And when his mum dies of cancer, his dad leaves Belfast and goes to live on his own in a little village in Cumbria.'

'How do you *know* all this?'

'That's what I'm getting to. I only know all this because of what happened to the dad. Finn doesn't have any siblings, not much family at all as far as I can tell, and his father is living all on his own, middle of nowhere. Then, out of the blue, his house burns down with him in it. Looks pretty much like arson, and the doors have been blocked shut.'

'When was this?'

'Well, they found the body... uh... let me see... yeah, 4 November 2001.'

A chill runs through Amber. Just five days before that weekend in the cottage.

'So then Finn stands to inherit all his father's money,' Ed goes on. 'Which puts a big flashing sign on his head as far as the police are concerned. Except he's got a cast-iron alibi the night of the fire — he's hundreds of miles away in London, surrounded by witnesses and CCTV. But then, well, you know what happens next. Last anybody sees of him is four days later, 8 November.'

Ed stops. There is silence on the line. He is waiting for Amber to speak. She can tell he is burning to ask her again about who this man was to her, about why he's been chasing down all his police contacts to get this dirt on a missing man from two decades ago.

'Did they ever find who did it? The arson?'

'Not as far as I can make out. You want me to keep digging?' A brief pause. 'And is there anything else you want to tell me?'

Amber hesitates to reply. She wants to ask Ed if he can tie the name to Benny or Mika or Sam or Genevieve, but she doesn't dare. Not yet. Not till everything else is exhausted.

'Amber...' She can hear the concern in Ed's voice and is aware of how long her silence has become.

She looks around at the archive and fears the truth as much as she craves it. She knows that each new piece of information Ed uncovers will start a trail that could lead eventually back to her. She can see in front of her a future where she will have to lie to Ed, and she will have to ask Ed to lie for her. Just as she has asked Kay to keep a secret that was not fair to share.

'Thanks, Ed, no. That's all for now.'

'But you are okay, aren't you?'

'Ask me again when you see me. I'll tell you, I promise.' And she hangs up.

She pulls herself from the floor and stumbles out of the archive, light-headed and her mouth dry. She holds tight to the railing of the stairs as she descends, and puts her other hand across her body as if preparing herself for the risk of a fall.

When she comes out into the studio and flicks the glass back to transparent, she sees how late it has got. Shadows are winning against the light; the clearing feels smaller; the woods are pressing in on her.

She gets out her phone and finds a message that must have come through whilst she was talking to Ed. It is from Johnny. It is full of support and love and emojis. She feels the searing stab of all the lies she's told him, knowing that soon the lies will have to end.

She swipes it away and starts a new message. It is to her tormenter

If I tell you everything, will you leave me alone?

There is nothing in reply. Only the crackle and swish of the trees. She types another message.

You can't frighten me anymore. I don't care who knows.
I'll tell everyone. I'll do it now.

She waits. Still nothing.

I'm not a coward like you.

But she is a coward. If she wasn't a coward, she would have told Kay and Ed everything. If she wasn't a coward, she would call the police right now.

A noise comes out of her mouth, a low moan, animal-like. Then she raises her face to the trees and shouts.

'Come on, you bastard!' Her voice is pathetic and child-like in the gloom. She sits down on the earth and wraps her arms around herself in a desolate embrace of her unborn child.

She isn't sure how long she is there. The present stretches and collides in her mind with the past: the knife in the intruder's neck, his blood flowing out across onto the cottage floor, her own naked body, and Benny's voice threatening a confession.

When she finally pulls herself up, she is dizzy for a second, and the circle of the clearing moves vertiginously around her. Then there is the crackle of breaking twigs and movement in the corner of her vision. She closes her eyes and bites down on the fear that is welling up inside her.

When she opens them, they are blurred with tears, and a red shape moves towards her from the trees like an old wound reopened. Her chaotic brain takes a moment to see first that it is a person, then that it is Yvey, wearing her red leather jacket and hoodie. She is moving uneasily, her shoulders turned in, her right hand holding her left wrist — perhaps in pain, perhaps just a gesture of protection across her body.

Yvey stops, looking up, realising there is someone in the forest in front of the studio. She squints towards Amber, who is caught in silhouette from the lights of the studio behind her. Yvey takes a couple of steps forward and pulls back her hood. She doesn't say anything, just draws a little closer as if still trying to see. The flesh around her left eye is red and swollen, and there is a raw graze across her cheekbone.

Then a new expression comes over Yvey's face. In that moment, her resemblance to Benny is gone, but there is another face that flashes in Amber's mind. She is thinking of the Lebanese boy, that look of fear and devastation on his face, but also one of righteous anger and a seed of vengeance.

Yvey looks for a moment as if she is about to speak, but then she dips her head, turns and runs back into the trees towards the house.

48

The phone in my hand feels like an explosive device that might go off.

It's unlocked. The screen is glowing. I managed to grab it whilst Yvey was using it, those busy little thumbs typing away.

I'm sorry I had to hurt her. I didn't expect her to fight so much or to be so strong. But at least she didn't see me. I wore my helmet. I felt cold when I put it on, suffocated, like I might drown in my own breath. I hadn't put it on since that night. The night I killed Benny. Yes, I can say it. I can admit it.

I tap the phone periodically to stop it timing out and locking. Then I get a grip of my thoughts, go into the settings and turn the screen timeout to its maximum. I still have to move quickly to explore what's on it before it's locked remotely.

I don't know what I'm going to find, but teenagers, they live their lives on their phones, don't they? If Yvey knows something about what I did to Benny, it's got to be on this thing somewhere. And it might tell me what she's been saying to you, Amber. And maybe what you've been telling her.

I hesitate again.

I don't know what I'll do with what I find. It's all got so out of control. All because I tried to help Benny. Because I was helping. It doesn't matter what Benny says, I was helping him.

It's not my fault what happened to Finn. But I should have known he'd mess it up. I should never have made the deal in the first place. Neither of us got what we wanted from it. All I got was nightmares about what I did. But I was doing my part of the deal. I've always kept my word. You can say whatever you like about me, but you can't say I'm not loyal, that I'm not true.

I grit my teeth and look back at the phone. I scroll through the screens, looking at the apps, trying to decide which to explore first.

Something catches my eye. There are two WhatsApp icons. Which I know must mean two accounts and a phone with dual sim cards. Yvey's real number and a second number. What's she been up to with those?

I swipe down from the top and see there's a WhatsApp notification. I tap it, and a message comes up on the screen.

If I tell you everything, will you leave me alone?

I start to scroll up the messages, a sickness rising inside me.

Amber doesn't hesitate to follow Yvey through the trees. The girl is running in a haphazard way, catching on the branches and ignoring Amber's calls.

They break through into the garden. Standing in the open French doors, the glow of the kitchen behind her, is Genevieve. She puts a hand up to her chest, and a cascade of emotions runs across her face — alarm, confusion, a flash of anger.

Yvey sees her mother, stops for a moment, then twists round and darts back across the garden. She skips over a flowerbed and rushes into the thick of the trees, quickly swallowed up by the branches and the darkness. Amber turns to follow her, but is stopped by Genevieve's voice.

'What the hell is going on?'

Amber is unable to speak for a moment. When she does, she is surprised at the boldness in her own voice when she speaks:

'What happened to Yvey's face?'

Genevieve shakes her head. 'I asked you what was going on. Look at yourself.'

Amber's eyes fall. Only now does she realise she is covered in dirt from the floor of the clearing. She runs a hand through her hair. It feels dusty and unkempt. She has no time to construct an excuse, and Genevieve is on a roll, her voice shifting into the high sharp tones of a disappointed head-mistress.

'Now, do you want to tell me what this is all about? Sam tells me you turned up unexpectedly and have been asking about Yvey. And now... this.' She waves a hand aggressively at Amber. 'If I'm honest, I thought you started acting a little oddly when you came to visit. But I let it go. I thought perhaps I was imagining things, that if you settled into the job, you might calm down. But I should have listened to my instincts.'

'Why won't you tell me what happened to Yvey?' Amber can't get the question out of her head.

'Because I don't bloody know. She says she went into the village to go to the shops and got mugged. But this is Radlow. People don't get mugged. She won't say anything else about it.' The hard lines soften a little. She steps forward into the garden. 'Honestly, I'm worried about her. She didn't come home last night till God knows what time.'

'She didn't message you?'

'Message me?' The suspicion is back on Genevieve's face.

'Radlow, it's not walkable from here, is it? Not along these roads.'

'What are you talking about? She goes everywhere on that bloody scooter Benny gave her.'

Amber nods, beginning to see. 'She still has it, then?'

'Of course she still has it.' Genevieve gives a long sigh of exasperation. 'You know what, Amber, if you're not going to tell me what's going on, I think perhaps you should go.'

'No, please, I'll explain. I'll try to. But can I ask you one more question?'

'Go on,' she says stiffly.

'Why did you ask me to do this job? No more lies.'

'Lies? I asked you for all the reasons I told you. Because Benny always–'

Amber cuts her off. 'It's been years. Why me, why now? There are dozens of people who could've done the job. Why did you bring me here?'

The impatience on Genevieve's face has not left, but Amber can't see even a flicker of guilt or malevolence. There is nothing that speaks of any grand plan playing out. The impatient look falls away with a sigh as she lowers herself into a moss-covered wooden chair by the back door. There is a heaviness about her movements.

'All right, I'm sorry. I haven't been entirely straight with you. It's foolish. You'll forgive me. I didn't tell you because it seemed... it seemed unprofessional. Your name was on a list; it really was. All of us at the Foundation wanted someone whose work connected with Benny's. And I've always felt the kinship in your photographs and his. I got talking to Yvey about it, and she said she loved your work. It felt like the first proper conversation I'd had with her since Benny died. She'd been so withdrawn. It was sentimental of me, I know, but she'd lost her father.'

'You hired me because your daughter thought you should?'

'I know, I'm sorry. It might seem like a strange decision, but she was set on it. She talked about your work for days, said how much she'd like to meet you. I thought it was a way... a way just to include her again. Something to cling to, I suppose. But now all this. What's happening between you and Yvey? No more lies.' The last words are pointed and thrown.

Amber pauses before she answers. She looks towards the woods, as if Yvey might re-emerge from them.

'You know Yvey thinks Benny was murdered?'

'Why would she think a thing like that? Have you been putting ideas in her head?' Genevieve's reaction is sharp and a little angry. But the defiance collapses quickly, and the form goes out of her shoulders. 'Oh, Amber, what's she been saying to you?'

Amber grits her teeth for a second, then finds the courage to reply.

'She's been saying she doesn't trust you. She said your mother says you weren't visiting her the night Benny died.'

'You're not telling me she thinks I have something to do with Benny's death? Oh God. Tell me Yvey doesn't think that. Tell me *you* don't think that.'

'Well, were you? Were you visiting your mother?'

'Of course I was. That silly girl. Look, my mother is nearly ninety, very senile. She thinks it's Christmas every second Tuesday. She wouldn't have a clue.' Genevieve shakes her head. She is smiling ruefully, the shape strangely out of place on her fallen face. 'Oh, I hoped this was all behind us. I'm afraid this isn't the first time she's fixated on a notion that wasn't true, that she's lied for attention.'

There is a quiver in Genevieve's voice, and all the parts of her that are weak seem to be winning against the parts that are strong. 'We tried, we really tried, Benny and I. But he was never here, and there was always so much work. She's such a bright child. Too bright, I've sometimes thought. The psychologists throw all sorts of words around with their large bills, but...'

She tails off and smiles weakly. It all seems slightly beyond what she is able to express. 'We thought we had it under control, we really did. Then last year, she developed...

I'm not sure what it really was... a crush, an obsession, some kind of unhealthy relationship with her art teacher, a young woman. It turned out Yvey had been inventing all sorts of stories about Benny and me to gain the teacher's sympathy and attention.'

'What sort of stories?' Amber asks, still not sure what she is hearing now is the truth.

'It really doesn't matter. They were all nonsense. And when it all came out, Yvey made some lurid accusations about her teacher, which of course the teacher denied. After that, Yvey...' Genevieve pauses, losing Amber's eyes again. 'She attacked her teacher. In the street outside her house, right in front of all her neighbours. We were lucky the teacher agreed not to press charges. She was badly hurt.'

Amber is shaking her head, the knowledge of Yvey's lies sinking in, yet still unable to imagine her as someone with violence in her. She thinks about Yvey's black eye and her story that someone attacked her. She looks at Genevieve and feels they are thinking the same thing, questioning everything Yvey has told them for days, even weeks.

'It's my fault,' Genevieve says. 'I tried to tell myself it was a good thing she seemed okay after Benny. But she isn't, is she? Just because she seems like that on the outside.' A tear is drawing a path down Genevieve's face. When she speaks again, there is a pleading note to her voice. 'Please tell me what's going on.'

'I'll try, I really will.' Amber feels she has finally begun to understand. The picture is not fully there in her head: bits of it are still burned away, patches of white light. But she can see large parts of it now, seeping into view, the chemicals coming through on the print. 'It's true Yvey has some explaining to do to you. She has some explaining to do to both of us. But that's okay. I do too.'

As she speaks, she wants the fear to lift. She wants the part of the frame she can now see to be all of the picture. She wants to be able to tie everything back to Yvey and be free from her secrets. At the same time, she still has that feeling deep within her, that relentless dread drawing ever closer.

The studio is in darkness. Amber was sure they would find Yvey here, but there is no sign of life as they break into the clearing. Amber feels Genevieve's eyes on her and keeps going towards the building.

As she slides back the glass door, she sees Yvey sitting cross-legged on the floor in the gloom, her trendy little satchel bag in front of her. She is in the same spot she sat and chatted as Amber started to get to grips with the archive. That was less than a week ago, but it feels like a different time.

Yvey curses at Amber when she sees her, but doesn't move.

'You're not allowed in here anymore. This was Dad's place. It's mine now.' Her voice is angry, pleading and uncertain all at the same time. As she speaks, she clutches her bag closer to her stomach.

Genevieve comes in behind Amber and turns on one light that glows from the far corner. Yvey sits up a little straighter and stares hard at her mother. The girl's face is now stern and motionless, but emotion bubbles and boils just below the surface. In return, Genevieve looks almost scared of her daughter, and Amber thinks about Yvey's teacher, attacked outside her own home.

Amber speaks first, bringing her out with a lie that can easily be punctured.

'Yvey, tell your mum about last night, how you told me your scooter was stolen.'

The girl's mouth stays tightly shut. Genevieve's face folds into a deep frown.

'Stolen? I don't understand.'

'That's what you told me, isn't it, Yvey?' says Amber. She is still tiptoeing towards the confrontation, because she knows it will also mean her own confession.

Yvey is silent, but her mother speaks. 'You promised me all the lies had stopped.' Her hands are in fists, her voice querulous. 'Are you lying about what happened to your face? Tell the truth.'

'I'm not the one lying.' Yvey's hand flies up towards her face. 'Someone attacked me. Amber's the one who's lying. She keeps on lying. Even now, she won't tell you the truth about her and Dad.'

'It's okay, Yvey, you can tell your mum what you know. You can show your mum your phone and the messages you've been sending me. Yes, it's all right, I know it's you. And you can tell us both what's really going on.'

Yvey looks down. 'I haven't got my phone. The mugger took it. I'm telling the truth, I really am. I was using it, and this dude in a bike helmet just jumped me, grabbed it out of my hand. I tried to get it back, but he punched me and pushed me over.'

Amber looks hard into Yvey, not trusting her words, but seeing that very real black eye, the blood spreading under her skin.

'Tell us what you know, Yvey. Please.'

'You won't believe me if I do.'

Genevieve has tears in her eyes again. 'We will, my darling. I promise.'

Yvey shifts like she wants to get up and run again. But then she shakes her head and starts to talk about how Benny was often up at night, pacing around the house. She talks about how Benny would go to his studio in the middle of the night, and how she used to creep out into the woods to watch him.

'It was a way of spending time with him.' Yvey dips her head and sniffs up a tear. The image that comes straight to Amber is the video from Yvey's Instagram: the lights full on in the studio, the magic glass open, the camera moving around the clearing, and the white-bright building at the centre like a burning beacon.

'After he got sick, he used to go there every night,' Yvey is saying. 'I guess he couldn't sleep — even more than usual. I couldn't sleep either.' She throws a sudden sharp glance at her mother. 'You never seem to have trouble sleeping, do you, Mum?'

Genevieve's mouth opens a little as if she is thinking of rebuking her daughter, but she holds her silence.

'He had this old metal box he would keep getting down from the archive. He'd get it out, look at it, then put it away. Over and over. I worked out where he kept it eventually, but it was locked, so I left it alone. He was looking at it the night he died. No, not died, not killed himself. It was the night he was killed. So, yeah, he had the box, but then he put it down and picked up the phone. I crept right up close. The door was a little open, but he didn't see me. I wish I'd never listened now.'

'What did you hear, darling?' Genevieve asks, shifting in her chair.

'I couldn't hear all of it. He kept moving around. But he

was saying it was time for the truth. He was talking to the person on the phone like they'd done something bad. Like Dad had too. How he should've gone to the police. And Dad was talking about someone else — a girl. Saying he wanted to take the blame before he died.' She stops and sniffs. 'I should have tried to record it,' she adds sulkily.

Genevieve is frowning at Amber, but Amber is still not ready to speak, still waiting to see where this all leads.

'Then Dad hung up, and he was looking at that box again. Then he... I think he tried to make another call that wasn't answered. Then he sent a text or put something else in his phone, I dunno.'

Amber knows what that text must have been. She knows exactly what it said:

I don't know if this is still your number. Can we talk?

'Then Dad came out and I hid. I thought he'd gone to bed, so I did too, but I couldn't sleep. A couple of hours later, I heard him go downstairs.' Yvey stops. Her eyes are scrunched up, and she buries her face in a hand that rubs and pulls at the skin. 'I should've talked to him. I shouldn't have let him go out on his bike.'

She is crying openly now. Genevieve moves towards her daughter and crouches down. She puts her arm around Yvey, who doesn't protest, but doesn't lean into the embrace, either.

'I went out of the house and watched him ride off down the drive,' Yvey goes on. 'Then I thought I saw a car's lights go past the end of the drive. Just, like, ten seconds after Dad went. I didn't really think anything of it then, y'know. I went back in. I went into your room, Mum. He'd left his phone by the bed. Maybe it was wrong to look, I dunno, but I did anyway.'

'I suppose you know my password too,' says Genevieve ruefully.

Yvey just looks at her with something approaching pity.

'He'd cleared the phone. His messages, call log, WhatsApp history, all of it. Why would you do that unless you want to hide who you've been talking to? Then it started ringing, and I saw who was on the caller ID. I should've answered it. Shouldn't I, Amber?'

Mother and daughter look at Amber. The similarity to Benny's face has fallen away from Yvey's, and for the first time Amber can see a resemblance between mother and daughter. Part of it comes from their shared expressions — faces full of questions and suppressed anger.

I feel exhausted by everything I've seen on Yvey's phone, but there's a sense of relief too. There's nothing in here that identifies me, not directly. There is that picture of Finn, but on its own, it isn't enough proof for anyone.

I still don't understand what Yvey wants from Amber, or what she really knows, even what her game is. Maybe I don't have to worry about her. From what I've heard, she's pretty cracked. Not a reliable witness.

Amber is a different problem. Is she really going to tell? I don't want to have to stop her like I stopped Benny.

Because I had to do what I did. I didn't have a choice. He brought it on himself.

Maybe I shouldn't have paid attention to a few words thrown out on a late-night interview that no one watches. But it went round and round my head. Then I got wind he was dying. Did he really want to clear his conscience? So I called him. I asked him what he meant, whether he was going to tell.

'Don't you think it's time to let it all out into the open?' he said. That was it. Then he hung up.

Did he mean it? Was it a joke? I started to think I shouldn't have called him. Had my call solidified an idea in his head? Had the fear in my voice pushed him over the edge — a drop of vindictiveness to go with his regret?

After that, he didn't return any of my calls and messages. Not for weeks, not until that night. Genevieve was away, but Yvey was there. I knew because I'd been watching him for days.

I messaged him again. I said I was going to come to the farmhouse if he didn't call me back. It was a bluff. I didn't want Yvey to see me any more than he did. But it worked. He called me.

I think deep down he was glad to speak to me. If he really didn't want to, he would have blocked my number. I knew I would wear him down eventually.

So now we could talk. It was the first time we'd spoken about it since it happened that wasn't in coded reference. I tried to draw him away from his mad idea of the truth, but he kept winding closer and closer to it. I told him he couldn't betray me, that he had to remember I'd done it all for him. I told him the truth wouldn't help anyone — not his wife, not his daughter, not the girl he'd been with that weekend.

The girl, the girl. I still didn't know who it was then, not for certain. But I know now. I can't avoid the fact anymore, not now I've seen what's on Yvey's phone.

'I can set her free from this,' Benny said to me that final night. 'I can make people understand it wasn't her fault.'

'It's way too late for that.'

'Is it? I was the one who wouldn't go to the police. I was the one who put that stupid idea in your head in the first place. That girl... that poor girl has lived with what she did for long enough.' Benny sucked in a breath. He had said too much.

'What she did? Oh, that's news. So you didn't even do it? She killed Finn. Jesus, Benny. I always thought you'd done it, that all she did was help clean up your mess. You've let her live with this all this time, and you think she'll thank you if you–'

'I'll call her. Right now, if I have to. We're the only people who know what happened there. I can take all the blame. If I die without saying anything, it will be with her forever.'

'You know it's not going to work like that.'

He couldn't find an answer, but I couldn't find any words either. I wanted so much to be able to say something that would stop all this from happening. I wanted to be able to press a reset button for Benny and me and wipe all of this away. Then I hated myself for that thought. And I was angry at him again, at this man who only ever took, never gave. A man who had lied to me and to himself, who wanted forgiveness, but didn't really care who his confession would hurt.

After he hung up on me, I sat in my car, the darkness of the country lane all around me. I played the conversation in my head again and again, trying to decide how much he really believed in what he'd just said. Would he really ruin all those lives — ruin my life — when his was already finished? I wanted to look him in the eye and know.

But it was too late for that. I couldn't take the chance any longer.

And here I am again. Sitting in my car in the same place I waited for Benny on his bike that night. Just a little back from the entrance to the driveway, half-shielded by a soft bend and a clump of trees.

I get out of the car, go round to the boot, and make sure my bag is packed with all the things I might need. If it comes to it. Best to be prepared. Somehow I have to stop all of this.

I get out my own phone, and I send a message.

'Was it you speaking to my husband that night?' Genevieve asks.

'No. I had a missed call and a message. I called back, but he didn't answer. I never spoke to him, I swear. I wasn't the person you heard him talking to, Yvey.'

Yvey looks crestfallen, and they are all silent for a moment. Then the girl speaks, her voice soft and sad.

'I remember when Dad first showed me your photos, Amber. And when he asked Mum to hang that one of yours in the hallway. I love that picture. You know what, your surname didn't even come up on his phone. It just said Amber. But I knew. I knew it was you. So when Mum started talking about maybe asking you to do the archive...' Her voice falls off, and Genevieve jumps into the gap.

'Why didn't you say something about all this, Yvette? To me, to the police? If you thought something had happened to your father–'

'Because I didn't know. I wasn't sure. Because you wouldn't have believed me.'

'That's not true.'

'Isn't it? *Isn't it*? You didn't believe me about Miss Richardson. None of you did. You still don't. *She's* the one who lied about what happened between us, the gaslighting bitch.'

Genevieve's eyes are full of doubt. She stands and walks away from her daughter.

Yvey's voice comes back softer. 'After what I found in the box, there was no one I could talk to.' A hand goes to her satchel and takes out a small brown envelope. It is stuffed full, the distinctive shining blackness of negative strips protruding from the open end. Moving with a studied slowness, Yvey pulls herself to her feet, hooks a few strips from the envelope and places them on the table with the lightbox.

Genevieve goes for them, but Amber is closer and quicker, grabbing them as if she has just won a round in a fast-moving card game. She has been watching Genevieve's reaction all this time, but it has been hard to discern, emotion hidden behind a hard frown of concentration.

'I'll explain, I promise,' Amber says to Genevieve, then turns her attention back to Yvey. 'Did you really think I had something to do with your father's death?'

'I knew you were lying.'

'Why didn't you just ask me?'

'I did. I kept asking you, and you kept lying.'

'Then why not show me the photographs and demand the truth?'

'Would you have told me? All of it?'

'I would've tried.' But Amber doesn't believe her own words. She knows she would have lied, made up a hollow story, tried to make it all go away.

'I thought if you trusted me, and if you were scared, then I could make you tell me. I didn't think you'd just keep on lying.' Yvey pauses, the steel gone from her face. 'But I'm sorry. I'm sorry I went too far. I'm sorry about scaring you. I'm sorry you fell. You just wouldn't tell me the truth.' Her voice is pitching deeper into the whine.

'And you had help, didn't you? Someone to send the messages when you were with me.'

Yvey laughs. It comes from nowhere, and the contrition is gone from her face.

'Man, you are well analogue. You didn't even think someone might be using a scheduling app?' She shakes her head as if she is disappointed in Amber, as if she has not turned out to be a worthy adversary.

'But what about the scans of the negatives? The man at my house? Was that Mika? How did you get him to help you?'

Yvey looks confused for a second. 'Mika? What? C'mon, you think I don't know how to scan a negative? Jeez.'

'And who was that who came that night to scare me at my house?'

Yvey looks down. 'It doesn't matter who that was. Leave him out of it. He doesn't know anything.'

'Who, Yvey?'

'If you have to know, he's just some guy who's had a crush on me. Boys are so basic. They'll do anything if they think they'll get some.'

Amber laughs. She can't help it. It's that slightly mad laugh. She almost wants to congratulate Yvey. She can see it all much more clearly from her point of view now: the frame, the subject, the intention.

First the simple questions about her and Benny, then the strip of negatives left among her work, just enough to unnerve her. Next, the photo timed to arrive just when Yvey was with her — the simple misdirection of a scheduled message.

I see you.

I see, and I am watching. Watching for a reaction, for a change in Amber's behaviour.

What happens next?

A question, a threat, an invitation to confess. Tightening the ratchet, seeing how much Amber would give at every stage.

Then the confrontation at her home. Was that the moment Amber was supposed to fold and tell it all? Because after that, the tone in the messages changed: the plaintive demands for the truth, the widening cracks of uncertainty. Not messages from someone who knew the truth and was using it against Amber, but from someone who was still desperately looking for it.

And in the end, Yvey's plan has worked in a way. Here they all are, just waiting for the rest of Amber's confession.

Amber looks at Genevieve. She has said nothing this whole time, nervously waiting as Amber extracted the truth from Yvey. Amber takes the negatives from under her hand and gives them to Genevieve. Silently, Benny's widow takes them, switches on the lightbox and begins to examine them.

Time stretches out as Amber waits for the reaction. Even at this distance she can see the reversed patches of light and shade in the negatives. She knows they are of her body, lying naked on the bed.

'This is you?' Genevieve says eventually. There isn't anger or shock in the question. It's flat, tentative, as if not really wanting to know the answer. She turns away from Amber and looks at her reflection in the studio glass.

'I'm so sorry,' Amber says to her, and she doesn't stop talking until she has told all of her story.

53

She has to get it out, every detail, every syllable. The affair, the cottage, the aftermath. When Amber talks about the intruder, she proffers her phone with the photo of the man illuminated on the screen.

Genevieve looks at it for a long time, bringing the image towards and away from her face, and tilting it as if it might give her a three-dimensional view into the past. But even when Amber says his name, there is no sense of recognition. Genevieve has no great revelation about who Finn Gallagher might have been to Benny.

Then Amber relates the events of the last weeks and days, bringing Yvey's stuttering confession into full view in front of her mother. It feels like a purgation and its own penance. The words hurt to say out loud.

When she finishes, no one can say anything. Genevieve looks shell-shocked. Yvey is shifting uncomfortably. The facts of Benny's death, his infidelity, the man Amber killed at the cottage two decades ago — all of it seems too big to grapple with.

Genevieve's gaze swings towards her daughter, who is

standing now, propped up against the desk where the computer sits. While Amber has been talking, Yvey has quietly slipped the envelope back into her satchel bag. She holds it now in one hand at her hip.

'Yvette, could you give Amber and I some time alone?'

'I'm not going anywhere. Don't you get it? I've been right all along. Dad was going to tell everyone about what happened at the cottage, but got killed before he had the chance. And why else was I mugged for my phone? Because someone's worried about what I know.'

Genevieve is lost for a response, as if still fighting with everything she has learned. Then abruptly she stands and in a quick motion grabs onto Yvey's satchel bag. But her daughter won't release it, and they are both pulling at it.

Yvey is shouting *No!* over and over like a stuck record. The bag slips from her hand, and she only has a hold on the thin strap. She tries to strike out at Genevieve with one hand, but it just lets her mother get a better grip.

Then Yvey is kicking, unbalanced. Genevieve gives a last tug and has the satchel. She backs off, putting the table between herself and her daughter. Yvey is looking around for something, a wild look in her eyes.

Then the girl is still again. Not defeated, but no longer on the offence. She stands with her legs apart, her breath beating up and down in her chest.

'Don't look. You can't.' She is defiant, but with an edge of pleading.

'Enough!' It's like a bark that comes out of Genevieve. And with it, all of her tense, poised control and gritty patience is gone. It is as if the shock wave of everything that happened all those years ago is only just now reaching her. 'Don't you ever tell me what I can and can't do.'

Yvey gulps at a response, but can't find anything. Then she is in motion again, running across the studio floor. She goes past Amber through the open doorway, half bouncing off the frame, the glass vibrating. Amber starts to go after her.

'Leave her!' Genevieve commands, and Amber freezes. Genevieve opens the satchel sharply and pulls out the envelope. She spreads its contents across the lightbox and turns it on.

There are strips and strips of negatives, perhaps a dozen films' worth. Genevieve is sliding her hands through them, then leaning into a strip to examine it. Then another and another. Frame after frame after frame.

'Bastard!' she breathes. She takes a handful of the negative strips and throws them out in front of her. They twist and flip in the air, falling to the table. Then she stretches out her hands into the fallen film and swipes them all off the table with a wordless shout.

The silence that follows thrums in the cold studio. Genevieve sits down at the desk and slumps forward a little.

Amber reaches down to the floor for one of the negatives and examines it on the light box. It is of a naked woman. Amber drops it and picks up another. Another naked form. She tries one more and already knows what's on it before she even looks. And there is something she notices about the poses. They are all just that — poses. Their faces are towards the camera. They are sitting, standing, stretching out in front of the lens. They all have in them what Benny's photos of Amber did not — that willing participation. She knows Yvey will have seen the difference too. She knows it will have fed her fevered questions and theories.

'Did you... did you have any idea? About all this?'

'I'm not a fool.' There is the cut of venom in Genevieve's voice. 'I knew what Benny was like. Everyone knew what he was like.' She shrugs as if all of secrecy is dead now. 'I wasn't always a perfect wife either. But we were a team, you know. Always a good team. You understand that, don't you?'

Amber nods, feeling a pang, wanting Johnny here with her, glad that he is not.

Genevieve waves a hand at the envelope still on the table. 'But that he *collected* them. It's just so humiliating. And the things he did to you and made you do. How do you grieve someone you love and hate all at the same time?'

'Did you never suspect about me and Benny?' Amber asks, a small flicker inside her clinging onto the idea that Genevieve has always known and has already forgiven her.

'Not you, no. I didn't put it past him. But you, Amber, no, I didn't think you would.'

'That's what Benny thought. He said you liked me too much to suspect.'

Genevieve grunts unobligingly. 'Huh. No, it wasn't really that. I did like you, that's true. But I've liked other women Benny liked. No, it was you and Johnny. I trusted that. I didn't think you'd betray him.' Her words twist into Amber. 'I thought you were–'

'Better than that?'

'Smarter than that.' Genevieve breathes out slowly through her nose, her lips pursed.

'I'm sorry.'

'Stop apologising. I don't want your goddamn apology.' The fight inside her is all over her face — a moment of searing grief and anger. But Amber recognises another feeling in there. It is a desire to know the truth about what happened all those years ago, and whether Yvey is right, that someone did kill her husband.

Genevieve gets up from her chair and starts to collect all the negatives together. She begins to lay them out on the lightbox again, examining them more closely this time. There is a methodical patience to how she seems to be recording each face. Amber doesn't doubt that there are friends of hers in here, enemies too. A portfolio of betrayal.

'Please, don't do this to yourself.'

Genevieve gives her a sharp look. 'You don't see, do you? I only just realised, but it's very clear now. It was late 2001, you said, at the cottage. The second weekend in November. Is that right?'

'Yes, that sounds right.'

'And it was a last-minute invitation, yes?'

'Uh... I guess. It was always last-minute with Benny.'

'That Sunday was the day I told Benny I was pregnant with Yvette. That's why I remember the date so clearly. It was *me* who was supposed to be at the cottage that weekend. Yes, he took me there too, you know.' She shakes her head. 'But I had to go away at short notice. I remember now when I saw Benny, he had bruises all over the side of his face. Some story about falling off a ladder, which was believable enough, given what a state this place was in. But the way you described what happened, how the intruder punched Benny away, then went for you. If he wanted to kill Benny, he wouldn't have done that. You can see that, can't you?'

Amber does see. The intruder had not knifed Benny and sought to make his escape. He had not killed Benny, then attempted to silence her. She sees the rest of the piece now, even before Genevieve says it out loud.

'That man Finn. He wasn't trying to kill Benny or you. He was trying to kill *me*. And he thought you were me. And my darling husband, that absolute shit of a man, was in on the plan. *That* was what he wanted to confess.'

54

Thursday, 23 August 2001

I was drunk, and I was angry with Gen. It's not a defence, but it's something you should know. Did I mean what I said that night? I meant it for the seconds I was saying it. I could imagine it. But there's a difference between meaning something and doing it. All the same, I did say the words.

It was months before it happened, before that weekend at Tim's cottage. Late August 2001, the end of that summer when nothing seemed to happen in the world. Before that day in September that burnt it all up.

I was drinking at a secluded little bar where no one I knew went. I was with an old friend. Drinks with her had become a quiet little fixture. She always said yes when I asked and never stood me up. I enjoyed the honesty I had found with her — in a relative sense of the word.

When I'd first known her, there had been a certain flirtation to our relationship, but it was an unemotional dalliance, as if every entendre had a layer of irony over it.

It was true we had slept together a couple of times in the first few years I'd known her. Careless, drunken couplings. After the second time, she had made a faltering suggestion we might make a regular occasion of it, but we both laughed it off when I reminded her I'd just got engaged. And we went back to how we were. I appreciated that kind of unusual constancy in my life.

I got another round in. The more I drank, the angrier I got about Gen. I'd had another stupid argument with her about that bloody farmhouse. I didn't even want to be talking about her, but my friend kept asking, probing into the state of my marriage. I should have left it alone. Because when Gen and I weren't living on top of each other, it worked well. We were a good team. But that summer, our lives were crushing together. I felt like one of those Japanese water-melons being grown in a box to force my well-rounded life into an ornamental square. I was becoming part of one of her collections.

And then there was Amber.

Nothing had happened with her by August. I had mostly seen her in company: those long boozy London dinners with that stringy would-be rock-star boyfriend of hers. But there had also been a few times of just her and me. Coffee, talk of photography and careers, aimless walks along the South Bank, neither of us admitting what we were feeling underneath.

I couldn't get her out of my head.

That night in the bar, I was trying to obliterate the feeling with alcohol. I must have thought it was also a good idea to obliterate it with sex. I know they say you shouldn't sleep with your friends, but I've always found it depends on the friend. I've found a lot of them can be remarkably civilised about it. The friend sitting opposite me certainly had been on previous occasions.

But I'm getting ahead of myself.

'If it's really so bad,' my friend was saying, leaning forward a little in her chair, waving the end of her cigarette, 'you should divorce her.'

'She'd take me to the cleaners, leave me with nothing but my debt. You don't inherit what Gen has unless your family is good at hanging onto money.' I made my hand into a claw.

'Well, if you can't divorce her and still want in on that inheritance...' She took a long sip of her vodka, then held the glass at her lips and stared at me over it.

Looking back, it feels almost as if she was willing me to say it, but that's only with the benefit of hindsight. We were the last people in the room, save for the bar staff and my own reflection looking back at me from a mirrored wall at the end of the room. I said it as half a whisper.

'I could kill the bitch, I suppose.'

MY FRIEND LAY next to me on the hotel bed. We were both on our backs, staring at the ceiling. I find it best not to make too much eye contact in these situations. The prelude to what had just happened was uncomplicated. We had stumbled from the bar and fallen into a cab. There had been little in the way of flirtatious overture. It was a simple offer, simply accepted.

'You could, you know,' she said now, lying on the bed.

'I could what?'

'What you said about your wife.'

I laughed hard. The idea felt like a release from my thoughts and my awkward sudden soberness.

'How would you do it?' my friend asked, barely missing a beat.

I propped myself up on the pillow, leaning into the grimness of the moment. 'I dunno, take her up to Tim's cottage for a weekend, kill her and dump her in the sea.' I thought for a moment, trying to visualise it. The thought gave me a heady mix of revulsion and catharsis. 'Kind of puts me in the frame.'

'Who's to say *you* have to do it?' She rolled onto her side and looked squarely at me. 'Everything's outsourced these days.'

I almost came back with a quip about how outsourcing was Gen's department and maybe she should commission her own assassination, but I kept the thought inside. The conversation and the serious, intense look on my friend's face were making me feel strange.

I rolled away, looking at the wall for a few moments, then heaved myself out of the bed. My head hurt, and the room rocked around me. I dressed in silence and made for the door.

My friend was still lying in the bed, still naked, nothing covering her slim form. She looked into me.

'See you soon? We'll do this again?'

'Sure,' I said. I already knew I had made a mistake. I just didn't know how bad it was.

55

AMBER

enevieve continues to sort through the negatives, laying them out in front of her like a strange game of patience. There is something a little missing in her face, as if the last few minutes have broken something inside her. Amber sits there dumbly, almost too frightened to speak. Genevieve breaks the silence.

'You can see now why my husband was so determined to cover up the murder. Not so I wouldn't find out about the affair, not because he was trying to protect you. Yvette was right. Benny was talking on the phone to someone he'd shared a secret with all this time.'

'But if he was expecting that man, why bring me to the cottage? If he knew about a plan to kill you, why not call a halt to it when you couldn't come? And Benny wanting you dead? Why not try again? You've been married for all this time.'

Genevieve shakes her head. 'I don't know. I can't explain. Back then, we were at our lowest. We would fight for days. It all felt like a terrible mistake. I'm sure even I threatened to kill him at least once. But I didn't mean it. Of course I didn't mean it. I never thought he might. But when I told him I was pregnant, he changed. He really did.'

Genevieve touches her stomach, as if her pregnancy with Yvey was only yesterday. 'Or I thought he did. But he loved our daughter. I'm sure of that.' But she doesn't sound sure and is close to tears again. She pulls it back, clamping down control on her emotions. 'So whatever he had cooked up went disastrously wrong. And afterwards... remorse, learning I was pregnant, I can't say...'

The emotion wins over again, and her whole body starts to shake, like someone shivering after a plunge into cold water. She hunches down over her knees for a second. Then, as if by a great force of will, her body stills itself.

Amber gestures at the negatives. 'Do you think the person Benny was talking to that night was one of these women? Is there someone you suspect?'

Genevieve looks defeated. 'I don't know what I was expecting to find.'

'But some of them are people you know?'

'A few. But you've seen them. They're all like you were. Young and stupid.' There is more sadness than venom in her words. She looks away from Amber, out towards the clearing — or rather just at their reflections in the glass, darkness now all around them. 'I shouldn't have let Yvette go off like that.'

'We have to call the police, don't we? About all of this.' Amber knows it is only a matter of time now. The process they are going through to try to find a grain of truth in these pictures is just putting off the inevitable.

'I am sorry, Amber.' Genevieve is shaking her head, but her tone is inconclusive. She gets up and walks towards the studio door. 'I can give you a little more time.' She casts a hand towards the computer and the scanner as if she is batting off a fly. 'But I'm finished here. There's nothing else I want to see. I need to find my daughter.' She goes out into the night, closing the door behind her as if sealing a tomb.

Amber sits in the silence, Genevieve's words echoing around her. *A little more time.* What did that mean to her? Amber has had so much of it: all these years and she's said nothing. What is she supposed to do with a few more minutes or hours? Run? Warn the people in her life what is about to happen to her? Take the same way out Genevieve used to believe Benny did? All of the years, all of the lies, all of the secrets are crushing down on her.

Slowly she starts to tidy up around her, as if sorting the archive is still her job. This displacement is all she can do to stop herself from collapse.

When the table is almost clear, she finds two more strips of negatives from the film Benny took, although she doesn't realise at first they are of her: there is no clear figure in them.

She holds them against the lightbox, her eye on the magnifier. Then she sees. They are of her body, but not all of her. They are taken from every angle and position, closer and closer, more and more intrusive. They are anatomical, like an autopsy or crime scene photographs. Benny has dismembered her with his camera.

She sits back, wanting to throw up. But there are two more pictures at the end of the last strip, these ones not of her. The first she immediately recognises as the hasty hip-level snap of Finn Gallagher.

After that, there is just one more. This one is less clear in negative — a series of geometric shapes. Amber quickly puts it through the scanner and sends it to the computer. It is a photograph of a door at the top of a short flight of steps. Off-kilter and imperfectly focused. Not a door Amber knows. It is not the cottage, not the farmhouse, not Benny's London pad. It is not the capture of a vanishing moment meant for eternity. It is just the last on the roll, haphazardly clicked.

Amber takes out her phone, trying to think what to do next. What is there left? In her notifications, she sees a message has come through whilst she was playing out the grim theatre with Genevieve and Yvey. It is Kay.

How you getting on? You need backup?

Amber puts the phone away, unanswered. There is nothing she wants to say to Kay, and no help her friend can give her.

She goes to turn the computer off for a final time. The last photograph is still there on the screen: fat white balustrades leading up to a door, and a thick white arch above it. The mid-grey tone of the black-and-white photograph could be any number of colours. There is a door-knocker at its centre, with a touch of Art Deco about the design.

She reappraises her first reaction, getting the same sense as seeing a piece of art for the second time and beginning to understand it.

She thinks about the Benny she knew: the man who would never flinch from an important shot. And of the Benny she has discovered through the archive and these stolen photos of her. Benny the obsessive, the compulsive, the disordered. Benny the man who thought he could possess people through images. All these negatives kept for all these years. Every single damn frame, like a substitute for memory or conscience.

She looks at the picture of the door, the sense she has seen it before now scratching at the back of her mind. It could be in London, the only place Benny was likely to have gone between leaving Norfolk and developing the film.

But it's the fact he went anywhere at all that twists in her mind. Why make a detour? Why shoot a final frame at all?

And the sense of something familiar grows. Familiar and recent. Something in the archive.

She goes first through the scanned images already on the computer. It's quick, *swipe-swipe,* across the screen.

As she searches, there is another sequence of questions going through her head about Yvey. Who was it who attacked the girl? Why take her phone? What were they looking for?

Amber refocuses on the images in front of her, but still there's nothing in them she can find. She looks in all the backgrounds, behind the main tableaus of action Benny has captured. Still nothing. But the idea of background sticks, and a sick feeling hits her.

She gets up and goes swiftly through the door at the back and up to the archive. She knows now the box she is looking for, and she knows the photo. It is that solitary shot that peeled back a little the lie about the depth of a relationship.

She feels sick again when she pulls the print from the envelope. The match between this photo and the last on the roll of Benny's film are clear to see: the Art Deco knocker on that door. Green in this colour print, a woman leaning against it with her sardonic half-smile and cigarette.

Amber hears a sound from downstairs in the editing suite. The hum of the sliding door, and footsteps on the polished floor.

56

BENNY

Sunday, 11 November 2001

I took Gen to Tim's cottage in the last weekend of September. It was a couple of weeks after that evening in the bar, and just before the time I spent in Afghanistan. I carried to the cottage the feeling I always get before I go into a war zone. *This time I might not come back.* It focuses the mind. It made for one of our better weekends. Finally we were away from the farmhouse and all that racket. I felt free again in the space of the sea and the sky. Sure, I thought about the words my friend and I had said to each other. But they felt distant and grimly comic in the bright sun and strong breeze. They were silent in the hours of careless sex.

In the weeks that followed, in the chaos of war, I didn't think once of that evening with my friend. The notion faded into absurdity. I'd not even heard from her, and I'd not made contact myself, either. I was still chewing on my mistake, my lack of discipline.

Then came the November trip to the cottage with Amber, and the man who came to change it all.

Those last moments of his life played in my head as I drove away from the coast on the morning after. What else was there to think about? I tried to consider the events leading up to his death, watching it all as if from his point of view. I could see him following us, thinking I was with my wife. I could imagine him tracking us throughout the weekend, trying to find the right moment. Did he run out of opportunities? Was he getting reckless when he broke into the cottage, desperate to finish the job?

The feeling about who he was felt implausible and unavoidable at the same time. I could tell myself he was a junkie or a drifter. I could construct a comforting lie that it was nothing to do with me: that someone from Tim's past had tried to catch up with him. I could tell myself it was coincidence that I had half-conspired to kill my wife. I tried to cling to that idea. I wondered how long I could. I wondered if I could just go home and never speak about it.

But I couldn't get away from how the man had behaved: getting me out of the way, warning me with the point of his knife to stay down, then going for Amber.

If I had any doubts left about who had sent that man, they vanished the moment my friend opened the door to me. Her eyes, fogged with sleep, almost lit up for a moment. But the sight of Kay Hamilton held no pleasure for me anymore.

'Benny,' she said, her voice rising hopefully.

I pushed straight on into her flat. It was nearly lunchtime, but she still had a dressing gown wrapped around her, a cigarette in a lightly trembling hand. I kept going through the flat, looking in the rooms, checking for signs of anyone else. The hallway was strewn with old papers, and the kitchen was piled high with unwashed dishes. I didn't know how to begin. The first thing that fell out of my mouth was disgust:

'You live like this?'

She was silent, for once the sharp casual riposte missing from her throat.

'Did you... did he...?'

Then my rage exploded, shooting out from me like a thousand flashguns firing. 'You stupid bitch! You stupid, *stupid* bitch.'

She fell backwards onto a chair, her dressing gown unfurling. I felt a great wave of disgust wash over me, and there was a seething silence between us. I was standing over her, my fists bunched. Then I backed away, pressing myself against the kitchen wall.

'Is your wife...?'

'I wasn't there with my wife, you idiot. So, no, Gen is not dead. And neither is...'

'Who?'

'It doesn't matter. It's none of your business who I'm sleeping with.'

'Then why do you always take such delight in telling me all about them? You think because you don't tell me their names, I think they don't exist?'

I didn't want to move towards where she was trying to drag the conversation.

'The only person who's dead is that amateur you hired.' I shook my head, grasping at a lost possibility. 'Tell me you didn't, Kay, please.'

But she didn't utter a word.

'Who the hell was he?' I bellowed the question, trying to focus on some solid fact.

'He's dead?' She looked pale. 'Did you call the police?'

'Of course I bloody well didn't. Tell me who he was.'

I thought Kay was going to throw up, but then a defiance

came back into her face. 'He was someone who understood something about loyalty. More than you ever will.'

'Jesus Christ, I didn't think you'd actually do it. And frankly, if you did, I thought you of all people would find someone who knew what they were doing.'

'So you did want me to do it.'

I couldn't speak. I just shook my head.

'You said. You said it. You wanted me to, Benny. I didn't force you to say it.'

'No, I–'

'All those girls, Benny, again and again and again. They last a few weeks, a few months, then they're gone. All of them a waste of time.' She had hauled herself up from her chair, hugging her dressing gown around her like a pathetic armour. 'And then you marry that stupid cow, and you *knew* it was a mistake. You'd trapped yourself and you wanted to escape. You were finally telling me that. I was helping you escape. Escape to me, Benny. That's what you wanted, really. I felt it. I felt it that night when you gave yourself to me.'

'It was just a fuck,' I said, but I could feel my blindness falling away.

'Tell me you didn't mean what you said. Tell me you didn't want me to act on it. I knew you did. I could see it.'

Then I could see too. I saw all of it. It wasn't a misunderstanding. My intention wasn't the important thing. Yes, I meant those things for the seconds I said them. I just didn't know how much they meant to Kay. I was giving form to something she had imagined for years. The desire had grown with every girl I slept with that wasn't her, and it had twisted into a new shape when I married Genevieve. My words had been a permission. A blessing. An instruction that only Kay could fully understand.

And I hadn't seen it, all this time. A blind spot, right in front of my face. Her reliability, which I never saw as devotion. Those eyes that fixed me when I spoke, in which I never saw longing or love. Her hard exterior, which I never saw as a defence. Even the sex — three times in a decade — had a casual indifference. And nothing I could say would change that.

I sat in my car for a long time after I left. I was parked right outside, looking up the white steps towards the green communal door of the big townhouse her flat was in. I was torn between going back in and driving as far away as I could.

There had been little else we could say to each other. Our asymmetrical guilt sat between us in the silence. I wanted her to speak, even if I couldn't. I wanted her to describe her feelings for me, to tell me how long she had entertained this idea, how she had planned it, the sequence of events she had thought would follow it. I felt it would absolve me for my part in it all. But she was never one for long monologues. She's always been about the sharp line, the quick response. Her response now was simple.

'We're never going to tell. Not anyone.' It wasn't a question. There was no doubt in it.

'No.'

And I left. I meant that 'no', at the time, almost entirely. I couldn't undo what I had done, and I couldn't ever forget it. Whether I ever told anyone else about it felt almost like a detail.

I looked across at my camera bag in the footwell of the empty passenger seat. I thought of Amber, her sleeping curves, the sheets down across her thighs. Her body became briefly a corpse again in my mind, then that corpse became Genevieve's.

I reached across, pulled the bag onto my lap and took out my camera. The counter said 36. One more picture left. It was an automatic act to photograph that door. Yes, the habit of finishing a film so I could preserve Amber in celluloid, but also to remind myself who was responsible for finally taking her away from me. And to remind me of my own stupidity.

I used my London studio to develop the film a few days later. I locked myself in the darkroom: that confessional where the only sin is to let the light in.

I got over my impulses to destroy the photographs. I knew the shots were incriminating. All of them, in different ways. But so many of my photographs are. So much of what is in that box is. I'm happy for someone to find it once I'm gone. Perhaps before I go. I don't regret for a moment keeping any of those negatives. I sometimes regret taking them, that's true. But I don't regret keeping them.

Record the truth; never let it go. Once, forever.

57

For a moment Amber feels in a state of suspended animation. She is looking at Kay and sees someone different from the woman she has known all these years. But it is a difference she does not completely understand. She cannot see the full shape of her friend's secret.

Amber has Benny's old photo of Kay in her hand. Like that last shot on the roll of Kay's door, it is proof of nothing, but she knows together they point towards the woman standing in front of her.

Kay breaks the silence. 'Sorry, sweetie, didn't mean to startle you.' Her voice is even but without light. Amber turns the photograph to face her body, and lowers it to her side. 'I didn't get a reply to my text. I was getting worried, thought I should come and see you were all good.'

'Yeah, all fine.' Amber goes for her phone in her back pocket, but it's not there. She looks over and sees it sitting next to the scanner.

'You must be tired.' Kay's voice is now in that register she uses for giving Amber advice. 'Let me run you home.'

Kay hasn't moved far from the sliding door. Now she twists

and glances out through it, but there is only darkness beyond. As Kay turns, Amber sees she has a small backpack on her shoulders and is wearing different clothes to the ones she had on when she gave Amber a lift. The smart, dark trousers have been exchanged for a pair of old jeans, and her shirt and jumper for a threadbare fleece. They look like clothes for getting your hands dirty, and they exaggerate Kay's slim but solid athleticism.

Amber tries to imagine her in a bike helmet, wondering if that would have been enough to disguise or confuse her gender, at least from Yvey, in the chaos of an assault. And she remembers the last message she sent, her declaration that she would tell everything, that she was not afraid anymore. Did Yvey read that? Or only Kay?

'Okay,' Amber says, trying to smile evenly, as if everything is fine, as if only hours ago she hadn't been talking to Kay about Benny's murder. She is aware of her own breathing. The studio feels very small around them, and the house very far away. 'I need to go back inside anyway, talk to Genevieve. I assume you're parked up at the house.'

'Genevieve? Oh, I saw her drive off.'

Amber nearly says out loud that she has probably gone off looking for Yvey, but stops herself. Something about Kay's shape has changed, as if all the pretence between them is falling away.

'I'm surprised you let Genevieve go,' Amber says, jumping with both feet into her suspicions. 'Don't you have unfinished business?'

'That's not how this is.'

'How is it, then? I told Genevieve everything, you know. About my affair with Benny, about how a man called Finn Gallagher attacked us at the cottage, and how I killed him.' Amber looks for a reaction in Kay, and its absence tells its story. There is no shock of revelation. 'I especially should have told you, shouldn't I? I should have said something a long time ago. And I really am going to tell everyone now. I've had enough of hiding in my own life.'

'I don't think that's a good idea.'

'Why not? What does it matter to you if this has nothing to do with you?'

Kay's face cracks a little. 'What is it you want me to say, Amber?'

'The truth would be nice. Because I think it's going to come out once I go to the police.'

'Amber, don't be silly.'

'Silly? Is that what you think I am? Do you still think I was a silly young thing who got fucked by Benny Raine? Were *you*? Is that what all this was about?'

'Amber, please, I don't want to fight. Let's just talk. That's all I've ever wanted from you. Someone to talk to.' There is a plaintive note in her voice, as if her mood is flying around all over the place behind her steady exterior.

'Let's talk, then. Let's hear it. Tell me you don't know anything about what happened in that cottage. Tell me you've never heard the name Finn Gallagher. Tell me you've never wished Genevieve harm, that you don't know anything about Benny's death. Go on, I'm listening. Talk.'

Kay shakes her head, the knowledge that denial is pointless now written all over her face.

'It was what Benny wanted,' she says, gritting her teeth. 'He pretended afterwards he didn't mean it, but he did. I thought I knew that man better than any of you, better than his wife. She was in the way, Amber, can't you see that? You *know* that, don't you. Tell me you wouldn't have got her out of the way if you could, when you were with Benny. You know how he made you feel when he was with you.'

Amber is shaking her head, but she can still hear the

distant echo of how she sometimes felt when she was with Benny.

'It was bullshit, though, wasn't it?' Amber says. 'It wasn't real. Not for him.'

'I loved him,' Kay says, her voice defiant, but then it falls. 'I thought I did. I thought he was the only man I ever loved. But I was wrong. He didn't care. He went through life pleasing himself, being careless with other people's lives.'

'How can you stand there and talk about being careless with life? You sent Finn to kill Genevieve, didn't you? I know about Finn's father too. Did you kill him? Was that the price you had to pay? Was that the exchange? Did you have a nice little alibi ready the night Finn came to the cottage?'

Kay smiles, looking for a moment impressed. 'I should have expected you to do your research, sweetie.' Her face pinches in. 'Look, Finn owed me. He was a small-time crook, but he was a good source. I always had plenty on him, but I looked after him too. I helped him keep his nose clean. He knew to be cooperative. And it was a good deal. His father was a bastard. The things he did to the boy, you don't want to know about. Finn deserved every bit of money he would have inherited. And I've always hated bullies. Genevieve is a bully, you know. She was one to Benny from the moment they met.'

'And Benny? What was he? You wanted to be with a man who would kill his own wife?'

'He said he wanted it.' Her voice sounds desperate, as if she is still convincing herself of something years later. And she starts to tell Amber a story about a drink they had together, about a night of sex in a hotel, about how he had given her a signal, how she was only acting as an agent of his will. As she talks, it is as if she is back in time, still feeling for Benny all the things she did. But even before she has finished, Amber knows that the story ends with Kay cast out of Benny's life.

When she does finish talking, Amber moves a little closer. 'And you killed him, didn't you? Because he was going to tell.'

She shakes her head. 'No, I didn't kill him, not really. He was dying anyway. I was just helping him on his way before he ruined everything. You of all people shouldn't mourn him. Think about what he did to you for all these years, making you carry a secret for all this time. He pretended he wanted to make it better for you at the end, but it was only ever about himself. I wasn't going to let him ruin my life. Not what's left of it.'

Her gaze hardens, and she flexes her shoulders. 'And I'm not going to let you, either.'

K ay's words lie like shattered glass between the two women. Amber finds her voice.

'Don't threaten me, Kay. Don't ever threaten me. I meant what I said, I'm not frightened anymore.'

Kay is scratching a hand through her short hair. She brings it down across her face, as if trying to wipe away the emotions roiling inside.

'Oh, Amber, sweetie, I'm not threatening you. I'm only trying to make you see sense. I wish you'd listened to me before. I tried to tell you not to come back here, to stop digging. I knew it couldn't do either of us any good. Don't you see now? You'll be throwing so much away. Think about Johnny. About the wee one. Just think for a moment. Nobody needs to know. Benny isn't worth it. You know that's true. And he's dead. Is that worth the rest of your life?'

'It's too late. Yvey knows someone killed Benny, and so does Genevieve.'

Kay looks unnerved for a moment. 'You trust that woman now, do you?' Then she hardens. 'I've seen what Yvey knows

— at least what she can prove. And Genevieve doesn't have any more proof than you do.'

'They know about Finn. They've seen what's on that film. Genevieve will go to the police if I don't.'

'Are you quite so sure about that? Are you sure Genevieve wants everything dragged out in the open, the truth about Benny to come out? Just think of the damage to the *brand*.' She drips the words, as if taunting the absent woman who she still despises.

'Don't be ridiculous.' But Amber doesn't feel confident Kay isn't right. She glances down at the photo in her hand and looks over at the scanner where the negatives are all laid out next to her phone. Scant evidence, and out of her reach. And Kay has Yvey's phone, that much is clear. Amber hopes that somewhere there are other copies.

Kay sees Amber's gaze, and her posture changes. Her legs are apart, and she is springy on her feet, like a boxer coming into the ring. She strides towards the scanner. Amber holds back, unwilling to try to fight her for the negatives. She just needs to keep her talking till Genevieve comes back. Kay swings the bag off her back, scoops up all the negatives and stuffs them roughly in. She picks up Amber's phone and turns it in her hand before depositing it in the bag.

'It's all a bit circumstantial, don't you think?' says Kay. She advances towards Amber, her hand still sheathed by the bag. 'You know we can destroy what little evidence there is, and you can walk away. I can walk away too.' She is closer now, and the bag drops away. There is something in her hand — the chromium shine of one of those expensive single-piece Japanese kitchen knives. 'That photo — give it to me.'

Amber nods slowly. She lets the photo go out of her hand, and it wafts down at her feet. She kicks at it, and it slides a little way towards Kay, who inches forward and picks it up. She looks at it and gives a small, melancholy smile.

'Why are we friends, Kay? All these years, if you knew who I was?'

The melancholy look is lingering on Kay's face.

'I didn't know. Not for certain. I've suspected, sure. You were always cagey about your time with Benny. It made me think, and it didn't take me long to find out when you were likely with him. At first I didn't like the idea. It made me feel all sorts of things I'd rather I didn't. But the more I thought about it... If it was you, then all it meant was that we'd both been Benny's victims. And we were both carrying part of the same secret, in our different ways. But I didn't have proof.'

She waves the knife. 'You want to know when I first really started to worry about it? It was that day we met in town after you'd spent the weekend here. You were being mighty weird, and I had this feeling, an intuition, call it what you like. So I kept an eye on you and on Yvey too. When did I have proof? Not till I saw those pictures on Yvey's phone of you at the cottage, that picture of Finn. And I don't want it to be you. I want it to be someone I don't know, someone I don't care about. It *hurts*, Amber. Don't you see this hurts me too? Don't you see I'm not angry with you? We're the same, Amber. He fucked us and threw us both away. And I've not done anything you haven't. Both of us have only killed in self-defence.'

Amber wants to argue, say it isn't the same what she and Kay have done. But she clamps that feeling inside.

'That's right, Kay, and we both need to face up to what we've done.'

'I don't want to hurt you, Amber.'

'You don't have to. Put the knife down, and we can talk.'

'What is there left to talk about?' Kay is shaking her head, and the knife lowers a little. 'I'm sorry, no. This is all —' she is grasping for the words '— all so lopsided now. You know how much worse it's going to be for me if you confess. How can I trust you'll keep quiet?' The knife stiffens in her hand.

'You won't do it, Kay. I know you won't do it. You won't hurt me. You won't hurt the baby.'

Kay keeps advancing, and Amber steps back, like a slow-motion dance being worked out. The fearful choreography stops as Amber finds her back to the door leading out of the main studio. She puts a hand behind her, and it touches the old heavy key protruding from the lock.

'Please, Kay, think.' Amber grips the key and pulls it out, clenching her fist around it behind her back.

'You can make this stop. All you have to do is never say anything, destroy all this.' She waves the bag, relaxing the knife again.

'If that's what you want. Okay, I'll do it.'

The look on Kay's face says she doesn't really believe Amber, but all the same, the knife is now right down by her side.

Amber takes the moment. She gives Kay as big a shove as she can manage, putting her off balance for just long enough. Amber doesn't strike her — she's not stupid enough to start that fight. And she knows there's no way she can run — she wouldn't make it out of the studio. Instead, she turns, pushes the door behind her and leaps through the space. She grabs the door as she passes and slams it at Kay, who is careering back toward her. It doesn't quite close. Kay's weight is on it. But from somewhere Amber finds her reserve. It is that same furious strength that saved Benny and killed Finn. And the door is shut. The key is in, and the door is locked.

She is in blackness, and the only sound is Kay hammering madly on the other side of the door.

59

The hammering stops. Amber calls out to Kay, but there's no answer. She gropes for the light switch, and as it flickers on, she feels for a moment safe. Kay cannot get in here, not through that old door. And Genevieve will be back: if not soon, then later. All she has to do is wait now. She tries not to think about what has to come after that.

She calls out Kay's name, but there is no answer. She assumes she must have run off, but a few seconds later, hears movement. It is the sound of things being dragged across the floor towards the door and of objects picked up and dropped close by. She doesn't understand what Kay is doing. Is she trying to barricade her in? What is the point of that?

Then she can see that whatever Kay is doing cannot be fully rational. Underneath her sometimes casual, sometimes needy exterior, it must be that Kay hasn't been functioning rationally for a very long time. Not when she tried to kill Genevieve, driven by some twisted idea of love; not when she silenced Benny; and not now, panicked by the threat of exposure.

Amber knows that last feeling. The sick feeling on the water, tipping in a small boat in heavy darkness, the blood from her hand coming through the bandages. The body falling beneath the surface to oblivion.

'Kay, listen to me! You're not thinking straight.' There's still no answer, but the noises stop. Amber presses her ear to the door. She hears a sound she can't place at first. Then she recognises it: the light splash of liquid. Then a small click, a pause, and a rapid *whoosh* like air being sucked out of the room. It is only when the sound is joined by a light crackle that Amber realises what Kay has done.

Amber turns the key and pulls open the door. A wall of flame greets her. It seems strangely cold at first, like when a fire is first lit in the hearth and the metal of the grate has not warmed. She sees the back of the sofa, apparently piled high with every piece of wood and paper that was in the room, all ablaze. The smell is chemical, with that almost alcoholic tang, and she knows that it has been dowsed in lighter fluid or petrol.

She tries to kick at the back of the sofa, but it won't move. She tries again, leveraging her other foot against the base of the staircase that runs up to the archive. It holds firm. It must be jammed in by all the other furniture in the room.

The heat is stronger now. The smell of burning leather and melting plastic, the crack and pop of metal and glass. As the smoke alarm sounds from the main studio room, Amber slams the door shut. She tries to think how safe she will be in here, and for how long. She looks up to the top of the door and sees that smoke is already seeping in around the old wood, and she remembers that old fact about smoke killing more people than fire.

She goes quickly to the end of the corridor and into the perfect darkness of the sealed studio. She finds the light and goes to the walls, running her hands along its white surfaces, trying to recall the studio building from outside — where the original windows were, and how it relates to the shape of the space she is in. But it all feels solid. No way out. Sealed like a tomb.

She runs back into the corridor. The smoke alarm has now sounded in here too. She rounds the bottom of the stairs, placing her hand on the door, already feeling the growing warmth coming through it. It's old wood. It won't be long before it catches.

As she runs up the stairs, she tastes the smoke thickly in her throat. She can't help but think about the baby now — the toxins in her lungs, in her blood.

She hurries through the door into the archive and slams it behind her. This door is modern and looks more fireproof. She should be safer in here for a little longer.

Again, she looks for an exit, but the walls are covered in nothing but the racks and racks of Benny's photographs and negatives. She tears the boxes off one set of shelves, and wrenches it away from the wall. It comes easily, not fastened to anything, and clatters down on the floor.

Unlike the clean white plaster of the studio downstairs, these walls are roughly covered. She thumps at the walls again, just as she did downstairs. This time she is lucky: a hollow sound comes back.

She bashes at the plasterboard and is surprised at how weak it is, or at how strong she has made herself in these moments of survival. Something animal pushing through. Then she has found something. There is an air gap here, around where a window frame creates space in its opening. She pushes her hand through and feels the cold caress of glass on her fingertips. Now the smoke alarm in this room activates — blaring at her like a screaming child.

She pulls at the plasterboard, great chunks coming off in her hands, until she can see the cross of the window frame.

She tries to pull it up, but it's stuck fast. Then she sees there is some sort of putty round the edges to seal it shut.

She can taste the smoke in her throat again and looks back at the room. The yellow light is dimmer still, and the air is more granular, like old film. She looks again at the glass. It is double-glazed.

She remembers the glass in the cottage, smashed with a stone from the beach, in thousands of tiny pellets at the intruder's feet. If she could break this, perhaps there would not be any jagged shards, perhaps she could squeeze out. She looks down at her body, not the shape it used to be, thinking about the baby inside her.

She takes off her jumper and wraps it round her fist. A deep breath and a hard punch. Her hand just bounces off it, and a deep pain cracks through her knuckles and up to her wrist. She screams a desperate obscenity and looks round the room, but there is nothing here to help her. She tries to think, but her thoughts are stuck, jammed by the screeching alarms all around her. All that comes through is a feeling that this is the end, that this is where she will die.

60

The temptation to give in comes over Amber like a drowsiness. There is almost a sense of peace to the idea that this might be the end. To no longer have to struggle, to lie, to keep half of who she is kept hidden away in a secret part of her mind. But the tentacles of the idea aren't strong enough. She knows it is partly the fire, the fumes, how her mind is not right, how none of this is right. She has to keep on going. For her daughter.

And it comes to her, her way out of this place.

She runs to the door and inches it open. The air in front of her is opaque. The smoke lapping in through the top of the old cottage door is thick now, acrid and chemical. She buries her mouth in the crook of her elbow and — eyes half-closed — stumbles down the stairs and into the photo studio. She looks around for anything of weight and sees a metal stool. She lifts it, and its base has a satisfying heft.

She is light-headed as she carries the stool through the corridor and to the bottom of the stairs. The smoke alarms chorus at her from all the different rooms. She tries not to think again about the fumes she is inhaling, of the carbon monoxide, of the damage it could be doing.

She has to drag the stool up the stairs, step by step, each movement feeling harder, her balance faltering. Unable to cover her mouth, she tries to breathe through her nose, but as the air comes back out of her lungs, it erupts in choking coughs.

Finally making it into the archive, she pushes the door behind her. It feels as if she has trapped as much smoke inside the room as outside. Without even thinking about her weight, momentum or the strength of the window, she lifts the stool and smashes it like a battering ram towards the glass and frame. A large crack appears across one pane. Another smash of the stool and the glass from two panes has splintered, flying out into the night. Her strength is going. She pulls the stool up again, but she fumbles, and it goes forward wildly, careering off the broken plaster and exposed window frame.

Just one more, maybe two, she tells herself. The stool in her arms, bracing it against her shoulder, rushing forward, leaning into it with her upper body to protect her belly.

Then she is through, the glass and wooden cross of the frame falling away. She drops the stool, sticks her head out and gasps at the cold night air. She looks down. It isn't so far. It's an old cottage, after all. Low ceilings, small stories. The ground underneath looks soft — a carpet of leaves over grass and mud.

You can do this, you can do this, she repeats to herself over and over.

She does her best to clear the bottom of the window of debris, picking sharp pieces of glass and wood away. Then she pulls her hands inside her jumper and grabs onto the top of the window frame. One foot is up on the bottom of the frame, then another. She pushes her feet through and is on her backside on the sill. The pain through the bottom of her jeans — glass and splinters digging into her — stops her hesitating. Arms off the top, then pushing at the sides of the frame.

There is barely any sense of falling, just the momentum of her push. Then her feet hit the ground, and she rolls instinctively. She has felt the impact on the soles of her feet and through her shins, but not in her body — less violence even than the fall outside her house.

Even so, she wraps her hands around her middle, as if she might be able to touch her baby, tell her she's all right. But there is only her own heaving breath making her body pulse.

She sits up and looks back at the cottage. Smoke is blowing from the window where she jumped, disappearing like breath into the sky above.

61

The woods are silent save for the hissing now coming from the studio like a pressure cooker on the edge of overloading. Amber is surprised to see it is almost in darkness. The lights in the glass structure are all off or burnt out, and the sliding door is closed. There is a glow coming from the glass end of the structure, but it doesn't look like a raging inferno. The main sign of the fire is the smoke coming from the broken window Amber has just escaped through. Perhaps it has burned itself out in the main room, with nothing else to catch in that bare space.

She doesn't have time to consider the fire for long. A high, sharp sound comes flying out of the darkness towards her — like the bark of a fox. Then it comes again, and Amber recognises its humanity. Then a third time — half scream, half call — and she knows the voice.

'Yvey!' Amber shouts into the darkness.

'Amber! Here!'

She has a direction on it now, and she makes towards it. She can hear more noises — they sound animal again, but this time like something moving in the undergrowth, grunting.

Then she sees. Kay is on the ground, trying to crawl forwards. Yvey is on the floor too, her arms wrapped around Kay's legs, her head twisting out of the way of kicking feet. The sleeve of Yvey's jacket has a slash across it, stained dark with blood. Amber runs round to Kay's head. Kay twists her face up. Her lip is split and swollen.

'Please, stop,' Amber shouts at her. Kay glances back along her body towards Yvey, then up at Amber again. Finally, her legs stop kicking. Yvey lets go and rolls back. Kay lies still for a few moments, then pulls herself up to a seated position.

Yvey gets to her feet, standing over Kay. When Yvey speaks, the phrases come out in gulps and spasms, her arms waving wildly.

'Went for a walk... saw the studio... she came at me with a knife... I managed to... Who even is she?'

'This is the person who killed your father.'

Yvey staggers backwards. For a moment, Amber thinks she is going to set upon Kay again. Yvey's foot stamps and swings as if she might deliver a sharp kick to her head. But then she blinks, as if someone has shone a bright light in her eyes, and turns away. She gives a shout at the forest — that animal sound again.

Amber tries to find something meaningful to say to Kay. But there is nothing that can convey what she feels. Instead she demands the return of her phone.

Expressionless, Kay gestures with her head, and Amber sees Kay's bag lying a few feet beyond them. Keeping her eyes on Kay, Amber goes to the bag and pulls out her phone. She unlocks it with her thumbprint and calls Genevieve. It connects in no more than a couple of seconds.

'You have to come back.' She can't find any words of

explanation. Genevieve is already talking rapidly over her, saying she's just got back into the house, how she drove to Radlow, then up and down the lanes, looking for Yvey.

'It's okay, she's here, just come out towards the studio,' says Amber, still unable to offer any sort of explanation. She looks over at Yvey, who has moved away, shaking her head, her hands going up to her face.

Their attention is only off Kay for a second, but it's enough. She is scrambling to her feet and running again, her feet slipping in the earth.

'Kay, stop. This is pointless. Where are you going to go?'

She doesn't answer, just keeps running. Yvey is already after her, and Amber follows. Kay and Yvey are both faster than Amber, who is exhausted and still coughing, and soon the colours of their clothes are fading to grey in the enveloping darkness.

Amber staggers on, and the quality of the gloom begins to change. She sees she is coming to the edge of the beech wood. It's as she spots the small hut she found with Johnny, still stacked with wood, that she sees the shape of Yvey crunching into Kay, and them both fall to the ground.

As Amber gets to them, Kay has managed to roll out from Yvey. Instead of attempting to run again, she goes for Yvey with a sudden ferocity. Like a trapped animal, she's lashing out, punching. And she's beating Yvey back — as if all the sinew in that tight athletic body is expending every last ounce of its strength.

Amber glances towards the large heavy logs and sees the axe leaning up against them. But, no. Enough violence.

'Stop it! Please!' Amber screams the words as she fumbles out her phone to call the police.

Kay steps back from Yvey, then goes towards Amber, who starts backwards. The phone slips from Amber's cold hands down into the mulch. She reaches for it, but Kay is going for it at the same time. They are on their knees, wrestling for the phone, looking right into each other.

Then Kay stops. Just stops. She releases her hands from the phone and sits down in the wet earth. It's as if it has finally hit her – there is nothing more she can do. She can fight and she can run, but there is no place left to hide her secret. She pulls her knees in tight to her chest, and buries her face in them.

'It's okay, it's over,' Amber says. 'For all of us.'

Yvey's form appears above her and Kay. Amber feels small with the girl looking down on them. This young woman, with the unnerving look of Benny about her, and the echoes of his gestures. Yvey gives what seems like a kindly smile, one of understanding. Perhaps one of forgiveness to Amber. But Amber is projecting. She does not know what the smile means.

'Who knows you're here?' Yvey asks. Kay knows the question is aimed at her. She lifts her face towards Yvey.

'No one,' she says, frowning.

Yvey nods to herself. There is something in her right hand, hanging down by her side. Then Amber sees. It is the axe from the pile of wood. And Amber sees too the single movement Yvey makes, pulling up sharply on the handle and catching it closer to the head. Both hands are on it, and it is up above Kay's head in a great angry swing.

'He was my dad, you bitch.'

The axe is travelling what feels like a great distance, yet coming down fast. Kay barely even has a chance to make a noise before it embeds itself in her skull.

Yvey's hands fly away from the axe as if it is electrified. The blade stays for a moment in Kay's head before the weight of the handle pulls it out. As the weapon falls, Kay's body crumples forward onto the ground. She is completely still.

The wound is a mess of red-black, half-covered in the leaves her head has fallen into.

Yvey staggers back. At first, it looks as if she is smiling. But the wide, grinning mouth is divorced from the rest of her body and face. Gaping eyes, hands wringing themselves together, a strange grinding noise coming out of her throat.

Then Amber runs. She doesn't know why. It isn't because she fears Yvey. It is just the pull of the urge to be anywhere but here. She runs in the direction of the house until she sees light flickering through the trees, and goes on towards it, like a deranged moth.

The studio is transformed. Where before only smoke was rising from the broken window, now flames are tearing out of it. The soft glow in the glass extension has caught again as the fire has reached to consume the wooden structure in which the glass sits. It is flooded with flame. Like a light-house, a burning beacon in the darkness.

There is a great crack as one of the sheets of glass splits in the heat just as Genevieve appears from the direction of the house. Her stricken face glows in the fire.

'The archive!'

Amber shakes her head. 'Let it burn.'

Genevieve stands speechless, her eyes wide.

'I think you should follow me,' says Amber, and she leads her towards the more terrible thing waiting in the darkness.

62

Time passes in pulses and waves, not a steady forward movement. It is a period of collective shock. It feels like a group hallucination, none of it real.

When Amber brings Genevieve to the scene of Kay's body, she looks as if she wants to scream, but no noise comes out. Moments later, she throws up into the leaves at her feet.

Yvey is shouting at her — *She killed Dad, she killed Dad!* — over and over, walking in deranged circles.

Amber puts an arm around Genevieve's shoulder, telling her she will call the police. But she feels a firm hand on her wrist and sees a desperate look in Genevieve's face.

'Wait. Let me think.'

'What is there to think about?'

The grip tightens. Genevieve shouts her daughter's name, and Yvey is finally silent. Mother and daughter hold each other's gaze. Yvey looks panicked, flittish, as if she might run off again. But under the power of her mother's stare, she collapses to the ground. She looks like a child, entirely helpless and innocent.

A change has come over Genevieve too. She is no longer displaying a face of shock. When she next speaks, she is back as the woman at the funeral: the one who hid her grief, the pragmatic widow asking Amber to come and visit her house. The woman bringing her unknowingly into all this.

'Who is she?' Genevieve asks Amber. 'What happened?'

In pausing gulps, Amber does her best to explain. She is still choking a little as she speaks, still trying to focus on whether she can detect movement inside her. She feels not quite present, not quite anywhere.

When Amber finishes, Genevieve repeats Kay's full name several times as if speaking a spell, and shakes her head. Then she turns directly to Amber and takes both her hands where they meet her wrists. She holds them firmly, pressing the fleshy pads beneath her thumbs, and brings them up in front of Amber. It was the way Benny had once done to her, the way Benny had probably done over the years to Genevieve. An act of discipline and control. But there is something else there. There is an element of pleading.

'Amber, please, no.' The look in Genevieve's face seems to say she has lost her husband, and tonight she has even lost any sense of who her husband was. She is not going to lose her daughter too. Amber understands what is about to come next. The woman who brought her into all this is about to try to lock her into it.

'I know what you're thinking,' says Amber. 'I know you want to protect Yvey.' She looks at the girl on her knees on the ground and has that same desire. In that moment, Amber doesn't care what happens to herself, but she sees the girl not much younger than she was when she killed Finn Gallagher, and wonders for a second how much the truth would serve justice. But she also knows that to try to protect Yvey, to force her to carry the secret for the rest of her life, will be worse. 'No, Genevieve. No.'

'We can bury the body here. There's so much land on the estate, places nobody ever goes.'

Amber can't find the words to answer. Yvey is silent too, looking up at Genevieve. The dynamic between mother and daughter has changed. It is as much from Genevieve's attempt to take control as Yvey's total submission: her need to be helped, to be saved.

Amber finds herself thinking about the incident with the teacher and how Benny and Genevieve had persuaded her not to press charges. They had made it all go away. But this is not like that. This cannot be made to go away.

'I won't make you help me,' Genevieve is saying to Amber. 'You don't need to be part of this, not again. You can walk away. You were never here.'

'Don't be stupid. People will ask about Kay. It's no secret she was my friend.'

'Say what you need to. Just say you never came here.'

'Sam was here. He saw me.'

Genevieve pauses, but not for long, as if what she says next is self-evident, as if the reassurance has been tested before.

'I told you, Sam's been with us a long time. He's extremely loyal.'

Amber remembers that feeling she had when she first arrived at the house — the headquarters of the Bayard-Raine empire. Property, art, finance. She hears Kay's withering certainty that Genevieve would want to protect her brand, and of all the things Freddie said about the Foundation's opaque business dealings. All those practices that hover on the border of legality. What else was there, just a little deeper, that Sam had helped protect? But Amber shakes her head.

'Whatever Sam's done for you in the past, this isn't the same. You do know that.' Amber throws a hand at the woods, towards the glow of the burning studio. She doesn't even need to speak about the fire. Even if Genevieve's faith in Sam were to hold, Amber knows she does not hold such power over the people who work for her that they can simply sweep away evidence of the inferno. The arson will be plain to see, however much it could be wrapped up in a story of some unknown vandal.

'I'm not asking you to do anything,' Genevieve says, her face not given up on the idea. 'I'm just asking for your silence. And whatever you need from me... from the Foundation...' She leaves the phrase hanging in the air, but the meaning is clear. Amber could name the price of her silence. 'Please, think. Beyond us, there is no one left alive who knows the truth — not all of it.'

Amber looks down at the grazes on her hands, smells the smoke on her clothes, and thinks about Ed. She knows he will not stop looking into Finn Gallagher — because he is too good a journalist. The dots will all join up eventually. And more than that, Amber knows that even if she could lie to some people, she cannot lie to Johnny anymore.

And it is clear now in Genevieve's eyes that, deep down, she too knows it is all over.

After that, Benny's widow barely says a word. She takes Yvey inside to administer her a stiff drink and some Valium. Just enough to keep her calm, perhaps to make her sleep.

It is the last Amber sees of Yvey, as she is guided away by her mother. Her hands are in front of her, and her head down, like a prisoner being led from the dock. Just before she disappears from view through the trees, she glances round at Amber. Her face is lost and still full of questions. Questions about the events that have led to these moments, about the act she has just committed, and about what is going to happen next. Teetering on a fulcrum between past and future. Then she drops her eyes. She knows Amber does not have all the answers after all.

Yvey and her mother go on into the woods, and Amber turns back towards the glow of the burning studio.

63

Four months later

The shifting sound of the foetal heartbeat on the monitor strapped to Amber sometimes sounds to her like the echo of a siren, sometimes like distant galloping horses. It changes with her daughter's movements and how well the monitor can hear her. Occasionally the rate drops right down, and a beeping alarm sounds. But it doesn't panic Amber now — she has learnt it is just the monitor latching onto her own heartbeat instead of her daughter's. Hers is the heart that beats at half the speed.

She is being induced. Her daughter is overdue, not ready for the world. Amber does not feel ready for her, either, but it isn't something you can prepare for, not really. Even so, she wants the process finally to start, so it can be complete. She feels trapped in a moment, full of all the things that have led to it and all those that will follow from it. Some of the mothers in the bays around her in the prenatal ward are like her, desperate for babies to come. Others are desperate for them to stay in a little longer.

The staff are all masked, gloved and gowned, in their attempts to protect themselves and her against COVID-19. The last months have been strange and awful, the rising tally of dead sometimes making the dreadful violence of that night at the farmhouse recede in her mind, sometimes bringing it starkly to bear.

She has been given the first round of drugs to induce labour, but nothing much has happened. She is waiting again. The last months have been full of waiting. Waiting for this new life, waiting for the next part of hers to start, waiting for justice.

AMBER DID NOT NEED to call the police. Genevieve did that. They came quickly, their blue lights strobing through the trees from the road, and Amber finally walked back to the house.

Genevieve calmly directed the police to the body in the garden as if they were contractors come to do some renovation on the estate. She informed them in a detached and efficient manner that her daughter had killed the woman who had murdered her husband and who had also tried to kill Amber.

The policeman looked at Genevieve with a studied scepticism, then at Amber, her face still sooty. So Genevieve explained about the studio, again in as few words as possible. She said nothing about Finn Gallagher.

Throughout this, Genevieve seemed half still in shock, half hanging onto the desperate pragmatism she had tried to bring to bear out in the woods. Whatever her mental state, there was certainly calculation in her words: just the simple and immediate facts, leaving all the space in the world for the more complex legal arguments that would need to follow.

Amber understood, too, that her confession would need to wait until there was a lawyer present. Indeed, at every stage since she first sat down in the interview room at the police station, lawyers have supervised her. They are lawyers that Genevieve has found and paid for. They are not people Amber could afford. It seems the offer of whatever Amber needs from the Foundation has held strong despite the truth coming out.

Amber is not entirely sure why she is being helped, and has not been able to ask. She has not spoken directly to Genevieve since that evening. Everything is conducted through the legal team. All she can suppose is Genevieve feels that throwing Amber to the wolves would not help her daughter. It is better if both Amber and Yvey are to remain as victims, unwilling executioners.

Amber's legal team have managed to convince the judge she is not a threat to anyone and have secured her a closely supervised bail. And they profess confidence — to her at least — that they have a reasonable shot with her case.

The story they intend to tell is one of Amber as a coerced victim from the outset: manipulated, bullied and terrified into keeping a secret by a powerful man, then almost becoming a victim of his vindictive former lover. This version of herself without much agency or guilt is not one she can entirely believe or disbelieve.

Or they can play safe and try to avoid the trial by getting the prosecutors to accept a plea of manslaughter, then attempt to bring all these mitigations to bear on the sentencing. But the legal punishment seems almost beside the point to her: no great or small amount of time in jail can wipe away what has happened.

As for Yvey, a plea of diminished responsibility seems a

likely route: the sort of plea that works well for those with wealth and influence and a phalanx of psychologists and character witnesses to call on.

Amber thinks about Yvey all the time: that final glance full of unanswerable questions, and the desolate space between her love for her father and the man he really was. Amber cannot begin to think how her unborn daughter will one day see her mother, and whether the love will one day be eclipsed by anger or disappointment.

It is late in the prenatal ward. The curtain around Amber's bed moves back, and there is Johnny, clutching coffees and pastries. He pulls his mask down and gives her his *how's it going?* smile. But he says nothing and sits in the big armchair next to the bed. He sips his coffee silently and scrolls absently on his phone.

There was no rage when he found out, partly because it took him a while to work out exactly what had happened. Then came a quiet astonishment, followed by a slow dawning that he had been a fool all this time. He tried to say he would have attempted to understand if Amber had told him the truth all those years ago, but they both knew those words were lies. She pressed him on it. It was important for him to be truthful now, as well as her.

'Would you have stayed with me, then? If I'd told you about Benny and given myself up to the police?'

'I don't know,' he admitted. 'I don't know.'

After that, there seemed no point for any further argument, any great declaration of blame and outrage. The truth was too seismic for that. He just shrank away, both from her and a little into himself. She knows they cannot go back. Circumstances will not allow it. It is not even about forgiveness. It is simply that the rupture is too large.

There is one promise Johnny is determined to keep. He will be their child's father, no matter what. He has been almost aggressive about that. Amber worries sometimes that he wants fatherhood too much, that the betrayal will grow inside him and become a hatred that he will use as a weapon to turn their daughter against her.

All Amber has now as a defence is the truth. An openness about everything she is feeling and thinking. Sometimes it has been too much. Sometimes Johnny has had to ask her to stop telling him the truth, to keep a little back. He doesn't want to hear about her infidelity or about how she chose not to tell him anything, even when she thought her and their daughter's lives might be in danger. *I'm not your therapist,* he threw at her in one moment of open anger.

But for now, he is here, waiting with her. And maybe it will all change again once their child is here, once she grows into a person with all her desires and needs and views on the world.

Amber feels a pulse of discomfort deep in her pelvis. A moment later, the feeling is gone. The child inside her moves, then settles, as if momentarily angry about the position she has found herself in. But there is nothing resembling the proper beginning of steady contractions. She thinks for the thousandth time about this new life about to start, and how it weighs against the ones ended, and the ones ruined. *One in, one out,* she can hear Johnny say, that day at Benny's funeral. But the ledger doesn't balance like that.

She reaches out a hand towards her husband, resting it on the edge of the bed. It is a few seconds before he takes it. She looks over at him. There is nothing she can say, nothing she has not tried to say in a hundred different ways. But perhaps their shared silence is okay. It at least has symmetry.

The midwife comes in, takes some more observations, and says they need to wait a little longer until the next stage of induction. She suggests Amber should try to get a little rest.

Amber nods. She would like that. She puts a hand on her belly and closes her eyes, hoping for just a small pocket of sleep. One without dreams, without images, and without any thought of the past or the future. No light getting in around the edges. Just a perfect darkness.

ACKNOWLEDGMENTS

Thank you to Brian Lynch for his sharp focus on story and structure, and to the team at Inkubator for making all this real.

My gratitude to Jon Rowe for making the connection, and to Francesca Cassidy-Taylor, James Castleman and Exposure Film labs for technical advice. Any remaining errors are my own.

To everyone who's supported me along the way, thank you for keeping me going. There are too many of you to mention, but I hope you know who you are. And to Lizzie, for everything.

And thank you for choosing this book. If you could spend a moment to write an honest review on Amazon, no matter how short, I would be extremely grateful. They really do help readers discover new authors, and writers go on writing

Credit
"Life is once, forever": Henri Cartier-Bresson, Interview with Sue Davies, 1973.

ABOUT THE AUTHOR

OCS Francis writes psychological thrillers and suspense novels that explore the darker corners of our lives and minds. He was born in Bristol and studied Human Sciences at Oxford. He has worked in academia, healthcare, television research, feature film development and as a telephone mystery shopper. He lives in Cambridge, UK with his wife and son. He relaxes by playing the piano and taking photographs.

You can find OCS Francis on his website.

www.ocsfrancis.com

Published by Inkubator Books
www.inkubatorbooks.com

Printed in Great Britain
by Amazon

67779546R00199